SCEPTER

Scott L. Collins

Scepter is a work of fiction. The events and characters described herein are imaginary and are not intended to refer to specific places or living persons. The opinions expressed in this manuscript are solely the opinions of the author and do not represent the opinions or thoughts of the publisher. The author has represented and warranted full ownership and/or legal right to publish all the materials in this book.

This book may not be reproduced, transmitted, or stored in whole or in part by any means, including graphic, electronic, or mechanical without the express written consent of the publisher except in the case of brief quotations embodied in critical articles and reviews.

Dedication

First to my readers, who give me the courage to wear my heart, or imagination, on my sleeve for the world to see.

To my wife, my beautiful bride, who first inspired me to put my stories down on paper. It was you who kicked open the door to my mind and convinced me that others would enjoy a look inside.

And to my two beautiful and wonderful boys, the inspirations for this book, who fill my days with laughter. I hope this book gives you the same joy you give to me every day.

Acknowledgments

I'd like to extend my thanks to those who helped make this book possible. First, to my two beta-readers, Bekki McQueen and Gary Collins, thank you for pointing out what worked and what didn't. To my fans who have been such a wonderful source of character names. Last, but certainly not least, to my editor, Shelley Holloway, who did such a wonderful job of polishing my manuscript up to a high shine. Thank you all so much for your contributions!!! Without you, *Scepter* would never have been published.

Chapter One

Waiting

They were coming. Argyle's men weren't here yet, but Daniel knew they were coming. Actually, he was surprised they hadn't shown up already. Pulling the deerskin coat closer around his shoulders, he sat in a chair by the fire and watched the flames dance slowly and methodically over the dry logs and sticks. The house was dark and quiet except for the crackles and pops from the fireplace, yet his heart raced. He'd been waiting, waiting for them to arrive. He was sick with dread knowing they were coming. They were coming for him this time. They would take him, and Aidan would be left alone. Knowing this was to be their last day together, Daniel had tried to make it as normal as possible for his younger brother. He hadn't even mentioned that it was his birthday, his fourteenth birthday. Up until a few years ago, that wouldn't have had a great significance. Times had changed. Now, fourteen years of age was when they came and took you.

Tears fell silently down Daniel's cheeks at the thought of leaving, of being dragged from his home, never to see his brother again. His chest ached as he tried to stifle the sobs building up inside of him. It had been bad enough when their parents were taken to the slave camps and he and his brother had been left to fend for themselves. Now Daniel was to be taken, and he feared for how Aidan would survive on his own. Aidan was only eleven and would now be alone. Though they both knew how to collect food and water and the like, who would take care of Aidan if he got sick or injured? Ever since their parents had been taken, they'd been there to take care of one another when the need arose. They'd never really searched out neighbors, keeping mostly to themselves instead, relying on their own skills and knowledge. While it had been the easy thing to do at the time, Daniel now questioned the logic of isolating themselves so thoroughly. There was nothing he could do about that now. It was too late. He'd failed his brother like he'd failed his parents. Fresh sobs rose in his chest. Daniel tried to be quiet as he wept, being careful not to wake his younger brother, but a few strangled cries escaped his lips anyway as he fought to ignore his breaking heart.

Aidan, for some reason, had retired to bed unusually early. Daniel wondered what he'd been up to. He'd acted strangely all day, speaking very little to Daniel and seeming to avoid eye contact with him. While Daniel knew Aidan was having a difficult time with what was to come, he'd hoped their last few days together would be happy ones, something he could look back on with fondness after being taken away. Instead, he felt almost completely ignored by his younger brother. Aidan had spent most of the last week off in the woods somewhere, leaving the house early in the morning and not returning until well after dark. Even then, he usually just grabbed a bite to eat and went to bed, giving Daniel little more than a grunt of acknowledgment before he disappeared into his bedroom.

Daniel thought about how much he would miss his younger brother and wished he'd been able to spend more time with Aidan over the last few days—that Aidan had been around the last few days to spend time with. That time was now lost, and the only thing the future held was a life of slavery in Argyle's mines. Pulling his feet up to his chest and wrapping himself even tighter in his coat, Daniel finally cried himself into exhaustion and slumped back into his chair, the need for sleep finally overcoming his fear of what lay ahead.

A sound outside startled him awake. Rubbing the salty remains of tears from his eyes and dropping his coat from around his shoulders, Daniel rose and moved quickly around the supper table to the front door and looked out. There was nothing to see but the dark forest that surrounded their modest house. No voices could be heard, no torches visible in the surrounding trees or further out on the rising hills. Not yet. Only the moon pierced the blackness of the night that closed in on Daniel. A scratch on the roof made him jump, and Daniel stepped outside to try to see what was making the noise. A fat raccoon froze and stared at him for a moment before continuing across the roof and jumping to a nearby branch that crowded the corner of the house. The animal waddled cautiously along the branch before disappearing into the leaves. Daniel turned his gaze toward the path that ran from the house and disappeared into the shadows of the forest and shuddered.

He could run, but that wouldn't do any good. If they showed up and he was gone, Aidan would be punished. He couldn't—wouldn't—allow his brother to be hurt because of his own cowardice. "I won't run from you," Daniel muttered to the empty woods. Scowling, he shuffled back inside and eased the door shut. He ran his fingers over his short, dark brown hair and stretched his aching neck from side to side as he made his way back to his chair. Daniel collapsed into it, emotionally drained from a long day of worry and fear. He covered himself once again with his coat and shifted uncomfortably before settling in. Falling into a fitful sleep, his dreams were filled with violent visions of the past.

Chapter Two

Tales

Even the youngest of children knew the story well. The Kingdom of Castiglias had fallen decades before, and the "Outsiders" were cast from the city into the surrounding countryside and mountains. After the murder of King Rai, only the "Elite" were allowed within the walls of the new kingdom, a kingdom now crumbling under the rule of the evil Argyle.

Though King Rai had been a young and unmarried man, he was considered a wise and noble king, one highly regarded for his knowledge and pursuit of justice. His only fault, if you could call it that, had been his trust in others. He'd failed to heed the multitude of warnings about his sorcerer's scheming. Why, one might ask, would a king so highly regarded for his wisdom fail to see the evil in his closest counselor? Well, Argyle had been his magical advisor for years. He had also been an advisor to Rai's father and had always served him with honor. Still, the time came when King Rai was told of secret meetings taking place between Argyle and some very rough and shady characters. Violent plots to murder the king so Argyle could assume the throne were said to be the topic of these meetings. Unable to believe his closest confidant would be capable of such things, King Rai had dismissed the accusations and focused his attention elsewhere. After all, Argyle had been instrumental in helping to negotiate treaties with the outlying kingdoms that surrounded King Rai's lands. What reason would Argyle have for securing the future of the kingdom, only to overthrow it? King Rai ignored Argyle's ongoing meetings with visitors from those lands, assuming them to be related to the treaties that had been signed and not to some treasonous conspiracy. Shortly thereafter, he'd suffered the consequences.

The battle for the city lasted only one morning. Most of the king's guards never even had a chance to fight and were captured while still in their beds, swords lying untouched in their sheaths. Others were slain where they slept.

The king himself was taken alive and dragged from his chambers to the center of the throne room where he was forced to the floor. Dressed still in his bedclothes, King Rai landed on his hands and knees, skinning them on the stone floor. He looked up, glancing first over his right shoulder, then his left. Surrounded by the new "Elite Order of the Guard," he rose to his feet and stood fearlessly next to the altar that dominated the center of the room.

The altar was a rectangular structure that rose to the king's waist. It was carved in jade and decorated with symbols of peace interwoven with ornate vines that wound their way around the base. In it was embedded the "Scepter of Harmony," a gift from the Fairies of the Wood. A hole had been drilled in the very center of the altar, and the base of the golden staff slid snugly into it, rising roughly a foot from the surface of the green table. Legend had it that the Scepter was the source of the tranquility and prosperity that had held the kingdom together for so many millennia.

The first human settlers in the region had endured many hardships to establish and grow their settlement. After their arrival, the people of that first village had been plagued with drought and disease. Crops were small, if they survived at all, and everyone knew they wouldn't last. The men had finally given up on their harvest and formed a hunting party to enter the woods in search of food for the coming winter. Javi, the chieftain, organized and led them into the surrounding forests. It was during that first hunt that they encountered the fairies in a war with a band of wandering goblins. Casting their own purpose aside, Javi joined forces with the fairies and led the settlers into battle with the goblins. The nasty creatures were no match for the well-armed humans, and the conflict ended quickly.

As thanks, the fairies later delivered the golden staff to

the settlement. The hilt of the Scepter was adorned with a cluster of gems: a ruby from the Lands of Sand to the south, an emerald from the fairies themselves who lived in the woods to the southwest, a diamond from the leader of the mountain clans to the northwest, and a sapphire from the king of Lethe, an island that controlled all naval activity in the Great Lake, which formed the eastern border. From that moment, peace and prosperity spread quickly, and almost immediately the small village flourished, quickly developing into a city and later a kingdom.

King Rai was a direct descendant of Javi, the first king to take the newly established throne. Standing before the Scepter that symbolized the noble history of his people, he wondered how this travesty could have come to pass. He'd been a fool to ignore the warnings and cursed himself under his breath.

"Beautiful, isn't it?" came a voice from behind him and to his right. King Rai spun and found himself face-to-face with Argyle.

"A present of purity and love to be certain," replied the king. "It is the source of all that is good in the kingdom. We are forever indebted to those that bestowed so great a gift upon us."

Argyle shook his head slowly, an evil grin spreading across his face. Brushing his long black hair from his forehead, Argyle raised his staff, and with a small enchantment whispered under his breath, small cracks began to form in the Scepter. King Rai watched in horror as the jewels broke out one by one and fell to the floor. He scooped them up and placed them gently back on the altar as his face flushed red with fury.

"That shall be the end of our relations with the gnats in the forest," Argyle proclaimed. Turning swiftly, he strode across the room to the throne and sat, smoothing his robes around him. He reached over and grabbed a lemon from a basket that sat next to the king's chair. Argyle took a bite and smiled. Some of the juice dribbled down the sorcerer's chin and dripped onto his shirt. He brushed briefly at the drops before relaxing back into the deep cushions of the throne. King Rai noted the change from Argyle's regular white robes to skin-tight, blood-red shirt and pants with a black cape that fell to the floor behind him. It brought to Rai's mind the image of a black widow. He shivered at the thought. "A new rule begins today," Argyle sneered.

The guards took their cue and began closing in on the king's position. Knowing what was to come, the king took action. In a last noble effort to defend his people, the kingdom, and himself, King Rai lunged at the closest guard and quickly disarmed him. A great battle ensued. King Rai moved swiftly and gracefully among the hostile mercenaries, blocking blows and delivering thrusts of his own. His training served him well as he shifted deftly between attacking and defending, using the open space of the room to keep is assailants at bay. But eventually the king was overcome. Breathing hard and bleeding, he placed his left hand on the altar to brace himself so he could keep fighting. He lashed out at his attackers, swinging his sword to and fro to keep them away, but they could sense his diminishing strength and stayed just outside his reach allowing him to waste what little energy he had left. At last, he dropped to his knees and collapsed, leaning his back against the altar. His lungs were racked with a series of violent bloody coughs. Wiping his chin clean and gasping for air, he drew a ragged breath and let out his last words.

"My people."

"MY people," Argyle taunted. He got up from the throne and tossed his half-eaten fruit to the floor. He crossed the room to where King Rai lay before the altar. "MY people," Argyle repeated as he knelt down in front of the wounded king. Rai saw a quick flick of Argyle's wrist, and his eyes opened wide in pain. He convulsed, his chest heaving in his struggle for life, and with one last shudder King Rai fell still.

Within the next few days, Argyle and his guards purged Castiglias of those the new king deemed unfit. Only the fairest, tallest, and strongest were allowed to remain. They were forced to pledge their allegiance to the New Order, and only then were they held to be part of the "Elite."

The rest were considered "Outsiders" and were forced from their homes into the surrounding countryside. They made homes where they could, building new houses, living in caves, anywhere they could find food and shelter. Some struck out in caravans to get as far away from Argyle as possible. Some gathered together, and new towns sprang up throughout the realm, while others chose to live a life of seclusion, opting to build by themselves out in the woods or prairies. The inconvenience of their isolation was a small price to pay for greater freedom and less intrusion from Argyle's men.

Disease took many lives, the worst being Witch's Breath, an often-fatal ailment that struck mostly children. The disease would begin innocently enough, just a bit of a cough and a fever, but it would quickly escalated as the person's temperature continued to rise and the phlegm grew thicker. Sometimes, the symptoms subsided and life returned to normal. And sometimes, just sometimes, those who survived developed special skills. Most abilities were for the most part trivial, such as being able to see farther or a heightened sense of smell. A blessed few of the survivors, however, were endowed with powers that held incredible potential. For those rare individuals, the indications of their newfound talent usually showed up within a month or two of the fever breaking. Aidan and Daniel's parents, Troy and Imogen, were lucky enough to be blessed with two such boys.

Troy and Imogen had been part of the second generation born outside the kingdom, which still suffered under the reign of Argyle. They'd had two sons, both of whom had survived early brushes with Witch's Breath. Daniel was now favored with incredible speed. He'd contracted the disease when he was only six months old, and his gift developed rapidly. He was running by the time he was nine months old, beating his father in foot races by age two, and the disparity only increased as he grew older. By the time he was ten, he could move faster than the human eye, becoming less than a blur, disappearing from one spot and reappearing in another. His reflexes were just as quick, and one of his favorite pastimes was catching arrows his father shot at him. Obviously it hadn't started with his father shooting them at him, but when he'd proven his abilities, it became a way to spend time together. His father never ceased to be amazed at his son's incredible ability, and Daniel never tired of trying to hone his skills. Together they spent many hours in a clearing not too far from their home, Troy firing arrows as fast as he could nock and shoot them, Daniel either dodging or catching them.

On occasion, Troy would use Daniel's ability for more than entertainment and send him to town or to a neighbor's house to retrieve something he needed in a hurry. The family's few friends grew quickly aware of Daniel's abilities and, while at their homes, he would usually linger for a bit to perform a stunt or two to demonstrate his skill. Nobody ever tired of seeing his various tricks.

Aidan's ability wasn't quite as well known to anyone outside the family. He'd caught the usually fatal ailment at the age of two, and sometime over the course of the next year, he'd developed a kind of psychic link with animals. When he was three years old, Aidan was outside playing in the yard in front of their small home when a hungry bear had wandered into the clearing in search of food. Seeing the small child, the bear charged, starvation eliminating its fear of humans. Aidan sat calmly in its path and looked into its eyes. The bear slid to a stop a mere foot from the toddler. The boy slowly reached out his hand and touched the cold nose. The bear knelt down to allow Aidan to scratch its head.

Their father had burst from the house, gun in hand. Drawing the rifle to his shoulder, he hesitated when he saw the bear roll onto its side and his child climb on top of it. He watched, mystified, as his son pulled on the bear's ears and nose while giggling uncontrollably.

Rare was the day that this same bear didn't come back to visit Aidan at their home, and the two developed a very close bond. Birds, rodents, wolves all seemed to respond to Aidan's look, his feelings. Eventually, at about the age of seven, Aidan could not only "touch their minds" as he liked to say, but influence their behavior. He described it to his parents and Daniel not as controlling them, but making them aware of his wants. The animals all seemed to desire nothing more than to make Aidan happy.

It wasn't much later that he discovered the most dramatic of his abilities. It was on the morning of his eighth birthday. After collecting water for the family, Aidan came across a squirrel in the forest. He could feel the poor animal's thirst as it searched out a small puddle of water from which to drink. Aidan gently set his bucket down to allow the creature to take a sip. Watching the squirrel, he realized that he was thirsty himself and so drank from the same bucket. With that small act, he discovered his fascinating gift. After taking his drink, Aidan sat staring at the squirrel, wondering what it was like to be one. Suddenly, his body tensed and the world went dark. He felt as if a hood had been thrown over his head. He clawed and struggled to get free. When he finally found daylight, he saw not his hand in front of him, but a paw. He looked at where his other hand should have been and saw the same thing. It took him a few minutes to figure out what had happened. He was now a squirrel! He chattered and ran. He climbed and leapt from tree to tree. He did all the things he'd seen squirrels do before dropping back to the forest floor and shifting back into his human form, exhausted and excited by his experience. He tried to change into a frog, but no luck. A dog? Again, no luck. Bear, wolf, bird? Nope, nope, nope. Squirrel? In a blink, he was back to being a squirrel. It took him about a week to figure out that the sharing of water with the animal was the key to his transformational abilities.

His parents had a difficult time keeping him out of the forest after that, as he spent any free time he had searching out new animals with which to drink. By the time his ninth birthday rolled around, he could transform into just about any creature in the woods. Only when he spotted a werewolf creeping though the forest outside his bedroom did he realize there were limitations to his powers. He could not make contact with the wild animal, nor could he feel its life force. After the animal had moved on, Aidan asked his parents about it.

"Werewolves are an abomination of nature," his father answered. "It doesn't surprise me that your gift doesn't work on their kind. They are the true embodiment of evil, killing for the pleasure of it, poisoning those they don't kill, and dooming them to the same miserable existence."

"Your father's right," his mother responded when he'd shifted his look to her. "They aren't natural. You should do what we all do and stay as far away from them as you can."

Aidan nodded in agreement. Still, he tried a few times more when he had spied them from the safety of his home. It never worked. Not surprising. He was shocked, however, when he discovered that werewolves hunted throughout the month and not just at night during a full moon as he remembered reading in a book. While on a stroll through the forest one summer day, he had spied one feasting on a small doe in a clearing below. He couldn't believe his eyes, but crept forward and confirmed that a werewolf was out in the middle of the day. He'd transformed into a squirrel and escaped into the trees when he saw a few more trying to sneak up on him. He made sure to tell his parents and brother when he arrived home, to be sure they knew to be careful, to keep up their guard at all times.

It had been a wonderful childhood. Both boys had shared in the household chores for as long as either could remember, but it never seemed unfair. Each member of the family did the tasks that were best suited to their abilities, everyone pitching in to make life easier for the others. When someone needed help, the others always chipped in where they could. Living away from others, it was important that each carry their own weight. Occasional injuries or sickness sometimes made things tough, but when that happened, the family always pulled together and made it through by trying to focus on their natural talents.

Their mother, Imogen, handled most of the baking and cooking, though sometimes Daniel chipped in as well. He wasn't as good as she was, but she was always thankful for the break and so he kept at it. He would sometimes just sit and watch her to try to learn something new, like some new herb or spice maybe. She also processed most of the meats brought into the house as she seemed to be able to make the best use of the meat and skins. She did most of the cleaning inside the house as well and tended to the small garden out back. They'd spent many years nurturing their plot, and it now actually provided almost enough food to feed the family. When she wasn't working around the house, Imogen focused her attention on her two boys. She was a loving, gentle, and kind woman. Forever patient with her two boys, they usually ran to her when they were hurt or scared.

Troy, their father, had been the one to enforce the rules, and although stern, he was always just. There was no playing of favorites. There was no goofing off when there was work to be done. A hearty respect for their father had kept them in line. Whenever either of the boys was feeling particularly "grown up," his strong physical presence helped remind them who ran the household. A farmer/hunter by necessity, he was a very muscular and fit man, lean and darkened by long days spent out of doors. The boys always marveled at their father's strength and seemingly endless supply of energy. He did a majority of the hunting, though Daniel began helping as he grew older. Aidan refused to do any hunting given his connection with the animals around them. After a few lengthy discussions, Troy had conceded the point. Troy also did the foraging since he'd grown up in the same forest and knew all the best places to look for the fruits and vegetables they couldn't grow in their garden. He took Aidan on most of these trips too. If unwilling to use his gift to hunt, Aidan could certainly use his gift to help them find other food by tapping into the nearby animals' sense of smell. But Troy's talents didn't end there. Having opted to live with as little contact as possible with others, Troy's carpentry skills were also ever developing. Their house was old, and Troy was forced to spend many an afternoon mending the exterior walls and roof. He'd also become adept at masonry when he'd built the fireplace and well, and his knowledge of medicine continued to grow as he and Imogen cared for two growing and active boys. He was a man of many talents, and he passed that knowledge on to his children.

But Troy wasn't just a man that labored all day and then went to bed. He played just as hard as he worked. Even after a long day working their small field and hunting in the woods, he always took the time to play with his sons. The boys had an unfair advantage in hide and seek, given Daniel's great speed and Aidan's ability to transform, and yet their father almost never declined a game. Mancala was another game they played together when the fatigue of the day or weather kept them inside. Most evenings were spent by the fire, reading one of the books that had survived the years since their ancestors had been exiled from the kingdom.

Though schools were no longer in existence, both Imogen and Troy were insistent that the boys learn to read and write. They were also taught to hunt, gather, and sew while constantly studying and practicing everything from farming to carpentry, and even medicine—anything that Imogen or Troy had knowledge in. From an early age, both boys could identify plants useful for treating various ailments, as well as identify breaks and sprains. They could even successfully treat most of them. This knowledge, for the most part, was born out of necessity. With the lands growing wilder and Argyle's men growing more ferocious, children needed to be able to take care of themselves from an early age, just in case. It was rumored that Argyle was collecting people to work as slaves in his mines, slaves to find the jewels to pay for his mercenaries, and slaves to find his precious cinnabar, which he used to strengthen his magic powers. And so Imogen and Troy taught the boys everything they thought would be useful, for rumor had it the time would come when both parents would be taken and would no longer be there for the two youngsters. To help in their studies, Troy would often trade part of their crops for books at the local marketplace. Though they didn't know it, their household had accumulated the largest library outside the kingdom. So they read.

Usually the boys would pass the book back and forth between themselves, reading aloud while their father whittled in his chair and their mother worked a piece of leather or sewed a new piece of clothing for her growing boys. They read adventure stories, botany books, medical books, stories of the heroes of old, anything and everything Troy could find for trade. It didn't matter, they enjoyed them all. Before retiring for bed, they shared their best and worst moments of the day. Then Troy and Imogen would kiss the boys and tuck them in to bed to rest up for another day of chores and fun.

All those moments that had become their lives ended the day their parents were taken. They had been kidnapped by a party of mercenaries and forced into slavery due to the continued decline of the kingdom. Daniel had been eleven at the time. A beautiful, bright autumn day had turned quickly darker with the arrival of the gathering party.

Daniel's mother had just finished the stitching on his winter coat. She sat in a chair by the front window to make use of the sunlight that tumbled in through the thick pane. She held the garment up for him to admire. A smile crossed her face when she saw his eyes light up.

"Thank you, Mother. It's wonderful." He grabbed the jacket and put it on. The soft fur of the coat would provide excellent insulation for warmth during the cold winters of the outside world. He bent down to give her a hug and froze when he saw the men approaching the front door. He didn't know at the time who they were, but when you lived a life away from others, any visitors you didn't immediately recognize were suspicious. He quickly pulled his mother to her feet and called for his father. Guiding his mother toward the back of the house, Daniel saw his father pass by one of the windows to his left, headed toward the men approaching the front of their home.

"Who are you?" his father inquired as he rounded the side of the house. "And what business do you have on my land?" Daniel heard a loud crunching sound and the thud of something heavy dropping to the ground. The maniacal laughter that followed turned Daniel's blood cold. His mother pushed past him and ran for the front door.

"Troy! Troy!" she yelled as she reached the door and

yanked it open. The men outside turned at the sudden movement, but did not even reach for their weapons as she lunged to her husband's side. "Oh, Troy!" she sobbed as she knelt next to him and pulled him into her arms. She pulled a scarf from her pocket and pressed it hard to the cut on the side of his head where he had been hit. Daniel stood in the doorway, frozen by what he was seeing. He watched as his father's eyes fluttered open and focused on his mother's face.

"Wha...?" he mumbled. He turned onto his side and tried to stand. Two of the soldiers stepped forward; each grabbed one of Troy's arms and pulled him up to his feet. They continued to hold him as he wobbled from side to side, unable to balance.

"You're coming with us, mate," came the gravelly voice of the larger of the two.

Daniel's mother leapt to her feet and pressed close to her husband's side. "No. No, you can't," she pleaded with his captors. Two more men approached her. As she turned to face them, the one to her left hit her hard in the stomach, dropping her to her knees gasping for air. Troy lurched forward reaching for his wife, but was yanked back. He was still groggy from the blow he'd taken to the head and was unable to free himself. Despite his protest and struggling, the men chained his arms and legs. One of the mercenaries grabbed a handful of Imogen's long black hair and pulled her to her feet next to her husband. Then they bound the two of them together.

Daniel regained his senses at the sight of his parents being restrained. He rushed the closest of the men, and while his speed allowed him to surprise the warrior, Daniel did not have the strength to overwhelm him. He attacked repeatedly, moving in and out of their ranks trying to find a way to take the man down and disarm him. Still young and not nearly as strong as his opponent, he lacked the power to do so.

"Daniel!!! Daniel!!! Stop it! Stop it now." He paused to take a breath and heard his parents yelling at him. He turned and looked at them, shocked at their request. "Go," cried his father, blinking hard to focus. "Go get your brother. Get him and stay away from here until we're gone. They're not here for you. You've got to go and find him. You've got to take care of him now. You're in charge. You can't save us, but you can save him." Daniel could see the agony in his parents' eyes at the realization that they might never see him again. Daniel saw movement out of the corner of his eye and turned just as one of the men hurled a large spear at him. Dodging quickly to his right, Daniel turned and caught the staff as it passed by him. Raising the weapon and extending his arm behind him, Daniel prepared to throw.

"No!" his father called. Daniel's eyes flickered to his dad who was now straining forward against the chains that held his wrists. "Go and get your brother. Leave now, run. Don't give them a reason to chase you." Daniel struggled with the decision. He couldn't just stand by and let his parents be taken, yet his little brother would be lost if nobody stayed behind to take care of him. Daniel couldn't risk being killed, not with their parents being taken away to slave camps. Daniel looked back to his parents, tears welling up in his bright blue eyes. "Go," his father stated, looking at him with gentle pleading in his voice. "Take care of your brother. Take care of yourself." Dropping the spear, Daniel began backing away. The men heckled him as he edged closer to the forest. Hatred burned in Daniel's tears, and they felt hot as they fell slowly down his cheeks. When he finally reached the trees, Daniel fled. He ran as fast as he could, searching the forest for signs of his brother who had wandered off in the morning in search of new animals.

On his third pass through a clearing to the south of the house, Daniel found his younger brother sitting, staring intently into the trees to the east.

"Shhhh," Aidan whispered as Daniel ran to him, slowing to a jog as he grew near. Turning to glare at Daniel for his continued crashing through the underbrush, Aidan jumped to his feet when he saw the tears streaming down Daniel's face. Aidan ran to him and caught him in his arms just as Daniel collapsed. Aidan lowered him slowly to the ground. "What is it? What happened?"

"They took them," Daniel choked out. "They took Mom and Dad." Daniel's shoulders lurched as he stared at the ground in front of him, sobbing and trying to catch his breath. "They took them and I couldn't...I couldn't stop them."

"Who took them?" Aidan asked, his eyes sweeping the clearing in the direction from which Daniel had appeared. "Why?" he asked, his lip quivering as the words started to sink in.

"Argyle's men. There were so many of them. I tried to stop them. I tried. Really, I did." Daniel finally raised his head and looked into his brother's dark blue eyes. "You have to believe me."

"What are we going to do?"

A loud moan escaped from Daniel as the feeling of helplessness overcame him. Sobbing convulsively, he grabbed his younger brother and pulled him into his arms. They remained in the middle of that field until well after sundown. It wasn't until the night chill shook them more than their crying that they returned to their home. Nearly three years would pass before Argyle's men returned.

Chapter Three

Aidan's Denial

The gathering party strode through the woods given one task and one task only. Because they were all heavily armed with swords, daggers, balls and chains, and other assorted weaponry, nobody challenged their authority. When they arrived to claim a child, the parents, if there were still parents, would fall to their knees sobbing and begging for their mercy, pleading for their child to be allowed to stay. But there was no denying the king's orders. Anyone who tried to flee from the gathering parties was hunted down and taken to the dungeons. While nobody was sure what exactly happened in there, continuous screams could be heard at the door to the underground jails and nobody came out alive. Those who fought back were subject to the same punishment. The soldiers came and took those on the list, leaving only the weak or infirm behind. While the few parents left on the outside were crushed to see their children go, none were willing to sacrifice their lives, or the lives of the rest of their family, to put up a fight that they would inevitably lose. The stolen children were locked in chains and forced to march with the rest, doomed to become slaves in Argyle's mines.

On this night, however, something unsettling was in the air. None of the men could quite put their finger on it. Their skins and leathers kept out the cool night breeze yet a chill worked its way into the hearts of the men. The woods seemed to be coming alive around them. Something, some things, lurked just beyond the light cast by their torches. The soft padding of paws could occasionally be heard, but the source was never obvious. Movement could be heard in the trees overhead, yet nothing could be seen in the corners of the flickering luminescence. The mercenaries at last saw the end of the path, the clearing that opened up beyond it, and the small home that stood in the center. The night became deathly silent. An uneasiness swept through the group.

"You hear that?" a burly red-haired soldier asked the man standing next to him.

"I don't hear nothin'," the other man grumbled in reply while he scratched at the fleas in his filthy beard.

"Exactly. Not the beat of a bat's wing. Not the howl of a wolf in the distance. I don't like this. Somethin' ain't right."

"Shut up and do your job."

As they entered the clearing, a small boy appeared on the roof of the house directly over the front door. His shoulder-length blond hair blew in the breeze as he spoke, his slender frame silhouetted in the moonlight, the light of which made his pale skin even whiter. He looked almost ghostlike standing atop the cottage, a specter of doom.

"My name is Aidan. This is my house. I know why you're here. You're here to take my brother, Daniel. He's all I have left so you can't have him."

The boldness of his tone brought a quick halt to the procession of men, not out of fear, but out of curiosity and amusement. A few chuckles filtered through the crowd of mercenaries. Aidan continued.

"Laugh if you will, but I'm warning you. You won't leave here alive if you try to take him. Leave now. Leave now and never come back. If you do that, I won't hurt you."

"What, might I ask, is one little boy going to do against the lot of us?" the commander asked in a stern voice, stepping forward from the rest of the men. A large sword was sheathed across his back and a deadly dagger strapped to his bare leg. Aidan had never seen a man this large, especially one with the scars to indicate a long and dangerous past. One poorly healed scar ran from just above his left eye down his face and across his throat. Aidan eyed it, but said nothing. He merely stared down from his perch on the roof, squaring his shoulders and raising his chin defiantly. It was then that they heard it. The forest coming to life. Five of the largest bears any of them had ever seen emerged from around the sides of the house, two on one side, three from the other. All took position in front of the door. Four mountain lions strode up on each side of Aidan and stood, hair raised, muscles tensed and ready to pounce. Wolves wandered into the clearing from the woods and paced nervously from side to side with growls rising in their throats. Their eyes, which seemed to glow as they reflected the moonlight, never left the men. Overhead, animals could be heard scurrying in the branches.

"This is absurd. I'm not going back to the king and tell him that I got chased off by a child and his circus." Drawing an arrow from his quiver, one of the men in the front stepped into the clearing, nocked the arrow and drew it back to its full length.

"Last chance," was Aidan's response. He glowered at the men, hatred filling his eyes, his hands clenched in tiny fists at his sides as he took a step forward to the edge of the roof. "You're making a huge mistake."

The man let the arrow fly.

Just as it was about to pierce Aidan's heart, a large bat streaked by, grabbed the arrow in its claws and disappeared into the darkness. Aidan trembled and then his clothes exploded into shreds around him. Where he had stood, now the largest of mountain lions perched. They saw his muscles tighten. He sprang. A frenzy of activity shook the very trees of the forest as every creature in the vicinity attacked. Birds swooped and pecked at the men, driving them forward into the clearing. Wolves, teeth bared, leapt into the group, scattering them, separating them to become easier targets. Only the bears stayed put, guarding the door to the house until it opened behind them.

Daniel had awakened from the noise and now stood in the doorway disoriented and confused. He stared in awe at the sight before him. Men screamed and ran in every direction, flailing blindly in an attempt to fight off the pursuing animals. Some stood to battle directly, but their efforts were in vain. They were taken down quickly and mercilessly. Only when the last man had been thwarted did the activity die down. Daniel watched a large mountain lion emerge from the forest edge and approach the house. The bears stepped aside as he closed the distance. It stopped about five feet from Daniel and quivered. In the blink of an eye, it transformed back into Aidan. Standing naked and covered in sweat and grime, Aidan burst into tears.

"I couldn't let them do it. I can't lose you too," Aidan choked out. He dropped to his knees, shaking with exhaustion, covering his face and sobbing.

"Let's get you inside, get you cleaned up and dressed."

"There's another."

"What?" Daniel replied, his eyes sweeping the clearing for any sign of danger.

"In the trees, a girl," Aidan gasped, trying to catch his breath. He pointed down the path in the woods. "She's bound in chains, so she wasn't attacked. I think she's a slave."

Daniel walked slowly to Aidan and gently helped him to his feet. "You get inside and get cleaned up. I'll go get the girl."

Aidan nodded and stumbled toward the door.

"And Aidan," Daniel continued. His brother turned. "Thank you."

Chapter Four

Introductions

Daniel walked quickly to the edge of the woods and peered into the darkness. Although he knew he needn't be afraid of the animals still lingering in the area, his heart pounded in his chest as he snuck farther into the shadows. He soon found a girl bound in chains as Aidan had described. She was filthy and appeared to be exhausted from the forced march. She stood trembling, hugging herself tightly and barely stifling the weeping that seemed to be inevitable. Her head was down and her hair fell in a curtain around her face. Daniel approached her slowly, trying to whisper reassurances as he went.

"Hello?" he breathed. "Are you okay? I'm not here to harm you." She didn't look up at him and only seemed to stiffen further. "Were you taken by Argyle's men? Is that why you're here? You're being taken to the castle?" Daniel kept his voice low and made sure to stay where she could see him. The last thing he wanted was for her to get hurt running through a dark forest with her wrists and feet bound in chains. If he used his gifts, he could get to her before she'd even realized he'd moved, but he didn't want to scare her anymore than she already obviously was. While certainly not an imposing figure to an adult, Daniel still stood almost a full head above the girl and had begun to fill out his frame, especially throughout his chest and arms. Trying to stoop a little to lessen the difference in size, Daniel asked quietly, "Did you see what happened to his men?"

At last she looked up at him, her hair parting just a little so he could see her eyes. She blinked a few times and looked around before answering. "I saw, but I can't believe it. This must be some horrible nightmare, and I wanna wake up. I don't like this dream. I wanna go home," she whispered in a high quivering voice. Her lip trembled and her legs became wobbly. Daniel rushed to her side and caught her just as she collapsed. He carried her gently out of the forest and into the clearing.

"You're going to be fine," Daniel assured her. "Aidan and I will take care of you. Why don't you come inside, and I'll get those chains off of you? Are you hungry or thirsty?" Daniel asked as he stepped through the front door and set her tenderly into a chair near the fire.

The girl nodded. "Water, please."

Daniel strode to the kitchen and returned with a glass of water and a large chunk of bread. He set them on the table next to her. "You look hungry," he explained when he saw the quizzical expression on her face. "Now, about these chains." He moved quickly across the room and began rummaging in a box on the floor. Crossing back to the girl, he placed a hammer and chisel on the end table before he walked out the front door. It seemed to her that Daniel had just left when he reentered the room carrying a small block of wood. This he set on the floor between her feet. "Would you like to take a drink or would you prefer I remove the chains first?"

"The chains, please."

Setting the block of wood below the chain binding her right ankle, Daniel set the chisel in place and struck swiftly with the hammer, freeing her right foot. The sound echoed through the house and the girl shrieked at the sudden noise. Daniel heard a muffled cry from behind the closed door leading to Aidan's room. With less than perfect grace, the door was torn open and Aidan came stumbling from the room.

"What on earth was that?" Aidan bellowed, eyes darting to the various windows while shoving his shirt into his trousers. They were big on him, but he wore his clothes large to reduce the tearing when he forgot and changed forms while still dressed. He'd also given up on shoes and switched to moccasins as they were much easier to mend. His mother had long ago drawn the line and refused to stitch his ragged clothing, telling him that if he was going to ruin it, he'd be the one to fix it. As a result, most of Aidan's clothes were overly large and crisscrossed with the jagged stitching of a child's hand.

"Relax," Daniel replied. "Just a little jailbreak." He looked up and smiled at the girl. She smiled back and Daniel felt his breath catch. Her large brown eyes seemed to look directly into his soul before she blushed and dropped her head. It had been quite some time since anyone other than Aidan and Daniel had been in the house, much less a beautiful girl. Feeling his face begin to flush, Daniel refocused his attention on the chains. With another crash of the hammer, her other ankle was free. Two more released her hands.

"Thank you..." she paused and smiled again. "I'm sorry. I don't even know your name."

"I'm Daniel, and this is my brother Aidan."

"Thank you, Daniel," she said quietly, giving him a small nod with her head. Daniel flushed again when she spoke his name. "And, Aidan," she murmured, "thank you as well. Thank you both for saving me. My name is Olivia."

"It's a pleasure to meet you," Aidan replied as he finished getting dressed.

Olivia held the water glass in both her trembling hands and took a long drink. She placed the glass back on the table and then tore into the food. She ate swiftly and finished off the hunk of bread, her appetite satiated for the time being. A small burp escaped her lips and she giggled.

"Sorry."

"Quite all right," Daniel answered. "You're looking better already."

Looking at the two boys, Olivia sat up a little straighter in her chair and tried to compose herself. She brushed her long dark hair out of her face and hooked it around her ears. She smoothed her wrinkled and dirty pants and blouse. "Now, I don't want to sound ungrateful or pushy, but would you mind telling me what happened out there? I still don't know if I'm dreaming or not, but I was wondering if you saw the same thing I did."

"Well, what exactly did you see?" Aidan asked while taking a seat next to her.

"Not much at first. It was dark, and they left me a little ways back into the forest. I could kind of see them at the edge of the clearing and could hear them grumbling and yelling something, but couldn't make out the words. Then the...the..." She trailed off, turning from the two boys. She fidgeted and stared into the fireplace though it wasn't the flames she saw as she looked back at the night's events.

"Then what?" Daniel asked, sitting down in front of her chair. She shifted and looked up at him. The intensity of her brown eyes startled him before she turned crimson and again dropped her gaze to her lap. Hiding behind her wavy brown hair seemed to give her confidence, and she continued.

"Then the forest came alive. It took them. I could hear their screams. I could see the shadows of the animals that dragged them away. What happened?" Her lip began to tremble again, and she clasped her hands together to keep them from shaking. She lifted her head and looked to Daniel, her face full of fear and confusion. Their eyes locked.

It seemed an eternity before Daniel could break eye contact and try to organize his thoughts. His mouth seemed far too dry to form words. Finally he was able to pull himself together enough to reply. "You'll have to ask Aidan about that. I was inside for most of the fight, asleep in the chair you're sitting in now. I didn't see or do much of anything." Daniel frowned and looked over at his brother. "Why don't you tell her what you saw?"

Aidan glanced from Daniel to Olivia and back at Daniel. He could see that something was bothering his older brother, but couldn't figure out what it was. Setting the issue aside for the moment, he looked back to the girl. "It happened exactly like you said. I saw the same things you did. I'll tell you more later." He shifted his gaze back to Daniel. "Right now I think we might want to talk about something I thought of while I was getting dressed. I meant to say something earlier, but I forgot about it when you broke her chain."

"What's that?" Daniel asked.

"He'll send more." Aidan saw both Daniel's and Olivia's heads jerk in reaction to his statement. "He won't let us get away with this. I don't know how long it will take him to know what we've done, but you know he'll find out. I think it might be a good idea to be gone when they show up."

"My sister," Olivia whispered.

"What?" Daniel and Aidan responded in unison.

"My sister. She's all alone. They'll go to my house first and find her there alone. We've got to go and get her. If they know that something happened to the gathering party, they might hurt her. Please, we've got to get to her before they do!" She jumped to her feet, reached out, and grabbed both of the boys' hands and started pulling. "Please, she's the only family I have left. One of Argyle's men escaped. He ran away when the fight started. He'll go back and tell Argyle. We've got to go!"

The boys exchanged a glance. "Of course," Daniel answered quickly. "But hold on just a moment." He reached out and took Olivia's hand in both of his and she stopped tugging. "First we need to get things settled here. Once we leave, there's no coming back. Why don't you two go get some sleep, and I'll start putting things together. Olivia, you can sleep in my room, and when I finish out here I'll sleep in Aidan's room with him."

"But my sister," Olivia began.

"It'll take Argyle's man a while to get back to the castle. We've got some time," Daniel explained, trying to soothe Olivia's frazzled nerves. "Really, think about how long it took you to get here. It'll take him about that long to get back." Seeing the logic in his statement, she sat back down in the chair with relief. "Do you think you can sleep?" Daniel asked. Olivia thought for a moment and gave a small nod of her head as she tried to stifle a yawn. The long march had obviously taken a lot out of her. "Let me grab some stuff from my room, and then you two should go to bed."

Daniel disappeared into his bedroom. Olivia could hear him moving about. Her gaze fell on Aidan. "Can you tell me more about what happened tonight?"

Aidan shifted in his seat. "It's hard to explain, and I don't usually tell people about my gift. I guess we're going to be friends though, so I should probably tell you about it." He paused. "We're friends now, right?" Olivia nodded and Aidan's eyes narrowed. His forehead creased as he concentrated trying to find the words to most accurately describe his abilities. "First, I can...change an animal's behavior."

"What?" Olivia asked, confused by his statement.

Aidan chewed his lip and tried again. "Daniel says I can control their actions, but it's not really like that. I can get them to do what I want, but it's not control really. I don't force them to do anything they don't want to do. I can sort of get inside their minds and show them what I need them to do and why. I don't like to think that I control them. It's just a special bond I can make with them, and it makes them open to helping me."

"That's incredible!" Olivia said. She still looked a bit skeptical, and Aidan could see she would require a bit more to convince her of the truth of his claim. She noticed Daniel had finished in his room and now stood in the doorway watching them, his right hand against his cheek, his fingers massaging his earlobe. She didn't acknowledge him as she still wanted to hear more. "Is that what happened tonight? You convinced the animals to protect you?"

"Well...sort of." Aidan stared into the fireplace.

"What do you mean?" Olivia asked. She reached out her hand and placed it gently on Aidan's arm.

"I did it to protect Daniel." Aidan looked up at Olivia. His eyes started to glisten as the old wounds were pulled open once again. "I couldn't let them take him. They took our parents, but we were too young back then to do anything to help them." His head fell forward and Olivia saw a single tear fall into his lap.

She saw Daniel's movement out of the corner of her eye and turned to him. Their eyes locked. Olivia shook her head slightly and he stopped, obeying her silent request. After a moment Aidan lifted his head. A new emotion now dominated his features: defiance.

"But not this time. This time I knew they were coming. This time I knew what they wanted. This time I knew what I could do. I couldn't watch them take the last of my family. When Daniel fell asleep, I snuck out. I didn't travel very far. I didn't know when they'd arrive, so I went and found every friend I could. Most of them were already here. I've been bringing animals closer all week. I brought in every animal I could make contact with and asked them to guard the house." A smile gently curled his lip. "It must have been scary for you." He glanced down at his hands twisting in his lap.

"It was," Olivia agreed quickly. "I didn't see everything, but from what I heard, and the few things I saw..." She trailed off.

Aidan nodded, still looking at his hands. "There's something else."

"Okay." Olivia turned in her chair and took both of Aidan's hands in hers, her eyes wide as she leaned closer. "Go ahead."

Daniel quickly stepped forward. "I think that's enough for tonight. It's time to get some sleep. Olivia, I'll get you a bucket of water to wash off with. If you want to put your clothes outside the bedroom door, I'll wash them tonight before I go to sleep and hang them near the fire to dry." Olivia's eyes burned into his back, frustrated and puzzled by his interruption, as he continued across the room to the kitchen. Aidan merely nodded and rose.

"I'll see you in the morning. If you need anything, we're right in there," he said, pointing to his bedroom. "Good night." Aidan gave her hands a squeeze and left for bed. Olivia gave Daniel a confused look before picking up her water glass and retiring to Daniel's bedroom to ready herself for the night.

Daniel spent the next few hours preparing and packing for the journey ahead. Although the road before them had not been entirely laid out, he felt they were in for a long trip and tried to plan accordingly. Food, water, and clothing were divided up into three separate piles. Not sure how much Olivia would be able to carry over long distances, Daniel was forced to guess. He decided to overestimate, since they could always rid themselves of supplies if she grew too tired. He gave her a pack that was roughly the same size he'd put together for Aidan, as she was just slightly taller than his younger brother. He then washed and hung Olivia's clothes as he'd promised. Last on Daniel's list was weaponry. He decided to take the bow and arrows his father had left behind. He'd always had an affinity for archery and thought the weapon would be useful if not in the event of being ambushed, at least for hunting. Realistically, there was only one other true weapon in the cabin. Although it had been a long time since the rifle had been fired, it once belonged to Daniel and Aidan's grandfather, and the boys had meticulously cleaned it once a month. Daniel decided to bring it along and see how Olivia handled a gun. Aidan had his own one-of-a-kind weapon. After going through the supplies and packs a second time, Daniel was satisfied and sat down heavily in front of the dying fire. Pulling his jacket on to keep warm, he tugged at the cuffs, which seemed to get shorter every day. His mind drifted back to the missed fight earlier in the evening before his eyes closed and he fell asleep.

Chapter Five

Preparations

Daniel awoke early the next morning and laid Olivia's clean clothes near the bedroom door before heading to the kitchen. They would need the nourishment for the long trek that awaited them. The smell of bacon and coffee soon filled the small home as Daniel began cooking up a very large breakfast.

Aidan stumbled from his room rubbing his eyes wearily and pulling on a long-sleeved shirt. Sitting down at the table, Aidan mumbled a barely audible thank you when Daniel set a cup of hot coffee in front of him. After taking a few sips, he got up and joined his brother in the kitchen. Aidan set his cup on the counter and hopped up next to it. He shifted around and cleared his throat.

"Where are we going to go?" Aidan asked.

"To Olivia's house, to get her sister," Daniel answered, looking at him as though he'd lost his mind.

"I mean after. After we go get her, where will we go? We can't stay there, but we can't come back here either. Where can we go that we'll be safe from Argyle and his men?"

Daniel stopped his cooking and turned to look at his brother. He ran his hand over his hair, which was short enough to stick up. He played with it, rubbing it back and forth for a moment as he pondered the question. He shrugged. "I don't know. I haven't gotten that far in my planning. All I know is that we need to go get her sister before Argyle sends someone to look for his gathering party. When his men don't come back, the next group to go out isn't going to show any mercy to anyone they come across. My guess is the first house that was visited by the last group was Olivia's house. We were the second. I think the next group will follow the same path. We can decide where to go after we get her sister out of harm's way."

Turning back to the stove, Daniel was mixing the eggs when he heard the bedroom door open. Both boys glanced over to see Olivia's arm emerge from the bedroom and pull her clothes inside. Moments later, she meandered out stretching and yawning widely. She flushed deeply when she realized both Daniel and Aidan were watching her, and dropped her eyes to the floor as she shuffled across the room. Daniel smiled to himself and poured her a cup of coffee as well, setting it in front of her as she sat down at the table.

"Who's ready to eat?" Daniel inquired. Aidan pulled out three plates, and Daniel piled them high with food. Olivia's eyes bulged at the amount of breakfast placed in front of her.

Daniel noticed the look on her face. "Just eat as much as you can," he commented. "It's going to be a difficult trip, and you'll need the energy. Plus, I don't know when any of us are going to get another home-cooked meal." Olivia glanced up at him at the last comment, but decided against addressing it. She picked up her fork and began eating. Daniel and Aidan both pulled up their shirt sleeves and then engaged in what could only be described as a feeding frenzy as they shoveled food from their plates to their mouths. After finishing his meal, Daniel walked to the sink, washed his dishes, and put them back in the cupboard.

"Why bother?" Aidan asked, pushing his now empty plate away from him and leaning back in his chair, one hand rubbing his full stomach. He tucked a lock of long blond hair back behind his ear before grabbing his coffee and taking a sip. "It's not like it's going to matter. We'll never be coming back."

"We don't know that for sure," Daniel snapped back. "I don't know if we'll ever get to come back. If we do though, I don't want my rotting food sitting in the sink." Aidan looked back down at his plate to avoid Daniel's glare. "I need to grab something before we go."

Daniel closed the cupboard doors, walked quickly to his bedroom, and shut the door behind him. He had wanted to retrieve one more item before leaving on their journey and had been unable to last night while Olivia was sleeping. From the shelf over his bed, he took down a game. His father had given it to him when he'd turned eight, and they had spent countless hours playing it together. Although he had played it with Aidan on occasion, it had primarily been something special Daniel shared with his father. He slid off the wooden lid, revealing the small bowls within, each filled with polished stones. Daniel picked one up and gently caressed it between two fingers. Dropping the stone back in the box and closing it, Daniel quickly wiped his eyes and left the room. After tucking it securely into his pack, Daniel looked back to the others. "Are you two ready to go?"

Both stood up from their chairs and followed Daniel's lead in washing their dishes and returning them to their appropriate places. Olivia followed Aidan back across the room to where the packs lay on the floor.

"Which one is mine?" Olivia asked, stepping up beside Aidan, her gaze moving back and forth between the two packs.

"Whichever," Daniel replied. "They both weigh about the same. We can move stuff around between the three of us once we get going and get a feel for what we're carrying. This is for you too," Daniel added, lifting the rifle he'd taken out the night before. Her eyes opened wide and she looked to Aidan for his reaction. "He's got his own protection," Daniel said, stepping forward and extending the weapon toward her. "My bow and quiver are by the door. We're all going to need something to defend ourselves out there. There are bullets and cartridges in each of the packs." Seeing the confused expression on Aidan's face, Daniel explained, "I didn't want to put them all in one pack in case it gets wet. As she uses up her supply, we can replenish it from our packs. We need to be careful. Also," Daniel remarked, looking back to Olivia, "you've got two bags in your pack. One is black and has regular bullets in it. The other is gray, and that one contains silver bullets, in case we run into werewolves. I also packed some of my mom's silverware. We can melt it down later and try to make some arrowheads. It'll be better if both of us are equipped to fight them off if we need to."

Olivia picked up the pack in front of her and hoisted it onto her back, shifting it to distribute the weight evenly on her shoulders. Taking the rifle from Daniel and bouncing a bit to settle the straps on her shoulders, she moved quickly to the door and outside. Aidan knelt down and picked up the other bag.

"Oh, I need to grab something real quick." Aidan announced before disappearing into the back bedroom. He came out a short while later and shoved something into a pouch he had tied to his belt. "Got it," he said. "Oh, and my sewing kit!" He disappeared into his room again and emerged, shoving the small kit into his pack. "I've got to keep myself looking proper," he laughed and walked out the front door to join Olivia.

Daniel scanned the room, partially to check for anything they may need to take with them, but mostly to take it all in one last time. He'd told Aidan he wasn't sure if they'd ever return to this home. Even if they did, he had a strong feeling it would never be quite the same.

Outside the house, Daniel stopped Olivia. "Can you shoot that?" Daniel asked pointing to the rifle she carried, "or do you need some pointers?"

"Is it loaded?" Olivia asked. Daniel nodded. Olivia lifted the rifle to her shoulder and aimed toward the path she'd taken to the house the night before. "See that yellow flower just to the left of the trail?"

Daniel's eyes scanned the forest floor where she was indicating. At last he spotted the small petals through the tall grass. Just as he started to say he'd located it, the blast from the rifle drowned him out. The flower exploded.

"Yes, I can shoot this." Olivia slung the rifle over her shoulder and proceeded across the clearing toward the path.

"Wow," Aidan murmured with a grin and set off behind her.

Daniel's chin dropped to his chest. Unable to find any

words, he followed.

Chapter Six

The Journey Begins

Crossing the clearing in front of the house, Daniel and Aidan walked on either side of Olivia as she approached the path through the woods. Olivia would be leading the way, at least for this leg of the journey, as she was the only one who knew the way back to her house. Eager to get back to her sister, Olivia moved swiftly into the trees, the boys staying close. Daniel scanned the forest looking for any signs of danger. Aidan, on the other hand, was completely at ease. Daniel glanced over at him, slightly annoyed by his nonchalant behavior.

"Keep your eyes open," Daniel warned.

Aidan snapped out of whatever daydream he'd been lost in and shrugged off Daniel's warning. "There's nothing around here that's dangerous to us. There are a few animals, but I haven't felt anything from them that makes me think there are any other humans around, or werewolves. I can't think of anything else we need to be concerned about." Aidan admired the woods that surrounded them. "We're safe in here. Nothing can get to us without us being warned first. Besides, Custos is protecting us." He reached his hand out and gently brushed a shrub as he passed it. A small lizard darted out from its hiding place and startled Olivia. A small cry escaped her lips before she could stop it, and a deep blush colored her cheeks. Both boys smiled to themselves.

Composing herself Olivia asked, "Who's Custos?"

Daniel glanced up at her. "He's Aidan's pet bear."

Aidan scowled. "He's not my pet."

Olivia's mouth hung open. "You've got a pet BEAR?"

"He's not my pet!" Aidan repeated. "He's just...a friend.

He's been my friend, well, forever. He's out there," Aidan motioned off to their left. "He's keeping an eye on us, keeping us safe."

"Was he there last night?" Olivia asked, searching the forest where Aidan had indicated.

Aidan nodded though neither of the other two saw. "He stood right in front of the door, guarding Daniel."

"Well, make sure to tell him thank you next time you chat with him, but I can take care of myself," Daniel grumbled.

"He was just doing what I asked him to do," Aidan replied. He caught Olivia's eye questioningly. She shrugged and shook her head.

"I don't need a babysitter."

"Okay." Aidan decided to give up and just walk. Obviously Daniel was in a bad mood and didn't want to talk.

An occasional comment broke the silence as they walked, but for the most part only the sounds of the forest could be heard: birds twittering, small animals in the trees, and the rustling of leaves in the morning breeze. The path widened and narrowed as it wound its way through the trees, Olivia constantly on the lookout for Custos.

"Can we stop for a rest?" Olivia finally asked, turning to look at the brothers following behind her, now in single file due to the thick brush that bordered the path. "My shoulders are starting to hurt and I'm getting hungry."

"I could use some lunch too," Aidan agreed. "It's been a while since breakfast, and I need a break. Let's stop at the next clearing, and we'll eat. That okay with you two?" Daniel nodded his agreement, since his back was aching as well. They came to a small break in the trees a short while later, and the three dropped their packs and stretched, trying to work the kinks out of their shoulders and lower backs. Aidan lay down and looked up through the trees at the clear blue sky peeking through. The grass tickled the back of his neck, and he tossed his head back and forth to scratch it before lying still. Closing his eyes and breathing deeply, he savored the smell of nature, the husky aroma of the earth, the sweet bouquet of the grass that swirled around him, the vibrant perfume of the flowers blooming in the nearby trees. Olivia sat down next to Aidan while Daniel pulled some meat, biscuits, and nuts out of their packs and handed them out. Sitting on a small rock, Daniel bit into a small piece of dried venison.

"How much farther is it?" Daniel asked.

Olivia looked up from her lunch. "It took us just over two weeks to march from my house to yours after they took me. I think we're traveling faster than the soldiers were, so I'd guess we'll arrive sometime in, I don't know, twelve days?"

Aidan sat up. "Twelve more days? I don't think Argyle knows what's happened yet, but I'd sure like to get to your place faster than that. We don't want them getting there first, and I'd hate to still be there when his next patrol comes through. They aren't gonna go easy." Daniel nodded in agreement while slowly chewing his food.

Olivia took a bite of her biscuit and added, "Well, one good thing is that we're going to turn east in about a week, toward the Great Lake. Then we won't be walking right toward his kingdom. I really don't see how his men can beat us there. I'm sure Argyle doesn't even know about it yet, and it's at least a two-week journey from the castle to our home." Aidan noticed her picking at her biscuit nervously as though she wasn't entirely convinced of her own words. She rubbed small crumbs between her fingers and tossed them mindlessly aside before picking off another piece.

"I'm sure you're right," he offered, glancing at Daniel behind her back. "How close do you live to the Great Lake?" he inquired, trying to sound nonchalant. Though unsure of what Aidan was getting at, Daniel eyed him suspiciously, catching the forced indifference in his tone.

"Oh, only about a half-day hike," she replied turning to face him. "We used to go there during the summer before my parents were...you know." Olivia paused and looked down at the food in her hands. "We used to have so much fun building campfires on the beach and sleeping on blankets in the sand." Daniel's concern over Aidan's question disappeared as he focused on how her face lit up with her recollection of her family trips, her brown eyes sparkling and her tan face flush with excitement. As she told Aidan all about the fun times they'd had, the games, the adventures, and more, Daniel found himself admiring the way her dark wavy hair shone in the sunlight. A small gust of wind caught a wisp of hair and blew it across her face as she laughed at some memory she'd been telling Aidan. Olivia caught it with her pinkie and pulled it away from her face as she turned to say something to Daniel. Embarrassed, he quickly dropped his eyes and dug mindlessly through his pack as though looking for something. He looked back up when she didn't continue.

"I'm sorry, what?" he replied, realizing he had no idea what she'd said that had prompted her to turn and look at him. The fact that she now sat with an expectant look on her face gave him the impression she'd asked him a question.

"I asked if you'd ever camped at the beach with your parents."

"Uh, no," Daniel answered, taking another bite from his jerky and inspecting his feet.

Olivia turned back to Aidan and continued talking. Daniel only caught bits and pieces of their conversation as his mind wandered back to Olivia's smile. Eventually the three finished their meals and stood to continue their journey. "Would you excuse us for just a moment?" Aidan asked, grabbing Daniel by the arm and pulling him toward the trees. "I have to, um, well, you know, before we go."

Olivia turned a brilliant crimson. "Oh, yes, go ahead. Good idea. You two go over there. We'll meet back here in a couple minutes." She turned and disappeared into the forest on the other side of the meadow.

"What's going on?" Daniel asked as they made their way farther into the woods. Remembering Aidan's look when he'd asked about where Olivia lived, he continued. "Why so many questions about where she lives?"

"I don't want to scare her," Aidan replied, "but I was thinking about Argyle. I don't know how he could have found out, but if he heard about what happened at the cabin..."

"What?" Daniel interrupted.

"Well, it wouldn't take them two weeks to get to her house. They could sail down Styx River to the Great Lake. You heard what she said. She only lives about a half-day's walk from the lake. That's travel with two children. How long do you think it would take Argyle's men once he finds out? It may take two weeks walking, but what if they sail? A day on the river, half a day on the lake, and then maybe a few hours to get to the house?"

Daniel tugged on his right earlobe, a nervous habit he'd developed as a child and had never been able to kick. He became concerned for Olivia's sister's safety as he processed Aidan's words. "You might be right, we need to hurry," Daniel agreed. "Let's push a bit harder and see if she keeps up. If she doesn't say anything, maybe we can cut our travel time down a bit. We should get started." He stepped behind a tree to relieve himself and Aidan followed suit. Back at the clearing the two boys strapped on their packs, helped Olivia on with hers, and handed her the rifle.

"Let's go," Daniel remarked, taking the lead on the path to try and set the pace. Aidan let Olivia fall in behind his older brother and followed closely in a silent attempt to get her to walk faster. The hours dragged on as the three trudged through the forest, stopping occasionally to take a drink of water. The breaks were quick and as infrequent as the boys could make them without arousing Olivia's suspicions. As night fell, the trail became difficult to navigate as the thick forest canopy cast deep shadows across the path, hiding roots and rocks that threatened to roll an ankle, or worse.

"I think we should stop here," Daniel announced, coming to a stop in the middle of the path.

"What?" Aidan asked. "We can't stop here. There's nowhere to lie down. What are we going to do, sleep in the middle of the trail?"

"No," Daniel answered, trying to stay patient though he was tired and hungry. "We can step off into the bushes and sleep there for the night. We'll keep going at first light."

"Why don't we just keep going until the next clearing?" Aidan argued. "That way we don't have to sleep under a bush. I don't know about you, but I'd be more comfortable stretched out in the grass."

"We don't know where the next clearing is Aidan. And with how dark it is, we can't see where we're stepping. We're not going to get there as fast as we need to if someone gets hurt. Besides, if we sleep out in the open, someone might see us. We need to stay out of sight until we can get to Olivia's sister."

"Lilly," Olivia interrupted.

"What?" both boys said simultaneously, caught off guard by her seemingly odd statement.

"My sister's name. It's Lilly. And I agree with Daniel. We don't know who's out there or if anyone is looking for us yet. I don't think anyone is, but I'd like to stay safe. We have to get back there."

Aidan looked at Daniel and then back to Olivia. "Fine," he finally agreed. "You get first watch," he joked, poking Daniel in the chest. "Call it a perk of being in charge." Aidan pushed his way through the bushes that lined the path, and disappeared. Daniel and Olivia followed. After a supper the same as lunch, Olivia and Aidan lay down and quickly dropped off to sleep, the physical exertions of the day having taken their toll. Daniel sat listening to the soft whisper of the breeze caressing the small leaves that surrounded him. He leaned back against the trunk of a nearby tree and struggled to keep his eyes open. Blinking furiously trying to relieve the dry, burning sensation, Daniel pulled his knife out of the sheath on his belt, grabbed a small piece of wood sitting near his leg, and began whittling, another pastime he'd shared with his father.

Chapter Seven

Wake Up Call

"Hey! Nice way to take first watch," Aidan whispered.

Daniel rubbed at his eyes. "Wha...?" he mumbled, forcing his eyes open. Aidan's face was mere inches from Daniel's. Startled, Daniel jerked back and smacked his head against the trunk he was leaning on. "OUCH!!!" he cried, pushing Aidan away from him and rubbing the rising knot on the back of his skull. "What's your problem?"

Aidan answered quietly, "You were supposed to take the first shift. You fell asleep." With that, Aidan stood up and stepped gently around Olivia who was still dozing. "I'm going to go pick some berries. I'd like something to eat other than jerky and biscuits. I'll be back in a bit. Why don't you wake up Olivia and see if you can find some water while I'm gone? My pouch is almost empty. I'll leave it with you in case you find some. We can eat when I get back and then get going. I've got a bad feeling, and I want to get going as early as we can." With the rustling of leaves as he pushed his way through the shrubs, Aidan disappeared quickly into the thick forest and soon his footsteps could not be heard. After picking up the knife he'd dropped next to his leg while whittling the night before, Daniel leaned forward and gave Olivia a gentle shake.

"Time to wake up," Daniel said softly. Olivia's eyes fluttered open. Not recognizing her surroundings, she bolted upright with a gasp, her eyes open wide as she jerked her head around.

"Where?" she started, before realizing where she was. "Oh, sorry," she mumbled and sat back down next to Daniel. She rubbed her eyes to try and clear the last of sleep away. "Where is Aidan?" she asked.

"Went out to find some breakfast," Daniel replied. "Guess he's already tired of jerky and biscuits," he joked. Olivia smiled. They talked about what lay ahead of them while packing up the few items they'd taken out the night before, and Aidan returned a short while later. He'd untucked the front of his shirt, forming a small basket in which he was carrying a sizable collection of fruits and vegetables.

"Breakfast is now served," Aidan announced while kneeling down next to Olivia. He dumped out a large quantity of raspberries and about a dozen baobab roots onto a small matted down section of grass. Daniel crawled closer and sat on her other side before grabbing some food. He quickly finished his portion of what Aidan had gathered and began putting on his pack. Aidan stood and followed suit while Olivia shoved her share of the roots into her pockets.

"What's the rush?" she asked, bending to pick up her pack.

"I'd like to get started before the day gets too warm," Daniel replied, stammering over his words in an attempt to sound normal. "I don't think we'll have as much shade today, and since we didn't go find any water to refill the pouches, we'll need to conserve it until we find a spring to refill them."

"Oh, okay," Olivia remarked and pulled on her pack. Aidan, standing behind her, gave Daniel a quick thumbs-up. Olivia fished the rest of her breakfast out of her pocket, pushed her way back through the bushes to the path, and followed Daniel northwest along the route back home. It was difficult to keep pace with the boys and eat at the same time, but she figured she needed the energy for another long trek.

The walk was monotonous and Aidan's mind wandered in the silence. He began probing the nearby woods for animal friends until he found what he was looking for. Aidan reached out to a young deer grazing a short ways off with its mother. He brought them both to the side of the path just north of where they were walking. Olivia gasped at the sight of the fawn and doe waiting at the edge of the trail.

She turned to Aidan.

"Can I pet them?" she asked eagerly. Her voice quivered with excitement and a smile played across her full lips.

"Of course," Aidan answered. "Just move slowly. I don't want to make the mother any more scared than she is already."

Olivia knelt down and extended her right hand, her palm forming a small cup under the fawn's nose. The deer dipped its head slightly and pressed its wet nose to her skin. Olivia giggled and placed her left hand on the animal's neck, petting it softly. It flinched at first, but then leaned into her touch as it became more comfortable. Olivia stared into its black eyes, sensing the intelligence behind them. She stood, careful to avoid alarming the doe who was watching her every move. Olivia ran her hand over the fawn's large ears and down its back, tracing her fingers between the white spots on its coat. When she finished, she gave the fawn a hug and slowly approached the doe.

"Thank you," Olivia whispered. "Your baby is beautiful." She again placed her right hand under the animal's chin so it could smell her. It nuzzled her right palm while she petted its muscular back with her left. She turned to Aidan, positively beaming with joy. "Thank you too. I really enjoyed this. They're incredible." She gave the doe one last caress before stepping back onto the path. The two deer bounced off through the bushes and vanished into the trees. Olivia grabbed Aidan and threw her arms around him, crushing him in her hug.

"Okay, okay." Aidan laughed when he finally escaped her clutches. "I'm glad you liked it. We better get going before Daniel scolds us for wasting time." Olivia glanced up the path to see Daniel standing with his arms folded across his chest watching them.

"You two done?" he grumbled.

"Yes," Olivia giggled.

"Good. Let's get back to it. There's still a long way to go."

Hustling after Daniel, Olivia turned her attention back

to Aidan. "So where's Custos?"

Aidan waved his hand off to their right. "He's over there searching for food. I sent him farther away so the deer wouldn't get scared."

"How come I haven't seen him yet?" Olivia asked. "Not much of a pet."

"He's NOT a pet," Aidan groaned. "He's just a friend of mine. He's one of the first animals I really connected with."

"So why isn't he walking with us?"

"Well, he is, kind of. He's just not walking on the trail."

"Why not?" Olivia asked, again searching the forest for Aidan's playmate.

"I thought he might, uh, scare you," Aidan answered. "So I asked him to stay away from us."

"I'm not scared," Olivia replied, puffing up her chest and raising her chin. "You can have him walk with us."

A grin crept across Aidan's lips. "Maybe later."

They hiked late into the evening, which fell quickly once the sun dropped below the peaks of the White Mountains. They stopped and ate a quick dinner before bed. As they laid out their bedrolls, Olivia and Daniel started at the sound of a snapping branch in the nearby woods.

"It's just Custos," Aidan commented, glancing into the darkness of the surrounding trees before lying down.

A large bear rambled out of the woods. Olivia gasped at the sight of the enormous creature strolling toward them. She froze in place, standing between her blankets and the small campfire they'd built. Custos shuffled slowly over to where she stood until his front paws stood on Olivia's bedding and he stood nose to nose with the girl. Olivia let out a high-pitched squeak when the enormous animal snuffled at her face, taking in her scent. Both boys laughed at the sound.

"C'mon Custos," Daniel chucked. "Don't scare her."

Custos sauntered over to where Daniel stood and groaned appreciatively when Daniel gave the animal a quick scratch behind the ears. After visiting with Daniel, Custos turned to Aidan and rose up onto his hind legs. He trudged slowly toward the younger boy and stood before him, front paws raised. Olivia gaped in awe at the nearly nine-foot-tall bear standing before her. It let out a terrible roar, and Olivia clasped her hands to her ears.

"Oh, now you're just showing off," Aidan laughed. He jumped forward and gave his friend a hug. The bear dropped its paws to the boy's back and purred. Not really the purring of a cat, but deeper, more primal. "All right," Aidan said, "lie down. You can sleep here with us tonight." Custos snorted and collapsed next to Aidan's blanket. Aidan sat down and leaned back against his childhood friend. Pulling the blanket over him and nestling into Custos's warm fur, Aidan smiled at the others.

"G'night."

Olivia dragged her blanket over to where Aidan and Custos lay. "Do you mind if I join you? You look pretty cozy there."

"Not at all," Aidan answered, patting the ground next to him. "Make yourself comfortable."

Olivia set up her bedding and dropped down next to Aidan. "Thanks, goodnight."

"Good night," Daniel murmured. "I'm going to put the fire out. It's warm enough, and I don't want to draw any attention to us." The other two nodded their assent, and Daniel snuffed the flames with a few handfuls of dirt.

It seemed they had just fallen asleep when the sun woke them up for yet another long day of traveling. Aidan would occasionally bring a different animal to the side of the path to break the monotony of the hike. Regardless, the long hours began to weigh on them all. The days seemed to grow longer and the walks harder as one day blurred into the next.

On the tenth day of their journey, the morning was unusually hot and humid. The air was thick and heavy, and they had all gotten a nasty collection of mosquito bites as they'd slept. Scratching at the bumps, they pulled their packs on and ate a meager breakfast as they walked. There was no breeze to cool them, and by the time lunch rolled around, they were all drenched in sweat.

"I've got to rest," Olivia groaned brushing her hair back

from her sticky forehead so she could see better. "And I need more water. I'm almost out." She lifted her pouch and shook it. The sloshing sound of the water let them know it was mostly empty.

"Me too," Aidan added. "We need to stop, and I have to get more to drink."

They spied a clearing through the trees just before noon and seized the opportunity to have lunch. Aidan sent Custos off to forage for food of his own.

Pulling off his pack and wiping the sweat from his eyes, Daniel told the others, "I spotted some fruit trees a ways back. I'll go back and get some for our lunch, and we can take some with us. No point in passing it up if we can get it."

"How far back is it?" Aidan asked. "Shouldn't we just eat, rest a little, and get moving again? We've still got a long way to go."

"It's only a few miles," Daniel replied. Daniel jogged across the meadow toward the path, taking a slightly shorter route back than the way they'd come. Approaching the edge of the clearing, Daniel stopped short, crouching as he slowly pulled his whittling knife from his belt.

"What are you doing?" Aidan called out. The younger boy and girl stood and started approaching Daniel's position. Custos stopped and raised his head, looking back toward the children.

Daniel waved them off and turned his head putting his index finger to his lips. The two younger children stopped and hunkered down as they scanned the tree line where Daniel stood.

Daniel looked back to the edge of the forest and at the collection of bones lying before him. He could see the trail not too far through the trees, but that small space was littered with bones of all shapes and sizes. The area was dim due to the foliage and thick hanging vines. Daniel's eyes searched for signs of danger. He could see nothing to explain the evidence of death before him. Still, the hairs on the back of his neck stood on end as he inched forward, his knife at the ready.

He stepped softly under the cover of the trees, carefully shifting some bones with his foot. He pushed a thick vine aside and peered farther into the gloom. Carefully, he tiptoed along, his eyes sweeping back and forth, searching for any evidence of what caused the graveyard that surrounded him. After finding nothing, he turned back to the others and shrugged.

"There's nothing here!" he called out.

"Uh, Daniel…" Olivia began. The vines hanging around Daniel had begun shifting and slithering toward him like dozens of snakes. Two grasped his feet and climbed rapidly up his legs to his waist.

Daniel jerked, but couldn't move as the creeper worked its way up his body.

"HELP!" he cried out, slashing at the vines. For all those that fell away, others found him. He tried to keep them from rising to his stomach and chest. He hacked and slashed. It was a losing battle. He could feel the vines beginning to squeeze. It was becoming more and more difficult to breath as one circled his chest and constricted. Daniel sliced at it. His knife caught it at an angle, pulling it from his hand, and it dropped uselessly to the forest floor just as Aidan plunged into the tree line.

Shifting to his bear form, Aidan swiped his powerful claws at anything that moved, opening a clearing for Olivia to make her way through. She screamed and her hands flew to her mouth. She stood in shocked silence at the scene unfolding before her. Daniel cried out as another vine snaked around his legs. Aidan looked back at her and roared before returning to the battle that held Daniel's life in the balance. Snapping out of her trance of disbelief, Olivia ran forward and followed closely behind Aidan until he reached the spot where the knife had fallen. More trailers from the plants dropped down around them, curling around their arms and legs in an attempt to capture even more prey. Custos came charging in with them, barreling this way and that and roaring ferociously as he, too, thrashed about.

Olivia sliced a vine that held her foot and lashed out at one of the many that were slowly strangling Daniel. Hacking through the highest one, Olivia heard Daniel gasp for air as the pressure on his chest was released. She worked her way slowly down his body while Aidan and Custos stormed around the area shredding any vegetation that came within reach. Once Daniel was freed, he and Olivia stumbled back the way they'd come until they again entered the clearing. The two bears followed closely behind while the creepers withdrew up into the trees.

Daniel and Olivia fell to their knees panting and watching the edge of the forest for any sign that the plants were attacking. Aidan stood with them for a moment before returning to where they'd dropped their packs. He grabbed his bag in his powerful jaws and wandered off with Custos to transform back into his human self and get dressed.

"Thanks for helping get me out of there," Daniel said, standing and helping Olivia to her feet. "I thought I was done for."

Olivia nodded. "Assassin vines. I'd heard of them before. I just didn't think they actually existed. We can stay away from them now that we know what they look like. Just so you two know, I've been told the fruit is deadly too, so don't eat that," Olivia announced as Aidan rejoined her and Daniel.

"Oh, I'll stay as far away from those as I can from now on," Daniel replied as he pulled his water from his bag and took a long drink. Aidan gathered his shredded clothes, shoved them in his pack and dropped it next to the others. With a long sigh he sat down and leaned against Custos.

"Yeah, and let's stay away from anywhere that's covered in bones. Not a good sign."

The other two nodded their agreement.

"So what exactly happened back there?" Olivia asked, looking at Aidan.

"Sorry," he stammered. "I wasn't sure how to tell you about that. I can do more than communicate with animals. I can change into them too. It's not something I've ever told anyone."

Olivia reached out and patted his hand. "It's okay. I'm glad you did it. It surprised me, but it's super neat now that

I think about it. We wouldn't have been able to save Daniel without it."

Daniel gritted his teeth. "Okay, great. Thank you both again. I'm gonna go get some fruit for lunch," he said, dropping the water pouch back into his pack. "I'll just go back the way we came in. Be right back."

True to his word, Olivia and Aidan had barely sat down with their meat and biscuit when Daniel reappeared with an armload of apples. Dropping one into each of their laps and a few in front of Custos, he set the rest down next to their bags and retrieved his own lunch. Taking a bite of his apple, he sprayed juice everywhere when he announced he'd also seen a spring when he'd gone to collect the apples. "I'll take the pouches back after lunch and fill them back up." Knowing their water supply was ample for the time being, the group drank freely and enjoyed soaking up the afternoon sunshine while finishing their lunch and rehashing the encounter with the deadly plants.

"And yuck, they stunk!" Aidan said. "If we hadn't gotten out of there, the smell alone might have killed me," Aidan added, laughing and patting Custos's broad side.

"Oh, by the way," Daniel replied, "thanks for saving me back there, again. I was a little short earlier, but truly, thank you."

"No problem," Aidan answered. "What are brothers for?" He cuffed Daniel on the shoulder and got back to work on his apple.

Daniel tossed the rest of his half-eaten apple aside, grumbled under his breath and took off to get a refill of their water. Olivia frowned as she watched him go, suspecting he was unhappy about something. Again, he returned much quicker than Olivia could have anticipated, and he was barely breathing hard.

"Amazing," Olivia stated, forgetting about her concerns. He lifted an eyebrow and looked over at her.

"What?" he questioned. "Why are you looking at me like that?"

"It's just incredible that you can run that far, that fast, and not even be winded. It's really impressive."

Daniel turned away in an attempt to hide the hot blush now climbing from his neck up high into his cheeks and shrugged. "It's a gift. Sometimes it comes in handy," was all he replied as he knelt down with his back to her and began shoving the extra apples into his bag. He finished and slung his pack back over his shoulders before heading toward to the path. "Let's go," he called. Aidan and Olivia scrambled to their feet, grabbed their stuff, and chased after him. Custos stayed put and finished the apples that lay on the ground before him.

"I know we're in a hurry, but what's the big rush?" Olivia asked striding up next to Daniel. He glanced sideways at her, but ignored the question and kept walking. "Hey!" Olivia said, grabbing Daniel's sleeve and pulling him to a stop. "Don't ignore me," she scolded. "What's the problem?"

"Nothing," Daniel assured her. "I didn't mean to ignore you. I just want to get there, that's all. The less chatting and strolling we do, the sooner we'll get to your sister." Aidan hadn't stopped when he'd gotten to where Olivia and Daniel stood. He'd wandered ahead of them and now stood staring off to the east side of the path. Daniel glanced at his brother and realized that Aidan still had not moved. Walking up next to his brother, he grew immediately concerned by the look on Aidan's face.

"What is it?" Daniel asked, taking a step back, pulling his bow off of his shoulder and drawing an arrow from his quiver. Daniel scanned the forest looking for the source of alarm on Aidan's face. Seeing nothing out of the ordinary, he looked back to his brother. Aidan seemed lost in thought, his eyes focused not on something in front of him but on something or someone far away. Daniel poked Aidan in the arm. "Aidan, what's wrong?"

Aidan blinked, his eyes coming back into focus as he turned and looked at his brother. "They've reached the ocean," Aidan murmured, glancing to make sure Olivia was out of earshot. She'd moved off the path and stood with the rifle at the ready. Though she was too far back to hear their conversation, she sat watching the two brothers. Aidan looked back to Daniel. "I felt a large flock of gulls fly across the path north of us. They saw ships on the water. I think it's them. I don't know how Argyle could know already, but I guess he does. His men are on their way to Olivia's house. I don't think we're going to make it in time," Aidan whispered, looking nervously toward Olivia.

Daniel glanced back to Olivia who was now watching them with a quizzical look on her face. She'd dropped the rifle to her side when she'd realized there was no immediate threat, yet she seemed to realize something was dreadfully wrong. She looked to Daniel, her frightened eyes searching his for some clue to what the boys were discussing. Daniel's mind was filled with images of what would happen if they didn't reach Lilly first. Whether it would actually happen the way it played out in his head was impossible to know for certain, but Daniel couldn't risk it. If Lilly was going to be saved, he'd have to do it alone. That was the only way to reach her in time.

Daniel shrugged out of his pack, but kept his bow and quiver of arrows. "Take Olivia west toward the mountains. I'll get Lilly and meet you at the mouth of the cave at Slieve Gullion. You remember the spot?" he asked Aidan.

"Yeah," Aidan answered. "The place we used to go with Dad."

"If I'm not there by the day after tomorrow," Daniel continued, "you'll need to keep moving. I'll try to track you from there and catch up when I can. Keep Olivia with you. I don't want her panicking and trying to follow me. Understood?"

"Yeah, I get it," Aidan answered. "You should go. I can take care of Olivia."

Olivia, overhearing her name, left the bushes and approached them. "What's going on?" she asked. "Why did you take your pack off?"

"There's been a change of plans," Daniel replied. "Aidan thinks Argyle's men are on the way to your house. I'm going to go on ahead, get your sister, and meet you at the base of Mount Slieve Gullion. Aidan, can you handle my pack?" Daniel asked, looking back to his younger brother.

"We'll need it when I get back."

"I can handle it for this trip. I don't think I can take it much farther. If we have to move on, I'll leave it in the cave for you."

Daniel nodded his agreement. While they were making their plans, Olivia stepped to Aidan's side. Daniel turned to face her.

"How do I get to your house from here?"

"What?" Olivia asked, confused by the question.

"How do I get to your house? I need very specific directions."

"Why?" she asked.

"I just told you. Listen, we don't have time for questions," Daniel replied, struggling to contain his frustration. "Just tell me."

Frazzled by his curt reply, Olivia relayed the directions to her home.

Turning back to his brother, Daniel continued their previous conversation. "Okay, then. I'll meet you at the clearing in two days." He patted his brother on the shoulder, turned north on the path, and disappeared. Aidan picked up the large pack and slung it over his shoulder.

"C'mon," he murmured to Olivia, "we've gotta keep moving."

Olivia stared at him in disbelief as she realized what was happening. "What? We're just going to let him go by himself to face all those men? He can't fight them all! They'll kill him, and Lilly too. We've got to follow him." Olivia stomped back to her bag and picked it up. Slinging her pack over her shoulders, she pushed past Aidan and marched along the path.

"You can't," Aidan pleaded, grabbing her arm.

"I'm going to get my sister," she answered, pulling away from Aidan's grasp.

"You heard what Daniel said. We're supposed to meet him at the mountain."

"And I told you I'm going to help. He can't finish off the lot of them, not by himself."

"He's not going to fight them," Aidan tried to explain.

Aidan ran his fingers through his hair, struggling to find the right words to convince her. "He's going to run and get there ahead of them. He's not stupid. He'll get your sister and will probably be at the mountain before we even get there."

"He runs fast, but he can't run that fast," she yelled. "Nobody can. Not that far. Not that fast. We've got to follow him."

"No we don't, because he can," Aidan promised. Olivia stared at him, confused. "He can run that far, and he can run that fast. You remember when he said it was a few miles back to the apple trees?" She nodded. "You remember how fast he got back." Again, she nodded. "You remember that he was barely breathing hard?" She didn't even bother nodding this time. "That's because he really is that fast. He runs faster than you can see, and he can keep running for a long time. I know you're scared, but he'll make it. He'll run himself into the ground to make it."

Olivia eyed him suspiciously. "He told me you said the men were on their way to my home. How do you know that?"

Aidan shook his head and looked down at his feet. "I don't for sure. All I know is that I felt some gulls up north heading away from where your house is. They'd seen a boatload of men. I'm pretty sure it's Argyle's men. I wanted to be safe and make sure your sister got out of there before they get there." Aidan kicked a rock off the path and into the bushes. Looking back up at Olivia, he continued. "If he runs like I know he can, he'll arrive in plenty of time." He saw the look of relief on her face. "Do you think she'll believe him when he tells her what happened, why he's there?"

Olivia's eyebrows furrowed as she pondered the question. "I think so. If he tells her how we met, I think she'll believe him. How else would he know me, what happened to me?"

"Good," Aidan answered. "That's good. Then she shouldn't have a problem going with him. Daniel won't be as fast with her, but he'll probably try to carry her on his back part of the way. I still think he'll make better time than we will though. We need to get moving if we're going to try and get to the meeting spot before them. Once we get there, we can decide how to get away from Argyle's men for good."

Hesitantly, Olivia agreed. "Lead the way."

Chapter Eight

A Tough Road Ahead

Daniel's journey took more out of him than he'd anticipated. After running for three straight hours, he was forced to stop and find food. His body had consumed its entire energy supply, and he had to replenish it. Taking a break at a creek that fed the main river far downstream, he drank deeply and then spent an hour or so fishing. He built a small fire to cook the fish that he'd caught, and he lay down for a quick rest while his food cooked. The smell of the trout filled his nostrils, and his stomach ached in anticipation of the nourishment he so desperately needed. He watched the smoke drift lazily into the afternoon sky before dissipating in the calm air. When it was done, he sat up and ate the fish directly off of the stick he'd cooked it on, barely giving it time to cool. He almost choked when he missed a bone and swallowed it. After coughing and hacking for what seemed an eternity, it finally dislodged. Gasping for breath and wiping the tears from his eyes, he placed the fish down on a rock and returned to the creek for another drink and to refill his water pouch.

He dipped his cupped hands into the cold water and was bringing them to his lips when he spied a wolf across the river from him. It stood completely still but was staring directly at him. His eyes immediately scanned the rest of the tree line, searching for the pack he was sure would be there. Sure enough, he caught a glimpse of four more prowling among the saplings. They were moving toward him, pacing this way and that, their grey coats blending in with surrounding brush, only their movements giving away their positions. They slowly closed the distance that separated them from him. Having left his bow back by the campfire, he was unarmed except for his knife. He didn't want them getting close enough to use it. The food he'd consumed was digesting, replenishing his dangerously low energy levels, but it wouldn't be enough for him to travel very far before he used it up. At that point the pack would catch him and take him down more easily than the prey they normally hunted. Whatever he did, it would have to be soon and it would have to be close. He racked his brain for a plan, anything that would buy him some time for his body to refuel itself.

In the blink of an eye, he dashed back the way he had come, returning to his fire. His bow and quiver lay next to the smoldering sticks and half-eaten trout. Snatching his weapons from the ground, he darted to a nearby tree and quickly ascended. He could hear the pack closing the distance behind him. As he scaled the sturdy pine, he looked down to see the first of the wolves arrive at the base. Leaping into the air, it lunged for his right foot as he pulled it up to a higher branch, but in his haste, his quiver slipped from his hand and dropped harmlessly to the ground. Daniel heard the snap of the fangs as the wolf's jaws closed on thin air. Soon, the rest of the pack arrived, circling the base of the tree. He climbed to a safe height and sat down to rest. Although he wasn't breathing hard, he could feel the toll the brief sprint had taken on his body. He hadn't eaten nearly enough earlier and would need more food, and soon.

As the wolves continued pacing beneath the tree, growling and yipping, Daniel began to feel impatient. He was losing valuable time. He should be back on the path by now. The men were coming and a few hungry wolves wouldn't slow them down. Yet here he was, stuck in a tree with no apparent way to escape. His best weapon, his speed, had been taken from him by his lack of nourishment. There were still three more fish, not counting the half-eaten one still sitting by the fire he'd passed just moments before, but they did him no good. His bow was at this point useless, as his arrows sat twenty feet below him tucked neatly into his quiver. Daniel slammed the branch he was sitting on in frustration.

Below him, he heard a clunking sound in the brush surrounding the tree. Startled, he looked around, trying to identify the source of it for he was sure it hadn't been one of the wolves. He was embarrassed when he realized it was from a few pinecones he'd dislodged when he'd struck the limb on which he sat. Looking around him, he saw many similar cones open and waiting to do their part to continue the cycle of life. *Great,* he thought to himself. *Here I am, trying to save Lilly and my best defense is a pinecone.* He slumped back against the trunk of the tree. The wolves continued to pace, stopping occasionally to look up at him. A few had wandered off the way they had come. Daniel presumed they were going back to retrieve his unfinished dinner. Grabbing a nearby cone, Daniel began plucking absentmindedly at the scales. Then a seed dropped out and onto the leg of his pants. A small groan escaped him.

"Of course," he mumbled to himself. Quickly he began pulling the scales off of the cone and collected the seeds in a small pile on his leg. Then he grabbed another and another. He ate the protein-filled nuts as fast as he could pull the cones apart and gather them. Within twenty minutes time, he'd filled his stomach with the nutrient-rich seeds that had surrounded him the entire time. Then he sat and digested, using the spare time to fill a small pouch in his shirt with extra seeds.

Now for the hard part, Daniel thought to himself. Watching the wolves below him, Daniel waited for his opportunity. When they'd moved what he thought to be a sufficient distance from the base of the tree, Daniel dropped. When he hit the ground, his right food landed on the edge of a root that branched out from the base of the tree. He heard a loud pop as his ankle rotated out, his foot folding under as the weight of his body hit the ground. A loud cry escaped his lips before he could stop it. The wolves turned. Daniel grabbed his quiver and ran. His ankle screamed at him with every step, a lightning bolt of pain shooting up his leg, almost to his knee. He knew he had to push through or a lot more than his ankle would be hurting when the pack caught up with him. Although he didn't cover as much distance as he would have liked before again growing tired and being overcome by the pain, Daniel was well out of range of the pack by the time he slowed to a hobble.

The sun had begun to set over the peaks to the west, but Daniel needed to keep moving for a while longer. If he could keep going for a few more hours, he'd be able to rest, get some more food, and get to Olivia's sister early the next morning. The journey seemed much more lonesome now that he was reduced to less than a normal walking speed. Without Olivia and Aidan with him, the darkness was descending like a thick woolen blanket, and he felt the steady throb of pain in his ankle. With Aidan and Olivia, he could distract himself by talking to them or just watching their movements. Without them around, his mind drifted back to the night of his fourteenth birthday, and darkness settled upon him, as did the night.

A tree branch snapped nearby and Daniel looked up, startled by the sudden noise. Pulled from his thoughts, it took him a moment to spot the fox darting away into the cover of the forest. He wasn't quite sure how long he'd been walking, oblivious to his surroundings as he relived the events of that night. Not knowing exactly where he was, Daniel decided to make camp for the evening and regroup. He needed to rest, and he needed food if he was going to get to Olivia's house by the next morning. Leaving the deer path he'd been following, Daniel collected berries and nuts in the small amount of moonlight that wandered its way through the canopy overhead. As he began, he ate most of what he found, but as he grew full, he pulled his shirt out of his pants and began dropping them in the makeshift basket. After filling it, Daniel dug a small hole in the loose ground, and dropped his collection into it. Lying down next to it, Daniel fell swiftly off to sleep.

The next morning came entirely too quickly in his opinion. Feeling groggy and exhausted, Daniel tried to ignore the sunlight dancing across his eyelids, but his body was insistent that it was time to get up, even if his mind revolted. It didn't help that his ankle had become very swollen since last night, and his shoe was now uncomfortably tight. Pulling himself into a sitting position, Daniel grabbed a handful of berries and shoved them into his mouth. Juice squirted out the left side and dribbled slowly down his chin. Daniel wiped it away with the back of his hand as he looked around and tried to get his bearings. After pulling himself up into a standing position to get a better view, he decided he'd have to find a hill that would allow him a better grasp of his surroundings. He knew he was getting close, but couldn't afford to get lost. He'd wasted enough time already dealing with the wolves. He quickly shoveled the rest of the berries and nuts into his mouth, hardly chewing before swallowing them. He then shook out his shirt and pulled in on over his head. Knowing he'd need more nutrients than his meager breakfast had provided, Daniel took an arrow from his quiver, nocked it, and began his hunt. Without many humans around, the options were plentiful. He initially sought a deer, but he knew he wouldn't be able to eat even a half of it, so he put his arrow away and caught a couple of rabbits by hand. Normally it wouldn't have been much of a contest, but with his sprained ankle, he'd lost much of his speed and agility. Despite the pain, Daniel had finally chased down two of the slower ones. After cooking and eating them, he felt at least partially alive and began the rest of his trip.

Daniel continued north, following the deer path he'd left the night before, when he came to a rise in the terrain. At the peak of the hill, he was able to verify his suspicions. He was still a few hours from where the path split off to the east toward Olivia and Lilly's house. He would leave the forest soon and would be on the plains. Hopefully, there would be a nice cool breeze coming down off the mountains and he'd be able to make the rest of the journey without having to stop for water. He ran. Pumping his arms, he pushed himself as fast as he could. Occasionally a branch or twig would lash out at his arms or legs as he passed, but he ignored the resulting scrapes and scratches. They were nothing compared to the agony in his right ankle. When the forest ended, he ran through the open fields. The grasses churned lazily as he flew through them. The fork in the path was as Olivia had described, and he took it without hesitation. He pushed himself harder, using every ounce of strength and speed he had left in him. He'd be there soon.

Just keep going. Just to that hill. Just to that stump. Just to that old burnt out barn. His mind picked out objectives and his body obeyed until finally there it was. Olivia's house stood at the top of the next rise. Daniel could see the faint wisps of smoke curling up from the brick chimney on the back side of the house. In an instant, he was standing at the front door. Not wanting to look threatening, he took off his bow and quiver and leaned them gently against the house. Taking one last hissing breath through his clenched teeth to catch his breath and settle himself, Daniel tried to slowly rotate his foot. Not a good idea. He gingerly set his foot back down and turned to face the door. As he raised his hand to knock, he caught a whiff of the cornbread and bacon that was cooking inside. The ache in his legs and torment of his foot were immediately forgotten as his nostrils flared and his eyes closed. He took another breath, savoring the scents. Then he opened his eyes, squared his shoulders, and knocked.

Chapter Nine

Hurry

"Who are you?" Daniel heard a small voice from behind the door inquire. "Why are you here?"

"My name is Daniel. I'm here to take you to your sister. We've got to get going."

The door flew open. A pale girl with long dark wavy hair, much like her sister's, stood in the middle of the doorway.

"What about my sister?" she demanded. "Where is she? How do you know her?" Lilly may have been cautious at first about opening the door to the cabin, but she had immediately slammed the door back against its hinges and come outside when Daniel mentioned her sister. Although Daniel was a good foot taller than she was, Lilly lunged at him, grabbed the front of his shirt, and tried to shake him. "WHERE IS SHE?" she yelled.

"Calm down," Daniel replied, pulling away from the small girl. "She's fine. I'll take you to her, just relax." He'd stumbled a few feet backward in an attempt to create some room between them. "She's with my brother. We're supposed to meet them tomorrow night."

Lilly still looked suspicious. Closing the distance Daniel had tried to keep between them, she poked him in the chest. "How do I know you're telling the truth? She was taken by Argyle's men. Why would she be with your brother? Who are you? What have you done with her?"

Daniel looked at her, then at the house, and then back to Lilly. He stepped to the side, again trying to create space between them. "Look, I can explain everything. Can we go inside? I really need to sit down, and if it's not too much to ask, I could also use some food. I hate to ask, but it smells incredible and I'm starving." He edged slowly toward the open front door trying to draw her along with him.

"Fine," she grumbled. "But if you're lying to me, you're in big trouble."

I can imagine, Daniel thought to himself, smiling at the thought of being subjected to Lilly's wrath. She was petite, but he could sense in her that she could be quite scrappy if you wronged her. Following her slow but deliberate gait back into the cabin, Daniel scanned the horizon before shutting the door behind him. He crossed the room to the kitchen and sat down at the table.

"Thank you." Daniel began gently rubbing his swollen ankle. After a moment, a heaping plate of food arrived in front of him. Daniel eyed her quizzically as he picked up a fork and began shoveling food into his mouth. He noticed her eyes were a hazy gray, like the sky just after a heavy storm. He also realized she never seemed to look directly at him.

"Are you blind?" Daniel stammered, his fork frozen halfway to his mouth. "I mean, sorry, I..."

"Yes I am. Do you have a problem with that?"

"No," Daniel blurted. "No problem at all."

"Good, then finish eating. I know I gave you a lot so you don't have to finish it. You won't hurt my feelings." Lilly sat down and her head dropped. "I just keep forgetting she's gone, so I cook for both of us. I'm not hungry anymore, so I gave you most of what I made. There's a little more on the stove if you're still hungry after that," she offered, nodding toward the plate from which he was scooping large spoonfuls of eggs and thrusting them into his already full mouth. He took a sporadic bite of bacon and biscuit as he went. Lilly went to the kitchen and returned with a cup of water, which she gently set in front of him. Sitting down cautiously at the seat to his left, Lilly sat patiently while he ate. Although slightly self-conscious about his table manners, Daniel's appetite won out. After thoroughly cleaning his plate, Lilly took it and refilled it with the rest of the food from the stove. Again, she set it down in front of him and sat down. This time Daniel was more civilized as his hunger pangs had subsided. Slowly and methodically he cleaned the plate again, finishing with a happy sigh as he leaned back in his chair.

"Okay, now tell me," Lilly insisted, leaning toward Daniel in her chair. Daniel's eyes popped open, stunned by her frankness. "I've been waiting patiently. I sat quiet while you ate and got some time to rest. Now I want to know what you know about my sister. I want to know everything." She scooted to the edge of her seat, teetering toward Daniel.

"How did you know I was done?" Daniel asked, ignoring her questions for the moment to voice his own. "And for that matter, how did you know when to refill my plate?"

"I heard your silverware stop scraping the plate. I guessed that meant it was empty," Lilly replied impatiently. "It's not important. What's important is my sister. Go on, tell me," she commanded.

"She came to our house a couple weeks ago," Daniel began. "She was with Argyle's men when they stopped at my house to take me." Daniel hesitated, not sure how to explain the battle that had then taken place. His eyes darted to the window as he searched for the words, words she'd actually believe. "There was a fight, a very large fight," Daniel tried, wishing he could come up with something better. "Argyle's men lost, but your sister was safe. I found her in the woods outside my house and took her in. She stayed the night with me and my brother Aidan, and we set out the next morning to come for you."

Lilly sat shaking her head as Daniel spoke. When he finally paused, she stood up from the table. She pointed to the door.

"Get out of my house," she demanded in barely more than a whisper. "Get out now. You think I'm going to believe you and your family fought off Argyle's men? They came by here first, remember? I know how many there were, how big they were, how many swords and axes. I may be blind, but I'm not stupid. I don't care how many brothers and sisters you have. There's no way you fought them off. I don't know why you came here or what you want, but I want you out of my house, and I want you out now." Lilly had edged her way across the room while she spoke and now turned back with a fireplace poker in her right hand. "Now," she repeated, waving the metal rod from side to side in front of her.

"Whoa, wait a second," Daniel remarked, his hands coming up defensively in front of him. "I'm telling you the truth. I know it's hard to believe, but it happened." Daniel maneuvered himself so that the table was between them. "When did she get taken by Argyle's men? She showed up at my house almost two weeks ago, so my guess is that they got here about a month ago? Am I right? They took her almost exactly a month ago." Daniel saw a slight pause in Lilly's pursuit of him around the table and so continued. "She's got brown hair just past her shoulders, wavy, like yours, and brown eyes. She's about four inches taller than you." Daniel rattled off as many facts as he could as fast as he could remember them. "She was the first one taken." Daniel was practically shouting now in an effort to convince her of his sincerity. He didn't fear the girl. With his size and quickness, he could quickly disarm her, but he wanted to do this right. He wanted to do it without having to restrain her or accidentally hurting her. "You don't have any siblings. She was worried about you because you're all alone out here," he continued as he made yet another turn around the table. She paused. "I know it's hard to believe. Here, let me show you something. It might help convince you that what I'm saying is true, that Argyle's men were beaten." Lilly stopped.

"Show me?" Her brow furrowed and her lip curled up into a snarl.

"Would you set the poker on the table," Daniel asked as he backed away and across the room. "I'm going to move all the way over here as far away as I can get from you in this room, okay?" He knocked on the wall next to him so she could hear where he was standing.

Lilly frowned, but did as he asked.

"Now, I'm going to take the poker," Daniel told her. She flinched toward the weapon. "Wait." The sincerity in his voice stilled her hand with just her fingertips on the handle. "I just want to show you what I can do. Maybe then you'll believe me." Before she could reply, the poker was gone from under her hand and Daniel again knocked on the wall so she knew where he was. Daniel now stood with the iron rod back where she thought he'd been standing the whole time. "Now check again for the poker."

She leaned over the table, her hands moving swiftly to the four corners, searching for the poker. "How..." she trailed off.

"I'm really fast," Daniel replied, speaking softly and moving back toward her. He set the poker back down at the fireplace as he walked across the room. "My brother has special talents as well. I don't have time to tell you everything about them right now though. Argyle's sent another group of men. He knows something happened. They'll come here first, and I don't think they'll knock politely at your door. We need to get going," Daniel told her. "We need to get going now. I don't think they're very far off. We're supposed to meet Olivia and Aidan at the base of one of the mountains. If we're going to make it by tomorrow night, we need to hurry."

Lilly shook her head, seemingly to clear her jumbled thoughts. "Tomorrow? We can't make it by tomorrow," she mumbled, slumping down into one of the chairs. "That's at least a four-day walk."

"HEY!" Daniel shouted, trying to snap Lilly back to the moment. "Argyle's men are coming. Now. Let's worry about how fast we can travel later. We need to be gone when they arrive." Daniel walked over to the front door and opened it, searching the horizon for any sign of the mercenaries he knew were on their way. He returned to Lilly and lifted her gently from her seat. "You need to pack. You're not going to be able to come back, so pack everything you'll need. If there's anything you think Olivia would want you to bring, grab that too." He gave her a small push toward the back of the house. "Do you need help?"

"No."

"Then hurry."

Chapter Ten

An Early Arrival

While Lilly packed her belongings, Daniel grabbed his weapons and stood outside in front of the house, scanning the countryside in the direction of the Great Lake. He wished he had some sense of where Argyle's men were, how long they had before his warriors arrived at the tiny house. At that moment, he became aware of a puff of dust rising into the air to the east. It slowly grew closer, and it finally dawned on Daniel that it was the mercenaries. They had landed and were on a path toward the house, kicking up the dirt he was now seeing. While not positive exactly how long he had before they were banging down the front door, he knew they had to get out quickly if they were to avoid a confrontation. Daniel stormed back into the house.

"Quickly," he yelled toward the back bedrooms. "They're coming!" He rushed to the back of the house to find Lilly sitting on the floor of one of the bedrooms methodically rolling and placing her clothing into a pack on the bed beside her. Daniel was shocked at how little progress she'd made in her packing. "What are you doing?"

"I'm putting my things together," Lilly answered as she grabbed another garment from her drawer and packed it gently in her bag. "Why are you so mad?"

Daniel snatched the sack from the bed and scooped all the clothes from the drawer into it. "If you need anything else, grab it now. We're leaving."

"Who do you think you are," Lilly raged, rising to her feet and searching for the pack in Daniel's hand. "Those are my things. Don't touch my stuff!"

Daniel grabbed Lilly by the arm and dragged her toward the front door, snatching up the rifle that stood by the entrance along the way. "They're on their way here right now," Daniel told her. "I can see the dust rising along their path from here." As he pulled her across the threshold, he stopped dead in his tracks. They were coming all right and this time they were coming on horses. He could already make out the individual riders as they galloped toward the house. Lilly reached out to her right and grabbed a long staff that stood leaning by the door. Daniel pulled Lilly around the side of the house and started off through the long grass. "We've got to run," Daniel shouted at her.

Daniel ran next to her, his ankle again beginning to throb. It was currently only a minor ache, but he knew that it would soon be alarmingly painful. As they hurried away from cabin, Daniel looked back over his shoulder. He could now hear the heavy beating of hooves on the earth as the men approached Lilly's home. Lilly was having trouble, stumbling along next to him. Realizing he was pushing her to do something dangerous, Daniel picked up the small girl and ran as fast as he could. He had to get them out of sight before they realized she wasn't at home. The pain was excruciating. With every step, he was in agony. He gritted his teeth, knowing he had to keep moving. If he didn't, they'd see him, and if they saw him, they would eventually catch him. That was unacceptable and so he ran. He turned a little to the south as they could use the cover of the forest to slow down without risking being seen. He wouldn't be going in at the same place he'd come out, but he would need to stop soon, and so he headed toward the closest set of trees. It took him far longer than his run this morning. Of course this morning he hadn't been carrying anyone. Once safely in the forest, he set her down and sat, trying to catch his breath while rubbing his ankle. It felt like it was on fire and although pressing into the flesh hurt, it did so in a good way. Lilly, looking skeptical, sat down across from him and laid her walking stick on her lap.

"How do you do that?" she asked, cocking her head to one side as she asked.

"Do what?" Daniel replied, groaning as he found an extra sore spot on the outside of his foot.

"Move like you do," she clarified. "How come you can run so fast?"

"I don't know. I've always been able to," Daniel answered, trying to catch his breath. "Just a gift I guess. My brother has one too. It's hard to explain so I'll let him do it." He leaned back against a tree while digging at a nearby weed. After a minute, he pulled it up and began gnawing on the root. "Sorry, I'm eating some roots. I need to eat a lot when I run like that," he explained when he saw the questioning look on Lilly's face. After finishing up a few more that he'd spotted nearby, he beckoned Lilly. "Let's keep going. I don't think they saw us so I'm not sure if they'll be following us or not. We'll walk for now so I can rest. Let me know if you hear anything, okay?" Lilly nodded in agreement. She then reached out and took his arm and they set off. They stayed off the main paths in an effort to hinder the men's abilities to track them, if they even were trying to follow.

After a few hours, the two took a short break for lunch near a creek. Daniel put Lilly in charge of starting a fire while he hunted. He'd skinned and cleaned a small doe just as the fire began dying out, leaving the hot coals to cook over. Daniel hung some meat over the fire pit and the two went to get some water while the food cooked. Daniel also took the opportunity to do a little washing up as he was feeling a bit grimy from all the running and sweating. By the time they returned to the fire, lunch was ready. The two ate heartily, Lilly because she hadn't eaten all day, Daniel because he needed to replenish his body after yet another difficult run. When they finished, there was still quite a bit left.

"May I have one of your shirts?" Daniel asked as he began carving hunks of meat off of the carcass.

"What for?" Lilly responded defensively, pulling her pack close to her chest.

"We need to take some of this with us." Daniel cringed in pain as he stood and turned to face her. "We need food more than you need five shirts," Daniel explained. "I need the shirt to wrap the meat in." She pulled the bag closer and began turning away. "Unless, of course," Daniel added, "you want me to put the meat in your backpack with all of your shirts. I guess we could carry it that way, too, if that's what you'd prefer." He squatted back down next to the carcass and continued cutting. A small shirt soon appeared on the ground next to his left foot. "Thank you."

"Hmph," was her only response.

He tore up parts of the fabric and wrapped the meat securely. It wouldn't last long in this condition, but he didn't need it to. Lilly had wandered off ahead of him while he'd been packing up. Daniel hollered after her. "We need to make some better time. We're supposed to meet Aidan and Olivia at the base of Mount Slieve Gullion tomorrow. If we're not there, they're going to move on. It'll be harder if we have to track them," Daniel finished as he caught up to her.

"I know you're really fast, but do you really think we can make it there so soon?" the girl asked doubtfully.

"I don't know," he answered. "We're going to give it our best shot though. Let's walk until you're tired. When you can't walk anymore, I'll carry you. We can do that off and on until we need to stop for the night or we get there. Agreed?"

Lilly nodded. "Doesn't sound fair for you, but okay. Let's go." Lilly set her stick in front of her and grabbed Daniel's free arm. Daniel walked next to her and, given the uneven terrain, was moderately impressed at the pace she'd set and the rhythm she'd gotten herself into. He listened to the repetitive sound of her footfalls, to her measured breathing. She trudged along for quite a bit longer than Daniel would have first guessed she was capable. When she got tired, he carried her again. They tore through the countryside, now sticking to paths worn by the animals through the dense trees and brush. While Daniel would have preferred to stay off of the paths, he preferred to not hit a tree at full speed even more. Self-preservation won out. The day wore on and the sun began its descent behind the distant peaks.

Daniel suddenly pulled up short and almost dropped

Lilly. As he'd come to a small opening in the trees, he'd noticed a house standing in the middle of it. He'd been able to stop himself just before bursting into the clearing where someone would have possibly spotted him. The small log cabin seemed to sag, and he could see a few shingles stood askew along the roofline. Although no movement inside could be detected, Daniel didn't want to risk it. He had no way of knowing if anyone lived there or what their reaction would be to his and Lilly's arrival.

Setting Lilly down quietly, Daniel raised a single index finger to his lips. "Shhh. There's a house." She nodded her understanding. He leaned close to her and whispered for her to stay put while he checked the place out. Daniel handed her the rifle he'd taken from her home. She squatted down while Daniel moved closer to the edge of the forest. In the blink of an eye and a rustle of some leaves, he was standing at the side of the house, just to the left of an open window. The shutters were only partially open, which hindered his view, so he hunched over and crawled so he was directly underneath. He slowly raised his head until he could just see over the sill. After a quick scan of the room Daniel stood and yelled for Lilly.

"Come on out," Daniel shouted. "The place is deserted. It doesn't look like anyone's been here in years."

Lilly stood up and walked slowly to Daniel's side as he made his way around to the front of the house. The door stood open and they entered. A thick layer of dust had settled over all the surfaces of the room. The sunlight that made its way in through the windows and still open front door illuminated the dancing particles that hung in the air. It gave the room a very warm feeling, except that the place was a mess. Two square windows opened up on each side of the combination kitchen/family/dining area. Pushed back into the far left corner stood a small yet handsome dining table. Partially blocked by the table was a good-sized rock and mortar fireplace. It appeared to have gone unused for quite some time. Daniel grabbed a broom that was leaning against one wall and gave the dining table a quick swipe to remove most of the top layer before pulling it away from the wall and setting down the pack of meat.

"Looks deserted. I'll be back in a bit with water and some berries if I can find them," he called back over his shoulder as he walked toward the door. "Stay inside and out of sight." He closed the door behind him as he went.

Setting her bag down on the floor, Lilly moved around the room running her hand over the surfaces, locating the furniture with her stick and outstretched hands. As Daniel had pointed out earlier, it appeared the place hadn't been occupied in some time. There was more to it than that though. The mess gave the appearance the home had been left in some hurry. Whether the owners had packed up and left quickly or whether the place had been looted by one of Argyle's gathering parties was difficult to say. Lilly's opinion leaned toward the latter as even someone moving out in a rush would treat their property with a little more respect. Her opinion, but who knows. She closed drawers and cabinets as she worked her way through the room. She picked up a couple of the overturned chairs and set them next to the table. Realizing Daniel was out gathering food and water for a mid-afternoon meal, Lilly went in search of some dishes on which to eat. She found them soon enough and set them out on the table. Thankfully they'd been in one of the few cabinets that had remained closed, and the layer of dust had been mostly contained to the top plate, which she'd set aside.

Opening the package of meat, Lilly set most of it on Daniel's plate knowing he needed the food far more than she did. While she was hungry, the amount she took would be ample, assuming he found some other vegetation they could eat with it. Wandering around for a while longer, Lilly found nothing else that interested her, so she sat back in her seat, opened her pack, and started refolding the clothes that Daniel had so carelessly shoved into it. She was mostly finished when she heard the front door open. Daniel entered carrying two buckets. He set them gently on the table and sat down in front of his plate.

"Found these buckets next to the house," Daniel explained. "Figured they'd be useful. One's water, the other is whatever roots, nuts, and berries I could find on my way to and from the stream. I was hoping they'd have a well. No such luck." Daniel got up from his seat and started opening cabinets. He soon found what he'd been searching for and returned to the table with two cups. He dipped them each in the cold water and set them on the table. Lilly finished folding her clothes and turned back to her plate.

"Thank you," she said softly.

Daniel had already shoved a large piece of meat into his mouth. He looked up. "For what?" he managed to say as a little juice dribbled out of the corner of his mouth and down his chin before he could wipe it away with his sleeve.

"For dinner," she replied hesitantly, "for getting me out of there before those men came back, for saving my sister." Her look held him. She couldn't see his face, yet it felt as if she were looking into his soul. He could see in her a strength that far exceeded her small stature. "I'm still not sure what's going on exactly, but thank you for everything." Tears welled up in her eyes and rolled slowly down her pink cheeks.

"Don't thank me yet," Daniel retorted. "We're not safe here. Not by a long shot." He picked up another large hunk of meat and took a bite. With his other hand he reached into the bucket nearest him and pulled out an assortment of fruits and vegetables. "Dig in," he told Lilly. "With any luck, this will be the last long stop before meeting up with Aidan and Olivia." With that, Lilly started eating. The rest of the meal was quiet as both sat in silence staring at their plates, an occasional scowl or crease of the forehead crossing their faces.

"We'll stay here the night and head out at first light," Daniel announced after they'd finished their meals. Lilly was in no mood to argue and was asleep in one of the back rooms within minutes. Daniel wasn't too far behind.

With the morning mist still drifting dreamily through the trees, Daniel and Lilly left the house and followed a thin trail north. "How far is it?" Lilly inquired as she followed closely behind Daniel. She would have preferred to walk next to him, but the size of the path prohibited it. It may have once been wide enough for two to walk side by side, but the years of disuse had allowed the plants to grow back.

Daniel turned his head so she could hear better. "It's still a bit of a trek to where we're meeting them. I took the liberty to backtrack a ways when I went to get water. I wanted to check our trail. I don't think Argyle's men saw us, or if they did, they didn't care. I don't think they're following us."

"So?" Lilly inquired, wondering what relevance that had on how far it was to Mount Slieve Gullion.

"If they're not following us," Daniel explained, "then we don't have to hide as much. Now we can at least take the main roads and trails. That'll save us some time and effort. You ready to pick up the pace or do you need more time to digest?"

"I'm okay," came the reply.

Daniel quickened his stride. "You let me know if I'm going too fast and I'll slow down."

Lilly again fell into a steady rhythm as she walked. Daniel called out the roots and rocks in the path as they approached them and helped guide her around them. A few times she felt a stitch growing in her side. She took a few deep breaths and tried to not let the pain show. She didn't want Daniel to think she was weak, so she gritted her teeth and pushed forward while trying to take deeper, more frequent breaths to relieve the cramp. It soon passed and the two kept moving. After having alternated several times between her walking and being carried, they emerged from the forest and back into the plains. The mountains loomed ahead of them as they hurried toward their meeting place. They made better time than anticipated, eating as they went. As the sun fell behind the peaks and cast their path into shadows, Daniel set Lilly down.

"Almost there," Daniel panted. "We can walk the rest of the way." Daniel stretched out his back and shoulders and started walking again on the path they'd been following. Lilly wasn't sure, but it sounded like he was limping a little, favoring his right ankle just slightly.

"You okay?" she asked as she hustled to keep his pace.

"What?" Daniel asked, pulling his gaze from the snow-capped peaks of the mountains.

"Your leg," Lilly explained. "Did you hurt it?"

"What...what makes you think I'm injured?" Daniel stammered.

"I can hear your limp. Are you okay?"

"It's fine," Daniel replied. "I twisted it on the way to your house. It'll be fine, just a little tender." The fact was his ankle was killing him. It wasn't getting any better, and wouldn't as long as he kept punishing it with long runs, especially long runs while carrying someone. Hopefully I'm done with that, thought Daniel to himself.

Chapter Eleven

Reunited

Daniel and Lilly arrived at the designated meeting place as the last of the daylight disappeared and the moon took over the illumination duties for the evening. Lilly took a seat on a rock with the rifle resting on her lap as Daniel wandered around making sure they were alone.

At the base of Mount Slieve Gullion there was a cave. The entrance was where Daniel, Aidan, and their father had spent so much time honing Daniel's skills. Aidan had come along, not to watch Daniel, but for the opportunity to encounter new wildlife. These meetings allowed him to work on his gift as well. The clearing was unremarkable. It probably wouldn't have been considered as such had it not been for the time the three had spent there. Daniel's running, stopping, and starting again had beaten down what little plant-life there was around the mouth of the cave where the trees had not been able to root.

Daniel picked his way around the beaten earth noting the marks on the trees from where the arrows shot at him had missed. At the far eastern side of the clearing, he took off and dropped his bow and quiver and sat down. His mind wandered back to earlier, more innocent times. He closed his eyes and on the backs of his lids watched the games he and Aidan had played here. He could see his father sitting to the left of the cave entrance watching them and laughing at their antics. He could almost hear Aidan's giggles as the two traded jokes. His ears perked up when he realized that he could, in fact, hear giggles coming from the path he and Lilly had arrived on. Jumping to his feet, Daniel ran to Lilly and pulled her to her feet as Aidan and Olivia entered the glade.

The two girls initially froze. Olivia was staring at Lilly as she began moving as swiftly as she could across the clearing. Each of their eyes began welling up with tears. Aidan looked from one to the other trying to anticipate which would speak first. The two sisters screamed at the same time and ran into one another's arms, chattering away like chipmunks. Daniel looked to Aidan and his eyebrow raised as he tried to figure out what the girls were saying to one another.

"What?" he mouthed to Aidan.

Aidan merely shrugged and walked over and stood beside Daniel.

"Glad to see you here," Aidan said. He gave Daniel a little nudge with his elbow.

"What took you so long?" Daniel teased.

Aidan rolled his eyes and wiggled out of Daniel's pack. "This thing was heavier than I thought. You can have it back. I'm tired of carrying your weight," Aidan replied with a smile. He took off his bag as well and dropped it next to his brother's. "Anyone chasing you? Or can we just stay here tonight? I'm tired of walking and my back hurts."

"I backtracked on our trip here and didn't see anything. I think we can rest here for the night," Daniel answered as he picked up his bag and carried it toward the mouth of the cave. "We should set up our fire over here just in case," Daniel called over his shoulder. He dropped the bag at the entrance, then sat down absentmindedly massaging his ankle. Aidan brought his stuff over as well and knelt down next to him.

"What happened to your foot?" Aidan inquired, a frown etched on his face.

"It's nothing," Daniel lied, looking away.

"Let's see it."

"What's to see? I twisted it a little. I'll be fine," Daniel replied, looking back at his brother.

"Let me see it," Aidan repeated. "We need it to heal if we're going to keep moving. I just want to see how bad it is." Aidan thought back to Imogen, their mother, who had trained as a nurse when she was younger, back when schools had still existed. She'd passed on her knowledge to both of her boys despite their age. She'd been convinced that everyone in the family should know as much as possible about their bodies. Many nights had been spent pouring over her old books—hers and the new ones their father had been able to acquire for trade. It was a good thing too. She was gone now and they couldn't rely on her to take care of them. Aidan's heart felt heavy in his chest. Pulling himself back to the present, he swallowed the lump in his throat and knelt down in front of Daniel.

Daniel pulled up the leg of his trousers and pulled down the sock. "Satisfied?"

A deep blue and black bruise wrapped the entire circumference of Daniel's ankle making it impossible for Aidan to see where the wound originated. The swelling was not a good sign either. At this point, if Daniel took his shoe off, it was unlikely he would be be able to put it back on.

"Where does it hurt?" Aidan asked as he reached out and gently grabbed Daniel's foot. He fingered it gingerly, trying to locate any possible breaks. Daniel hissed through his teeth. "Right there I guess," Aidan said to himself. He continued examining Daniel's ankle, gently rotating it to see range of motion while pressing and massaging various places until he was at last satisfied. "Doesn't look too bad," he offered up at last. "Well, I take that back. It does look bad, but I don't think you broke it. I'll go get our dinner. You stay off your foot. That needs to heal." With that, Aidan walked away.

"We've got a little bit of meat left over," Daniel called after his brother. "It's in Lilly's pack."

Aidan raised his hand and gave a brief wave to acknowledge his brother's comment and kept walking.

Olivia and Lilly, having at last composed themselves, sat down facing one another where they had been hugging and talking. As Aidan approached the edge of the dell, Olivia called out to him.

"Where are you going?" she hollered.

"I'm going to find some dinner," he called back.

"Would you please come over here first?"

Aidan meandered across the clearing until he stood next to the two girls.

"Aidan, I'd like you to meet my little sister Lilly. Lilly, this is Aidan."

Aidan leaned down and offered his hand. "It's my pleasure. I'm glad Daniel got to you before Argyle. It's nice to meet you."

"Thank you. It's my pleasure as well," Lilly responded, putting her hand out.

Finally realizing why Lilly had moved so slowly across the clearing when he'd arrived with her sister, Aidan took her hand and gave it a firm shake, his eyes wide with surprise at what he'd missed.

"And thank you for saving my sister from those men. I'm still not sure how you and your brother did it, but I'm happy you did." She stood. "What can we do to help?"

"Don't worry about it. I can take care of it," came Aidan's reply, hesitant now that he knew of Lilly's disability.

"I'm sure you can take care of it," Lilly shot back. "I'm going to do my part here if that's okay with you. How about Olivia and I get firewood? We can build the fire and have it ready for when you get back. I'm sure you've figured out that I'm blind, but I'm not useless."

Caught off-guard by her forcefulness and with no support coming from Olivia who eyed him awaiting his reply, Aidan could only summon a one-word answer in response. "Fine," he mumbled and made his way into the dark forest in search of dinner.

When he returned, he found a comfortable fire waiting for him at the entrance to the cave. Not wanting to fill their shelter for the evening with smoke, they'd built it just outside for better air circulation. Aidan and the two sisters quickly prepared a stew with some of the leftover meat and the vegetables Aidan had brought back. At last, with dinner warming over the fire and the remaining meat drying nearby, Aidan, Olivia, and Lilly joined Daniel in the cave.

"Since dinner won't be ready for a little while," Lilly began, "I'd like to hear how you two saved my sister. I've never heard of anyone fighting off Argyle's men."

Aidan looked over at his brother. Daniel did not meet his gaze.

"Daniel already told me a bit of what he can do," Lilly continued, "but I don't think running fast is going to scare Argyle's soldiers away. What's the rest of the story?"

Again, Aidan looked at Daniel. This time Daniel seemed intent on picking at something on his pants and didn't seem interested in the conversation.

Aidan looked down at his own feet crossed in front of him. "I...I'm not sure how to begin," he stammered.

"Why don't I tell her my story, and then you can fill in the rest?" Olivia offered, seeing Aidan's unease. "Besides, this will be my first real time hearing it all too." Noticing the surprised look on Lilly's face, she continued. "That first night, after they saved me from Argyle's men, we talked. I think there's still more to the story that I don't know, so hopefully I'll get to hear the rest." Daniel flinched, but she went on. "I think we can talk about that tonight. I'd like to figure out what each of you can do." Aidan nodded his agreement so Olivia continued. She told the story of how she was taken from her home, chained, and marched across the countryside until she at last stood in the woods near the boys' home. She told of the sounds of the animals in the forest around her, the cries from the men, the growls, shrieks and snarls. She related the feel of the air swirling around her from the beating of unknown numbers of wings and the movement of large animals passing around her. She spoke of the sudden silence when the last of the men stopped screaming. Standing in the dark, she was sure that she would be next. Terrified, she stood alone, waiting to be attacked. That was when Daniel appeared and took her into his home, freed her from her chains, and tried to settle her down. Lilly sat dumbstruck through the whole tale. She didn't utter a word until her sister had finished.

"Wow," was all she could muster when her sister finally fell silent.

Olivia turned to Aidan. "Your turn."

"Why don't we eat dinner first," Daniel interrupted.

"The stew's ready, and if we wait for Aidan to finish, the vegetables will be soggy." While what Daniel said was true, Aidan sensed in the comment something more, a bitter edge.

He's probably just tired, Aidan thought to himself, and pushed up to his feet. "I'll get yours," Aidan told Daniel, placing a hand on his shoulder to keep him seated. "You need to stay off that ankle for now."

Aidan, Olivia, and Lilly cut the meat for dinner into smaller chunks, dropped them in the stew and filled the wooden bowls Daniel had brought from home before sitting back down in their previous spots.

They ate in silence for a while savoring the hot delicious meal. When everyone had had their fill, Aidan took the rest of the pot and dumped it at the edge of the cave.

"What are you doing?" Olivia asked. "That will attract animals."

"That's the point," Aidan answered and laughed as Lilly's eyebrows shot up. "I'm expecting a guest for dinner." Custos wandered out of the woods and lay down next to the pile of meat and vegetables, pawing through it and finishing off the scraps.

"Who is it?" Lilly asked. "Shouldn't you introduce your friend?"

Daniel and Olivia suppressed their snickers as Aidan led Lilly to where Custos was feeding.

"Lilly, I'd like to introduce you to Custos, my oldest and most trusted friend."

"It's lovely to meet you," Lilly stated. She extended her hand.

Aidan linked his mind with Custos's and prompted the animal to raise its large paw and drop it into Lilly's outstretched hand. Lilly jumped back and the others burst out laughing.

"What? What's happening?" Lilly shouted over the ruckus. "It's not funny!"

Both of the boys fell immediately quiet, ashamed, and the color rose in their cheeks. Olivia, on the other hand, only laughed louder.

"It is funny," she choked out. "You should have seen

your face." Olivia gasped for breath. "Custos is a bear. Aidan's gift is with animals." Olivia's peals of laughter finally petered out into giggles as tears streamed down her face. "That was priceless."

"Not funny," Lilly repeated, though Aidan could have sworn he caught a glimpse of a smirk play across her lips. "Anyway, it's very nice to meet you Custos." Lilly gave a quick curtsy and then turned back to where the others sat. When dinner and clean up were out of the way, and with Custos tended to, Lilly insisted that Aidan tell his portion of the story.

"Nobody outside our family knew about my gift until the other night. The night the men came to our house to pick up Daniel, that is," Aidan began. "Afterward, I told... or rather showed Olivia, so now I guess I should tell you. I don't want to scare you when I have to use it." Looking directly at Lilly, Aidan pressed on. "I can communicate with animals."

"No. It's more than that, come on, tell her everything," Olivia interrupted.

"Give me a minute... I'm getting there," Aidan said. "I can...influence their behavior." Aidan stopped when he saw the look of confusion on Lilly's face. "I can control them, if that's what you want to call it. I can get them to do what I want. It's hard to explain. That day last month, Daniel's fourteenth birthday, I knew Argyle's men would come. I couldn't let them take him away. He's the only family I have left." Aidan saw Daniel shift uncomfortably next to him. Still, he went on. "I spent the day gathering my friends. Every animal that I found in the area I sent back to our house to guard him. There were quite a few by the time I was done. I'm sorry I didn't tell you what I was doing, Daniel. I thought you might try to stop me." Daniel said nothing, just nodded slowly. "Daniel fell asleep in the house, and I snuck out through my bedroom window and climbed up onto our roof. All my friends were there. Bears, wolves, mountain lions, birds, bats, you name it and it was probably somewhere in the woods around our house. They waited with me, quietly."

Lilly was leaning forward, captivated by his every word. Olivia reached up and brushed a small curly lock of hair out of her eye, hooking it behind her ear, and whispered "Go on."

"When the men showed up at our house, I warned them." Aidan shook his head at the memory. "They didn't listen. I told them what would happen. I tried. You have to believe that."

"Okay," Lilly said calmly, trying to ease the anxiety she could hear the anxiety in Aidan's voice and encouraging him to continue.

Olivia was watching her sister, ready to deal with her reaction to what was coming next.

"They just didn't listen," Aidan continued. "They laughed at me. One of the men in front drew an arrow and shot it at me. One of my friends took care of it, but I knew we were in trouble and needed help. So… I changed forms."

Aidan waited to be sure Lilly heard and understood, but what he saw on her face was expectation. She was waiting quietly for him to explain, so he did. "Using my gift, I changed into a mountain lion and attacked Argyle's men." At that, Lilly gasped in total shock. "I'm sorry," he hurried. "Maybe I shouldn't have said anything. It's hard to explain to other people. That's why I've never told anyone until now. How do you tell someone that? How can I expect anyone to believe me? Even if they do, they'll think I'm a freak. We're all outcasts as it is. I don't want to be an outsider to the outsiders."

Lilly realized how distraught Aidan was and reached out with a calming touch to show she was okay. After a moment, he asked, "Are you sure you want me to go on?" Lilly nodded, so he pressed on. "We… the other animals and I attacked them. We didn't stop until they were all gone. All except one as it turned out." Aidan looked up, his eyes glistening. "They should have listened to me!" he shouted. "I didn't want to have to do that!" His hands curled into tight fists in his lap as he told the rest of his story. "When it was over, I came back to the clearing in front of our house. That's when Daniel came out. I told him about Olivia, how she was standing chained in the forest. He went to get her while I went inside to clean up and put some clothes on. When I came back out of my room, Daniel had started breaking the chains off. We told her a little about ourselves that night," Aidan went on, giving a small nod of his head toward Olivia. "I just didn't tell her everything. We left the next day to come get you, Lilly, before Argyle found out about it and sent more men," Aidan finished. He let out a long sigh and slumped back against the rock behind him.

"How?" Lilly asked. "How do you do it?"

"I don't know," Aidan mumbled. "It started a long time ago. I can get them to do what I want pretty easily. I've been able to do that for as long as I can remember. A few years back is when I found out I could change into them. I have to share water with them for that to happen though."

"You can control and turn into any animal you want?" Olivia inquired.

"Not any animal, just the ones I've shared water with. And I can't control werewolves. My parents told me it's because they are an abomination. I don't know," Aidan trailed off.

"Wow," Olivia exclaimed, casting a quick glance at her sister.

"Aidan," Lilly stated forcefully, "I just want to say that I don't think you're an outsider. You have a gift, and it helped save my sister. Thank you. If there's ever anything I can do for you, I want you to tell me. Promise?"

Aidan rolled his eyes. "Sure."

"Promise?" she insisted.

"Yes," he finally conceded.

"Good. Daniel, is there anything else you can do? I think you should tell us everything right now so we don't have any more surprises. Argyle's men will have some for us if they're still looking for us. Mom and Dad used to tell us stories about him. He doesn't sound like a nice man, so I'm sure he's still coming."

Daniel, who had been leaning back against a large boulder during Aidan's story, sat up straight. His right hand moved unconsciously to his ear and he started massaging it.

"Nothing you haven't seen already. I can move quickly. That's about it."

"Lilly can find stuff," Olivia interjected.

The two brothers turned and looked at her.

"What does that have to do with it?" Lilly asked.

"Well, we're talking about gifts, right? Lilly can find stuff."

The two boys turned their attention to the younger of the two sisters.

"It's no big deal," Lilly remarked, shy to the sudden attention. "She's making it sound important, but it's not."

"Am not," Olivia said defensively. "She doesn't go looking for an item when it's lost. It's like she's drawn to it. Growing up she always found things that had been misplaced. She doesn't go searching in drawers and under the beds. When you tell her what you're looking for, she walks right to it. It's like she knows. To tell a secret, I used to hide stuff just to see if she could find it. She did, every time."

Lilly's face fell into an open-mouthed gape. "You what?!"

"Oh, settle down," Olivia chortled. "It was all in good fun. Besides, maybe it'll come in handy."

"I don't get it," Aidan interjected, shaking his head. "Aren't you...well, blind?" he blurted out.

"I am," Lilly answered calmly, "but I'll still find anything you hide out there." A mischievous grin spread across her lips.

"I've got to see this," Aidan said, rising to his feet. "C'mon, get up!" he urged impatiently, pulling on Olivia's shirt sleeve.

Daniel was pushing himself up, favoring his injured ankle. "No," Aidan said, putting a hand on Daniel's shoulder. "You just rest and watch. Olivia, go grab one of Daniel's arrows. We're going to hide it. I want to see if Lilly can find it."

"You're kidding, right?" Lilly asked as she stood. "I was just teasing. We don't have to do this right now."

"Not at all. I want to see this," came Aidan's reply. "You wait here with your back to us. We're going to go hide it and see if you can find it."

"Oh, she'll find it alright," Olivia remarked as she returned with an arrow.

"Let's go then."

Lilly moved over and sat next to Daniel, her back to the cave entrance. "This is pathetic," she grumbled.

"He'll get over it," Daniel said with a smile. "He's just curious. He'll settle down when the novelty wears off." Daniel chuckled. "Don't be surprised though if over the next couple of days he's moving your stuff around just to watch you look for it." Daniel and Lilly chatted for a few minutes about nothing until the two others returned.

"Okay," Aidan announced, "let's see what you can do."

Lilly pushed herself up, grabbed her walking stick, and wandered out into the clearing. She shut her eyes, focusing her mind on the arrow. Aidan could see her eyes moving back and forth under her closed lids. After a moment, she opened them and started to the south tree line. She stepped over a log and dug her hand into a small pile of leaves on the other side. Aidan stood, his jaw dropped open, as she straightened back up with the arrow in her right hand.

"Amazing," was all he could muster as she swaggered past him and tossed him the arrow. He caught it with his left hand and turned to follow her back to the cave where Daniel sat. "That was incredible," he stammered as he sat down next to Lilly and opposite Daniel. "How do you do that?"

"I don't know," she replied. "How do you turn into an animal? I just focus on what I'm looking for and it's like I'm pulled to it." Lilly tossed a strand of hair out of her face. "It's always been like that."

"Amazing," Aidan repeated, shaking his head in disbelief. "I didn't think you'd ever find it, but you walked right to it."

The four sat in silence for a moment before Aidan spoke up. "So now what?"

Daniel shook his head. "I don't know." He looked to the two sisters as they, too, shrugged.

"No idea," Olivia responded.

"Let's figure it out in the morning then," Daniel

remarked. "I need to get some sleep. It's been a long day."

"I agree," Aidan replied. "Let me check out the rest of the cave to make sure there's nothing in there we don't want to sleep with, snakes and stuff," he explained seeing the confusion on the girls' faces. "I'm not very good with reptiles yet. They're...different. Then you three can get ready for bed while I throw some more wood on the fire. I'd like that meat to be ready by the morning so we can take it with us."

"Good idea," Lilly grunted as she stood up. "I'll take care of the fire though while you check on things. Olivia, why don't you give Daniel a hand." Lilly grabbed some wood and headed over to set the logs on the embers while Aidan went searching in the cave.

Olivia offered her hand to Daniel. He shook his head. "I can do it myself," he grumbled, trying to struggle to his feet. His ankle throbbed as he tried to put weight on it and he fell back down into a sitting position.

"I know you can," Olivia replied, "but I can help you too. You've helped me plenty already. Helping you stand and walk inside is the least I can do."

Daniel looked up into her face.

"Take it," Olivia ordered, again offering her hand.

Daniel gave in and grasped her forearm while she did the same to his. After pulling him to his feet, she wrapped his arm over her shoulder and helped him hobble slowly toward the entrance to the cave and closer to the fire just as Aidan caught up to them and Lilly wandered back.

"Nothing back there that'll hurt us," he announced as he grabbed the bags and hauled them over to where Olivia was assisting Daniel as he sat back down. The light from the fire cast an orange glow that penetrated into the cave only about ten feet. It was just enough to allow the three to see what they were doing as they moved their packs around and settled in for the night.

"Goodnight," whispered Olivia.

"Goodnight," came the chorus from the other three.

Chapter Twelve

A Bold Decision

The morning came in a flash, and Daniel woke to the sounds of Olivia, Lilly, and Aidan moving around the cave. His eyes felt like they had sand in them as he tried to rub the sleep out of them. He sat up and started massaging his stiff ankle.

"How's it feeling this morning?" Aidan asked as he repacked his bag.

"Sore," Daniel muttered, "but I can walk on it."

"Good," Aidan replied, sitting down across from Daniel. He called back over his shoulder to the two girls. "When you two are done over there, you wanna join us?"

After a few minutes of organizing their things, Olivia and Lilly sat down with the two brothers. "What's wrong?" Olivia asked as she sat down to Aidan's left, her sister across from her.

"Decision time," Aidan responded. "Where to now? We can't go back to either of our homes, so where should we go? What do we do?"

The four young outsiders looked at each other, glancing from side to side, waiting for someone else to speak first.

"We could go back to a house that Lilly and I stopped at on our way here," Daniel offered. "It looked like it had been deserted for a while. We could hole up there for a bit."

Aidan chewed his lip as he contemplated Daniel's suggestion.

"How long do you think we can stay there?" Olivia inquired.

Daniel looked over at her. "As long as we want, I would guess. I don't think the people who lived there are coming back anytime soon from the looks of the place."

Lilly nodded her head in agreement. "But..." she started.

"But what?" Daniel broke in, catching the stern expression on Lilly's face, clearly annoyed by his interruption.

"BUT, how long do you think we can stay there before Argyle's men find us? They're bound to come through there and if they do, do you think we can fight them off?"

Daniel was taken back at her bluntness. "Well, maybe they won't find us," he finally managed to reply. "There's no reason for them to look for us there."

"True," Lilly shot back, "but maybe they will. I don't think we can just hide and hope they don't come looking for us."

"What do you suggest?" Aidan asked, tossing a small rock into the air and catching it.

"I think we go there for a little while, just to rest up and let Daniel's foot heal. Then we leave."

"And where will we go from there?" Daniel grumbled.

"Then I think we should go fight."

The three others stared at Lilly, the same flabbergasted expression on each of their faces. It took a moment for Olivia to respond.

"WHAT?"

"I think we should go fight," Lilly repeated in a matter of fact tone. "Argyle's men have been coming out here and taking us as slaves for a long time, too long. I think it's time we fight back."

"How on earth do you expect us to fight Argyle's men?" Daniel stammered.

Lilly's eyes flickered in his direction before staring straight ahead of her. "The same way you did last time."

Daniel froze, his jaw clenching in an involuntary reflex. His eyes dropped to the dirt in front of him.

Olivia sat staring at Lilly, dumbfounded at her sister's suggestion.

"It could work," Aidan offered, giving Lilly a little wink of encouragement, forgetting that she couldn't see it. Lilly smiled and blushed anyway at his compliment. Aidan continued, watching the rock rise and fall in front of him.

"We could follow his gathering parties and ambush them," he suggested. "With the four of us working together, I think we could do it." Aidan turned to Olivia. "I saw you shoot back at the house. We could loop around and get in front of them. We could find a spot where they have to cross an open area. We could hide you at the far side, somewhere high up for a better view. You could do some real damage from a distance. I could do my thing with the nearby animals and with Daniel's speed he could move in and out of their group before they even knew what hit them."

"What about me?" Lilly asked, a little pout in her voice. "What do I do while you three are attacking them? Just sit by and brush my hair?"

Aidan was caught off guard by the question and only half mumbled a senseless answer.

"You get to help us find them," Olivia offered, picking up the planning where Aidan had been kicked off track. "We'll need your help to figure out where they are. Plus, you can reload for me. I'll be able to help a lot more if I can shoot, hand you the rifle, and shoot again." Lilly sat up a little straighter as she realized she would be able to be of assistance.

"Well, when do we leave?" Lilly asked, the excitement evident in her voice.

"Now hold on a minute," Daniel interjected. All eyes turned to him. "It's all fine and dandy that we got the best of Argyle's men once. I think it's a bad idea to go searching them out."

Aidan glared at his brother. "What do you suggest we do?" Aidan asked.

"I...I don't know."

"We can't go to the little cottage and hide forever. They'd catch us eventually. What, you scared?"

Daniel was on his feet in a flash and on Aidan before anyone else could react.

"Take that back!" Daniel screamed at the top of his lungs, pinning Aidan to the ground beneath him. The girls struggled to pull Daniel off.

"What? Was I right? What are you afraid of?" Aidan

answered, his voice rising in anger at Daniel's hostility.

Daniel punched him once in the face and was pinning his arms down again before Aidan could even suck in a breath at the sudden pain flaring across his left cheek. "Take it back," Daniel yelled.

"No." Again a flash of pain seared his cheek. Aidan could feel his eye beginning to swell. "You think hitting me will change anything?" he seethed, his anger rising with Daniel's. He knew he'd hit a nerve and pressed further. "You can hit me all day, but it won't change the fact that you're being a coward."

Daniel let out a bellow of rage and disappeared. The dust kicked up in the air lightly along the path that he'd followed and then settled gently back down to the earth. Aidan sat up and wiped his now bleeding nose with his sleeve. Both girls glowered at him with sour expressions.

"What?" Aidan asked, pushing himself to his feet. "Why are you looking at me like that?"

"Are you serious?" Olivia replied. "Why did you do that? He's your brother."

"Brother or not, we're better off without him if he wants to run and hide."

"NO," Lilly yelled. She reached out to find Aidan's arm and turned him to face her. "No, we're not. He saved me, and so I owe him. And he also has an incredible gift. We need that. In case you didn't notice, his gift can come in handy in a fight. I don't know what you look like, but it sounded like he punched you hard, and you're probably hurting a little. He can do that to them too. Now I don't know what your problem is, but you'd better fix it." With that, Lilly let go of his arm and fumbled around until she found her pack and a rifle. "Now let's get on the road to that house. Hopefully he'll meet us there when he calms down. You get to carry his bag since it's your fault he took off." Aidan mumbled something under his breath, grabbed Daniel's sack, and pulled the straps up onto his shoulders.

"What was that?" Lilly asked, turning and stepping close. "What did you say?"

"Nothing," Aidan answered.

"If you have something to say to me, say it so I can hear it. If not, you need to learn to keep you mouth shut, or I'll make you look worse than Daniel did. Understand?"

"Yeah, whatever," Aidan stammered, taking a step back, hand up defensively in front of him.

"Good, come on sis," Lilly called to Olivia who stood with her hands over her mouth, trying to hide the smirk that was curling up at the corners of her lips despite her best efforts.

Olivia picked up her stuff and joined her sister. "Let's go."

Olivia and Lilly stopped briefly outside the cave to pack the meat they'd left on the fire the night before. The heat from the fire had thankfully been sufficient to dry the meat properly, giving them a few day's worth of food if they needed it. The trip took them most of two days. They stopped a few times during the days to eat and to allow Aidan an opportunity to rest. Carrying the two packs had obviously started to take its toll on him given the pace Olivia was setting. He didn't gripe though, and no muttering could be heard. The breaks were for the most part silent, broken only by the sounds of chewing and swallowing and instructions as to who would gather what to eat or drink. They arrived at the cabin shortly before dusk on the second day, the dining room in the same condition Lilly and Daniel had left it previously. Lilly and Olivia began cleaning up while Aidan went to get a couple of buckets of water.

At the creek, Aidan took some time to undress and bathe. The water was cold and a shiver ran through his body. He was filthy so he jumped in anyway and gave himself a quick scrub. Washing his face took a bit longer as he cleaned off the dried blood from his nose and gently washed over the huge knot that had formed on his left cheekbone. His winced as the pressure of his fingers glided over it.

"Coward," he mumbled and climbed back out of the creek and onto the leaf-strewn shore. He stood for a while allowing the cool breeze to dry him off. He closed his eyes and projected his mind out, trying to find some of his animal kin. There was an abundance of wildlife in the area. He could feel them in his mind, moving around him. He was moving from creature to creature when he came across a frightened doe. She was being chased. She splashed along the banks of this same creek, farther to the west of where he now stood. He probed more. He sucked in a shocked breath when he realized what she was running from. It was a pack of werewolves and they were headed straight for him.

Aidan reached down and grabbed his clothes, leaving the buckets of water behind as he ran wildly for the cottage. The cramp that developed in his side was barely noticeable as the adrenaline surge pushed him forward, faster, harder. His feet slammed on the bare earth in some places, on thorny weeds in others. They didn't slow him down. Even the bristly shrubs that tried to catch at his thighs and shins barely registered in Aidan's thoughts. The only thing that bothered him was his eye. The swelling made it difficult to see, to judge distances. But he couldn't slow. He could feel the deer getting close. He caught a glimpse of the house through the trees and his heart leapt. The last hundred yards passed in a flash as he rounded the house and burst in the front door, slamming and barricading it behind him.

"Close and lock the windows!" Aidan yelled at the two stunned girls behind him. Aidan quickly pulled on his trousers and ran to a nearby window. As he shut it, he called back over his shoulder. "There are werewolves outside. They're on the trail of a doe and she's going to be passing by here any moment." He ran to the next and slammed it shut. The two sisters snapped out of it and started scrambling around the room securing shutters as Aidan was doing. Although the windows to the two small rooms at the back of the cabin were locked, they shut the doors to the bedrooms as well.

Aidan collapsed into a chair near the front door, sucking in air as fast as his lungs would allow. He felt like his heart was going to burst.

"Oh!" Olivia cried.

Aidan jumped up and scanned the room, looking for the source of her alarm until he realized she was looking at him.

"What's wrong?" Aidan panted.

"What happened to your feet? And your legs?"

Aidan looked down and saw blood oozing from numerous cuts on his feet. Thin lines of crimson had also started appearing and spreading on his pant legs. He sat back down in his chair and leaned his head back, trying to slow his heart rate and breathing.

"I guess I got cut up a bit. I, uh, didn't have time to get dressed before I ran back," he croaked, his dry throat making it difficult to talk. His blood rose into his cheeks as he continued. "Although you probably already noticed that when I came in." This time it was the Olivia's turn to blush.

"Won't they smell the blood?" Lilly whispered.

Aidan's eyes shot open. He hadn't thought of that. Of course they would smell the blood and that would bring them to the house. "Oh, no."

Aidan reached out to the doe, trying to track her progress through the woods. He found her soon enough, still racing along the creek. This time she was without pursuers. They'd stopped chasing her a short distance back. Still, she ran on, fear still driving her legs to keep going. Aidan pulled back and broke the connection.

"They smelled me," he told the girls, his eyes still closed. He opened them slowly. "I'm so sorry."

Olivia grabbed the rifle and started digging in her bag.

"What are you doing?" Lilly asked, hearing her sister digging frantically through her stuff.

"Daniel gave me silver bullets," Olivia replied, without even looking up. "Ah ha!" she exclaimed, pulling a small grey pouch out of her pack. She immediately started loading the rifle.

"You can't go outside," Lilly cried, grabbing at Olivia's arm.

"I'm not going outside," Olivia answered, pulling her arm away. "There are slots in the window coverings. It's not just to let light in." Lilly moved her hand to a nearby wall and felt her way to a window, inspecting with her fingers the cross-shaped openings Olivia had been referring to. "I can shoot through those. If I can see them, I can shoot them."

The three jumped when they heard the first howl from the approaching wolves. Olivia pulled the ramrod out of the rifle and moved to a nearby window. She set the end of the weapon in one of the crosses and waited. The three were absolutely silent as they listened for the sound of the pack.

A rustle in the woods outside alerted them to their arrival. Olivia pulled the butt firmly to her shoulder and readied herself. Aidan moved stealthily across the room and looked out the window opposite Olivia. After a moment, he turned his head back toward Lilly and murmured that the wolves were moving around to Olivia's side of the house. Lilly leaned over and whispered to her sister. Olivia nodded her head.

The blast from the rifle was deafening in the confined space of the cottage. Aidan's ears rang as he ran across the room and looked out another window.

"I missed," Olivia growled as she picked up her bag of silver bullets and dug out another. She tore open the paper with her teeth, primed the pan and dumped the remaining powder and ball into the barrel. She shoved the paper down in last and used the ramrod again to pack the bullet down. She again raised the rifle to her shoulder and slid it into the cross, searching for another target. Lilly slipped around her and pulled out another few cartridges to try and help her sister reload faster. Grabbing the other rifle, Lilly went through the same loading process Olivia had just performed. She dropped the ball in, but it didn't feel right so she dropped it back out and started over. After a few attempts she tossed the gun on the table in disgust and went back to standing by the window with Olivia.

"What's wrong?" Aidan asked.

"The shot is the wrong size for the barrel," Lilly replied. "She can't use that rifle."

"Great," Aidan mumbled. He stood by, watching and feeling helpless as Olivia shifted her stance to get a better view off to her right.

The next crack of the rifle was followed immediately by a loud yelp from outside. Aidan hurried to a nearby window and looked out. He couldn't see anything except a softly swaying bush at the edge of the tree line. He glanced over at Olivia who was already reloading. A small smirk rose on her lips.

"Got one," she announced. "He was poking his head out of the bushes when I saw him. He fell back when he was hit. How many more are there?" she asked looking at Aidan.

"I don't know," Aidan answered, shaking his head. "I can't feel them like I can other animals. I'd guess at least four or five based on the howls that we heard earlier. I can't be sure though. What can I do to help?"

"Why don't you take a look out those windows over there and tell me if you see any."

Aidan stumbled across the room after kicking a nearby chair and sending up a large cloud of dust. "I don't see anything on this side," he coughed, waving a hand in front of his face to try and clear the air.

There was a loud crash at the front door that shook the very frame. Both girls cried out and Aidan stumbled backward, catching himself on a bookshelf.

"What was that?" Lilly asked. A snarling from the front of the house answered her question.

Again the werewolf threw itself against the house. The top of the door splintered but held.

"It's not going to hold much longer," Aidan announced. "Keep your eye out for a target. Shoot anything that moves. I'm going to try to barricade the door."

Olivia was focused out her window again, weapon at the ready. Aidan pushed the table across the room and flipped it onto its side before pushing it against the door.

"Maybe they went away," Lilly whispered hopefully. There was another impact against the house and the table trembled. "Maybe not."

"Keep quiet," Olivia whispered. "Another one is creeping out from the tree line close to where the first one went down." Olivia let out a long breath and gently squeezed the trigger. Another cry indicated she'd hit her target. Aidan ran across the room and looked out. Sure enough, the werewolf lay about twenty feet from where Olivia had said she'd hit the other one. Two more moved slowly into the clearing, their muzzles twitching as they explored the scene. The larger of the pair, probably the leader, let out a long howl and charged back into the brush. The other followed. Aidan caught glimpses of three others as they joined the leader.

"Looks like they're leaving now," Aidan cried.

Lilly gave a little jump and pumped her fist in the air. "Yes!"

Olivia leaned the rifle against the wall next to her and walked slowly to a nearby chair. Her knees seemed to wobble beneath her and she collapsed into her seat.

"You okay?" Lilly asked, moving to her sister's side.

Olivia nodded. "I...I just need a moment. She looked at Aidan. "I was so scared."

"We're safe now," Aidan said gently, walking to her side and kneeling down next to her. He put his hand on her shoulder. "We're safe. You drove them off. Good job."

Olivia nodded as she took a couple deep breaths. "You think they're scared off for good?"

Aidan paused. "I think so. I don't think they're used to being hurt."

"Except by silver bullets," Lilly interjected.

"Except by silver bullets," Aidan agreed, looking up at the younger girl. "But I don't think they run into those very much. I think they're gone for good," he told Olivia, pushing himself back up to a standing position. "Excuse me for moment."

Aidan walked gingerly to one of the bedrooms and closed the door quietly behind him. Olivia's eyebrows raised in a silent confusion of what he might be doing, and she whispered her question to her sister. Lilly shrugged and started putting cartridges of silver bullets back in the small bag. Aidan emerged a few minutes later. Olivia noted a small figurine in his right hand that he massaged between his thumb and forefinger. He stood in the center of the room turning slowly in a circle, his eyes raised to the ceiling.

"It's hard to tell exactly where they are, but I think they moved off pretty quick. I get a few weak feelings from some animals north of here that I think might be the werewolves passing by. I'm not really sure. I'm also getting something weird from the west. I don't know. That's all I can get. If they were closer, I think I'd be feeling something stronger from the animals nearby."

"I guess that will have to do," Olivia responded, noting that Aidan seemed distracted, not completely focused on the location of the werewolves. "You think they're far enough away to risk going back down to the creek and getting our buckets of water? We really need to do something about your legs."

Aidan looked back down at his crimson-streaked pants and was about to answer when the front door exploded inward, tipping the table and sending it careening across the dining room floor.

Chapter Thirteen

A Cold Welcome Home

Aidan leapt forward at the sound, transforming instantly into a mountain lion. The girls cried out and jumped. Olivia reached for her nearby rifle. Aidan stood in the middle of the room, a low rumbling emanating between bared teeth, the hair on his back bristling on end, a torn shirt slowly swishing side to side around his furry neck. His nose twitched and he stopped growling. The doorway stood empty, only small leaves dancing into the room on a light breeze. Aidan's hackles settled back down flat, and he turned slowly around to face the back of the room. The girls' eyes followed his gaze.

"Daniel!" Olivia shouted. She ran across the room and threw herself at him. He caught her delicately in his arms and gave her a hug.

"What's going on here?" he demanded, his gaze locked on the large cat still standing in the middle of the room.

Lilly felt her way around the overturned table and closed and secured the front door as well as it could be considering the damage done to it. "Werewolves," she hissed between clenched teeth. "And then you almost scared me to death barging through the door like that."

Aidan grabbed his bag in his teeth, dragged it to one of the back rooms, and dropped it in front of the door. He let go and pawed at the handle. Olivia giggled nervously, let go of Daniel, and went to open the door for him. Aidan dragged the bag into the room and kicked the door shut behind him. A few moments later he appeared, again human.

"I should make you mend these for me," Aidan commented as he picked his pants up off the floor. He untied the small bag from a loop on his pants and tossed the torn clothing he'd been wearing before his transformation at Daniel. The clothes hit Daniel's arm, but he made no effort to catch them. Instead, he strode to a nearby window and looked out. Aidan stooped down, grabbed the figurine he'd dropped and slid it nonchalantly into his pouch.

"I heard the shots. I wasn't sure if you'd made it here yet or not." He was still facing away from them, but Aidan and Olivia could both see his chin drop to his chest as he continued. "I ran as fast as I could to get here. I thought maybe you'd been caught by some of Argyle's men."

Aidan let out a snort and stopped immediately at the vicious glares cast at him by the sisters.

Daniel turned and looked at Aidan. "I know you don't respect me, but you're still my brother. I wasn't going to stand by when I thought you were in trouble. I thought I was going to be sick on my way here, imagining what would happen if Argyle's men caught the three of you. From now on I'm going with you." Daniel held up his hand when he saw the smiles appear on the girls' faces. "Don't misunderstand me," he continued. "I still don't agree with your plan to attack Argyle's gathering parties. What's gotten into you?" Daniel asked, turning to his little brother. "You were angry and upset after they attacked you at the house. Now you WANT to pick a fight?"

Aidan dropped his eyes for a moment before looking up to meet Daniel's gaze. "I realized it's not our fight," Aidan answered. "This isn't our fight, it's theirs. I didn't want any of this. I didn't send Mom and Dad away. I didn't come to take you away, or Olivia. He did. Argyle and his men. They started the fight and they won't stop. The only way we'll be okay is if somebody stops him, but nobody's fighting back. It's up to us I guess. That's why I want to fight, to end it, to finally be safe."

Daniel shrugged. "I hope we can. I don't know if that's possible, but I'd rather go with you than sit out there by myself, wondering what's happening with you. It made me crazy today. I'm certainly not going to subject myself to that forever. I'm in. I'd rather fight alongside my brother than lose you."

Olivia jumped back into Daniel's arms and squeezed him tightly. Lilly shuffled over and gave him a hug as well.

"We're glad you came back," Lilly said softly. "It'll be better to have you with us."

The two girls turned icy stares toward Aidan. Olivia gave a small cock of her head to indicate he should say something.

"Yeah, I guess," was all he could muster as he meandered over to the front window and looked out. "I'm going to go back down to the creek for the water buckets. You two can tell Daniel about our adventures while I'm gone." He opened the door and cast a glance back at Daniel before closing it quietly behind him.

Once outside, Aidan sauntered around the side of the house and walked tentatively to where the closest of the werewolf bodies lay. Squatting down beside it, he tried to get any feeling he could from its lifeless body. If he could get any kind of unique feel for them, he could help the others steer clear of the wolves' paths in the future. Nothing. He got nothing from it. Neither good or bad. Disgusted, Aidan grabbed the hind feet of the animal and pulled it farther into the woods away from the house. Predators would not come for this feast, nor would any scavengers. He grabbed the other as well and dragged it to the same spot hoping it would be far enough away when the carcasses began to decompose. He didn't plan on staying for long, but he wanted those bodies as far away from the cottage as possible in case there was a hot spell in the next few days.

After wandering back to the creek, Aidan again took the plunge into its icy currents to clean off the feeling of filth he'd had since handling the werewolves. He scrubbed his hands pink in the frigid waters until he was at last satisfied he'd cleansed himself. He took his time putting his clothes back on, wincing as he pulled his shoes back on over his still oozing feet. He then filled the buckets with water and hauled them back to the cottage. He walked slowly as the last of the daylight had disappeared behind the mountains while he'd bathed. Tree roots and rocks marred the path he'd chosen, and he was forced to choose his steps very carefully to avoid spilling the water or twisting an ankle. *One gimpy traveler is enough,* Aidan thought to himself with a smile.

Daniel, Olivia, and Lilly looked up when Aidan opened the door. Lilly was telling Daniel about Olivia's shooting as the wolves attacked. Aidan placed the buckets next to the kitchen sink and sat down at the table with them to listen to the rest of her story.

"And then she got a second one!" Lilly exclaimed. "I didn't get to see anything obviously, but I could hear it. And then they all just went away! It was so exciting," she finished, a little out of breath at the recollection of the fight.

"It's a good thing you were here," Daniel said, casting a quick glimpse toward Aidan. "The girls never would have known they were coming if you hadn't gotten back here so quickly to alert them and lock the place down." His voice dropped to a grumble. "Good job."

Aidan shrugged, seeming to inspect something on the table in front of him. "They probably wouldn't have even come up this way if they hadn't smelled my blood. They would have just kept on chasing that deer and passed right on by."

"No," Daniel retorted a little too forcibly. He paused and collected his thoughts. Aidan looked up, his eyebrow cocked, waiting for his brother to continue. "They would have stopped for you if you hadn't run back. You saved yourself, and I feel pretty certain you saved Olivia and Lilly too." The girls nodded their agreement.

"You'd have been a goner for sure if you hadn't come back," Lilly added.

"I really don't want to think about that too much," Olivia said. "Let's just be happy that everything turned out okay."

"Agreed," Daniel responded, rising to his feet and slapping the table with an air of finality. "Now, Aidan, why don't you take one of the buckets of water back into that room with you. You can clean out the worst of your scratches with that. I'll go try to find some yarrow so they don't get infected. Olivia, would you and Lilly unpack the bags. I think we should stay here for at least a few days so we can heal and come up with a plan for our attacks. I'll be back as soon as I find something for Aidan's cuts." Aidan had already grabbed the bucket and was on his way to the room as the girls stood. Daniel marched to the door and opened it. "Block this behind me, just in case," he announced as he shut it. "I'll have to fix this tonight when I get back," Daniel noted, shutting the door and watching it swing back open. Olivia slid a chair under the handle after Daniel left and joined her sister at the table, pulling various items out of the bags and organizing them based on where they should go.

Daniel knocked on the front door just as the last few items were being pulled from the packs. Lilly set down the bullets from Daniel's pack with the others and tottered her way to the front door to let him in. He entered carrying a bouquet of small feathery white flowers.

"How's the unpacking coming along," he asked as he crossed into the kitchen and grabbed a small wooden bowl. He began grinding the flowers and stems of the plant into the bowl using a rock he pulled from his pocket.

"Good," Lilly answered. "We've got everything out. Now we're just working on putting it away.

"Excellent," Daniel replied. "Thank you for the help," he offered, looking up from the bowl. "I appreciate it."

"You're welcome," Olivia responded with a smile. "When we're done here, we should probably start thinking about dinner. It's getting pretty late."

"Yeah," Daniel agreed, getting flustered by her gaze and dropping his eyes back to the plants in front of him. "I had a hard time finding these in the dark. Let me finish with this, and I'll go back out and find some fruit. We still have meat left over from the other night, right?"

"Of course, it's right here," Lilly said. She ran her hands over the items in front of her before finding what she was looking for and picked up a large bundle from the table.

"Great. We'll have that and whatever I can find outside."

Daniel added a little water to his bowl and ground the flowers into a thick paste. When he finished, he took the foul smelling concoction to the closed bedroom door. He knocked gently. "I've got the yarrow for you," he announced.

"Come in," Aidan's muffled voice called back.

Daniel opened the door and stepped inside, closing the door behind him. After a few minutes, he and Aidan returned to the main living area. Olivia smirked at the smears of paste that now marked Aidan's exposed legs.

"Ha ha," Aidan remarked, knowing what she was smiling about.

"I like the new look," Olivia chortled. "Very zebra. Or, since you seem to be fond of cats, very tiger."

Lilly laughed out loud before clamping her hands over her mouth and sitting down, embarrassed by her outburst. "Sorry," she muttered.

Aidan rolled his eyes, but didn't respond. He just wasn't going to win this battle. Best to let them get it out of their systems.

"I'll be right back," Daniel announced as he left.

The three worked together and cleared their gear off the table, then set it for dinner. They'd also found a couple of full lanterns in one of the back rooms and brought them out to the table. Aidan fumbled with them in the gloomy room. After a few unsuccessful attempts, he finally managed to light them. They filled the room with a warm and welcoming glow. When Daniel returned, he grabbed a chair from the back room and leaned it against the front door to keep it closed while they ate. Content the door would stay put, Daniel dumped a small pile of berries into a bowl and set it on the table. "Sorry there's not much. I couldn't find them in the dark."

"It'll be fine," Olivia said. She reached for his glass and poured him some water. After she'd finished pouring for the other three, the meat made its way around the table, followed by the berries. "There," she announced. "A meal fit for a king, or queen," she added as she reached across the table, giving her sister's hand a squeeze.

The topic of conversation turned quickly to the events of the day, and Lilly again recounted the details of the attack and Olivia's shooting prowess. Aidan chimed in at times with observations of his own, but the majority of the speaking was done by the two girls. Olivia watched Daniel throughout the meal, sensing in him a growing frustration as the story unfolded. It wasn't anything tangible that he did. There were no clenched fists or jaws, no flared nostrils, just a general sense that something was bothering him. He sat, eyes on the table while he gently squeezed his earlobe between his right thumb and forefinger. Olivia realized he did that quite frequently, usually when lost in thought. She smiled at his little quirk and looked back to her sister. When Lilly was done with the story, Olivia quickly changed topics hoping to pull Daniel back into the conversation and out of whatever funk he'd fallen into.

"How about we play a game after dinner," she suggested. "Something to take our minds off of the stress of the day." Daniel looked at her quizzically. "I think I saw some games in the cupboard."

Olivia got up from her seat and crossed the room to the kitchen. She paused and looked over at Daniel before opening the cabinet. He'd dropped his head down and now appeared to be inspecting something in his lap. A scowl crossed Olivia's lips and she turned back to inspect the shelves.

"We've got Mancala," Olivia announced proudly.

"I'm done," Aidan quickly responded. "I'll sign up for doing the dishes. You two can take turns playing Daniel."

Lilly raised an eyebrow. "Why's that?"

"I think I may have beaten him once in all the times we've played that game together. I'd rather do the dishes and go to bed than have him beating me all night long." Aidan stood from his chair and began clearing the table of dishes. Lilly helped.

"Olivia, why don't you play first. I'll help Aidan and then I get to play the winner," Lilly offered.

"Sounds good to me," Olivia replied. She sat back down at the table across from Daniel. His mood seemed to have improved dramatically. A sly grin played on his lips as he took the board and small stones from the box. His eyes gleamed as he divided the pebbles among the appropriate cups.

"Ladies first," Daniel mocked, sweeping his hand over the table.

Olivia rolled her eyes and reached forward. Taking the stones from one of the cups, she started dropping them one at a time into the following indentations.

"Your turn."

Daniel grabbed a pile of his own and began plopping them into the bowls as well. Daniel was the first to capture a stone. Olivia frowned, but took her turn. Back and forth they continued until at last Daniel claimed victory.

"Good game," Daniel said, standing and giving Olivia a bow over the table.

"Thanks." Olivia stood and wandered over to the kitchen. "Your turn," she told Lilly. Lilly dried her hands and went to join Daniel at the table while Olivia stayed to help Aidan finish up.

"He's pretty good," Olivia said while grabbing a plate to dry. Aidan snorted.

"He should be. He's played it enough."

"Oh?" Olivia prompted. She tried to act nonchalant in the hope that he'd continue.

"Daniel used to play that all the time with our father, back before... back before our parents were taken." Aidan glanced over at Olivia and then back down into the sink. "They'd play it for hours, just the two of them." He shook his head.

"Didn't you ever play with them?"

Aidan finished rinsing the last plate and handed it to Olivia to be dried. Grabbing another towel from the counter, Aidan turned around and leaned back against the sink while drying his hands.

"I played every now and then," he answered, "but I didn't like it as much as they did. Usually I just read with our mother. Plus, when you lose every time, where's the fun?" He shrugged. "I still play with him every now and then, but not very often. It seems like he's getting better and I'm getting worse. Usually I just take it out when he's in a bad mood. Something to try and cheer him up." He glanced back at Olivia, then tossed the towel back onto the counter. "Well, I'm going to call it a night," he announced. "I'll share the room on the right with Daniel. You two can share the other. I'll go get it set up for you before I go to bed."

"I can take care of that," Olivia replied. "I'll take care of it while I wait for my turn again. Thank you though."

"Okay. Goodnight all," Aidan called back over his shoulder as he meandered to the bedroom.

"Goodnight," they replied in unison.

Olivia had barely finished making up the beds when Lilly came in to let her know that it was her turn. "He throttled me," Lilly huffed as Olivia passed her on the way out of the room.

The games continued late into the night, Lilly and Olivia taking turns being beaten by Daniel. Lilly kept her hand on Daniel's to feel where he was placing his stones and keep track of the pieces. That slowed the process some, however they both enjoyed the competition too much to stop. Some games were closer than others, but Daniel remained undefeated at the end of the night, a huge smile plastered on his face as they chatted and played. Things finally settled down and they decided to call it a night. Daniel put the game back in the cupboard and pulled out some tools to try and fix the door. The girls grabbed one of the lanterns and headed back to their bedroom.

"Goodnight, Olivia. Goodnight, Lilly. Thanks for the games. It's been a while since I got to sit down and play Mancala."

"Goodnight," Lilly answered through a yawn.

"Goodnight," Olivia replied as she walked to the back of the cottage. "Oh, and Daniel?" she said, pausing and turning to face him.

"Yes?"

"I will beat you."

Daniel smiled. "I look forward to it."

Chapter Fourteen

A Time for Healing

The next morning, Aidan awoke to the smell of bacon. The fragrant meat immediately caused his mouth to water. Rolling out of bed and pulling on his pants and shirt, he opened the bedroom door and shuffled into the kitchen. Daniel stood at the stove cooking breakfast. He glanced over his shoulder at his younger brother before turning back to flip a slice of sizzling bacon.

"Morning," Daniel remarked.

"Where'd you get the bacon?" Aidan asked. He pulled a chair over from the table and sat at the end of the kitchen counter. Daniel flipped another slice and pulled back with a hiss when the bacon popped and splattered hot grease on his hand.

"I went out this morning when the sun came up," Daniel answered, rubbing the back of his hand. "I found a wild boar and traded it to a farmer for some supplies. I figured we could use some food in this place if we're going to stay here for a few days."

"Sure smells good," Aidan commented before letting loose a tremendous yawn.

Daniel smirked and pulled a few pieces out of the pan and put them on a plate. He slid it down the counter toward his brother.

Aidan caught it at the end. "Thanks!" He hooked his hair with his pinkies and pulled it back behind his ears before picking up a slice, blowing on it, and shoving it in his mouth. It tasted as good as it had smelled. Aidan grabbed the other two pieces and sent the plate back down the counter to Daniel.

"Listen," Daniel murmured, dropping his eyes to the

stove in front of him and busying himself with cooking more bacon. "About our fight, I'm sorry I hit you."

Aidan swallowed his mouthful of bacon. "It's alright. I probably deserved it." Aidan pressed slightly on the bridge of his still swollen nose. "Besides, I think I look pretty good with a nose pushed a little to the left."

Daniel looked over at his younger brother. "Sorry, I just lost it. If it'll make up for it, you can get a few shots in on me. I won't even fight back." Daniel put the fork he was using down on the counter and stood, arms out to his sides, palms up in a defenseless gesture.

"Oh, cook the bacon," Aidan huffed. "I'm not going to hit you. I'm already in trouble with the girls for the things I said back there. What do you think they'll do if they come out and I'm hitting you and you're not fighting back? I'll tell you what they'll do. First they'll beat the heck out of me. Then Lilly will go find a pack of werewolves to bring back here. This time they'll lock me outside. Heck, Olivia might even shoot at me while I'm trying to get away. No, sir. I'm going to sit here and eat bacon if that's all right with you. I'm sorry for what I said. You're sorry for hitting me. Let's just move on."

Daniel nodded. "Okay. Here're a couple more pieces. When you're done, why don't you run out and refill the water buckets. I'll cook up the eggs and put out the fruit. We can have breakfast when you get back. Wake up the girls on your way out."

"Wait a second. First bacon, and now eggs and fruit? Where did you find all this stuff?"

"I told you," Daniel answered. "I got up early. I found the pig in the forest. There's a blackberry patch not too far north of here that I missed last night in the dark. The eggs are from the same farmer as the bacon. It's a ways off, but an easy enough run for me."

Aidan looked at him disapprovingly. "You'd better rest that ankle for a couple of days. You need it to heal, and it's not going to if you keep running around on it."

"I know, I know. I'll try and stay off of it today, now go get the water. And don't forget to wake Olivia and Lilly on your way out."

Aidan got up and slipped his moccasins on, then walked to the closed bedroom door. Pressing his ear to the door, he knocked lightly. "Time to get up," he called. "Breakfast is almost ready."

A muffled and sleepy voice called back. "Ugh, it's morning already?" There was the brief sound of creaking bedsprings before things again went silent. He knocked again. "Okay, we'll be right there." Aidan could hear the creak of one of the beds as someone's weight shifted. He heard Olivia mumble to her sister to get up.

Satisfied that they were getting out of bed, Aidan grabbed the buckets and started another trek down to the creek. When he returned, Daniel was serving up plates while Olivia and Lilly set the table. Aidan took the pails into the kitchen and grabbed some pitchers. After transferring the water to them, he took the pitchers to the dining table and set them down. Olivia and Lilly grabbed their plates, and Daniel grabbed the other two. He handed one to Aidan and sat down.

As the other three ate, Daniel picked at his food. "What's on your mind?" Aidan asked through a mouthful of eggs.

"Just trying to figure out how we're going to fight Argyle's men." Daniel replied. He dropped his fork with a clank and looked up from his plate while wiping his mouth on his sleeve.

"I don't think it'll be a problem," Aidan answered back, reaching over and grabbing some of Daniel's bacon, before shoving it into his mouth. "Lilly can probably find them. If not, I'll try to get a feel from the animals where they are. Once we find them, we'll fight."

"I don't think it'll be that easy," Lilly retorted. "Now that Argyle has lost one group of men, the next ones he sends out will be harder to fight. They'll probably be bigger and have more weapons. You took the first group by surprise. I don't think they're used to anyone fighting back. At least not anyone with your special gifts." Aidan's chest swelled while Daniel seemed to shrink in his chair. Olivia noticed the differing reactions, but Lilly didn't and so continued. "The next groups will be ready. They'll know something happened to the others, and they'll be extra careful."

Daniel nodded his agreement. "I think we need to put together several plans of attack, based on the different areas where we might find them. What if we don't have a good place to hide Olivia and Lilly? If we don't have cover for them, they'll be easy targets. What if there aren't many animals around? Your gift to turn into whatever you want will come in handy, Aidan, but we'll need more support to keep the men busy with diversions other than you and me."

Aidan looked like he'd been slapped. "I hadn't thought of that, any of that," he conceded. He pushed his plate away and sat back slowly in his chair, a frown creasing his brow.

"That's why we need to talk this out," Daniel responded. "If we all talk it through, we should be able to come up with alternative scenarios for whatever happens." Daniel finally started in on his breakfast while the others pondered what he'd said. Olivia and Aidan looked back and forth at one another across the small table while Lilly sat and quietly finished her breakfast. None of them seemed to have any answers to the problems Daniel had just posed.

"Do you have any suggestions?" Olivia asked Daniel after a minute of silence.

Daniel nodded his head and swallowed his mouthful of food. "I think we need to try and fight them on our turf. We can set traps for them."

"How are we going to do that?" Lilly inquired. "We'd have to know where they're going and get there before them."

Daniel shook his head. "Not necessarily," he answered. "We just have to get an idea of which direction they're headed and set a trap near where they're going. Aidan and I know a lot about the lay of the land all around here." Daniel saw Olivia's eyebrows rise up in confusion, and so explained, "Aidan's done a lot of flying and running around as different animals, and I've done my own share of running around these forests and hills. We figure out a good place to attack and bait them in."

"Bait them in?" Olivia exclaimed. "And just how are we going to do that?"

"I'll do it," Daniel replied. He could see the shock on the others' faces and so pressed on. "We'll find a location we can defend, with a place where Olivia and Lilly can hide and shoot, and where Aidan can bring in his friends to fight with us. Then I'll go out and bring them back." He could see the doubt in their eyes. "I'm the one with the speed. There's no way they can catch me. I'm not worried about them shooting at me either. They can't hit me. I'll run slowly enough that they can chase me, not catch me, and I'll bring them back to you three. Hopefully that will give us the advantage we need."

"I don't know if I like that idea," Olivia responded.

Daniel turned to face the older of the two sisters. "It's the best we can do," Daniel replied. "We can't send you or Lilly out as bait. We could send Aidan. He'd only be safe, somewhat safe, in one of his animal forms, so he'd have to change. They're not going to chase a mountain lion into the woods, but they will me."

Aidan nodded his agreement. "Daniel's right. He's the only one who can do it. And we'll need to search out our own places to fight whenever we can. It's our best chance of beating them."

"And what if they find us somewhere else, somewhere that we don't expect, where we haven't set a trap?" Olivia asked. "What then?"

"Then we run," Daniel answered. "We get out. I don't want to try and fight them when they have the advantage. Maybe Aidan and I can keep them busy while you two get out, or we can carry the two of you away. But I don't want to get into a fight unless we're the ones to initiate it. This is going to be hard enough, dangerous enough. We need to be as careful as we can. If that means we pass on a couple of fights, so be it."

Aidan opened his mouth as if to say something but then shut it.

"What?" Daniel asked.

"Nothing, forget it." Daniel stared at him. "Really, it's nothing."

Lilly spoke up. "Let's not try to figure it all out right now. Why don't we finish our breakfast and take the rest of the day to have fun and stock up our supplies? We can do all our planning tomorrow and the next day if we need it. Let's just enjoy ourselves."

Olivia coughed and cleared her throat. "She's right. No point in making things more serious than they need to be. I think we'll be stuck with serious soon enough."

Daniel and Aidan quickly agreed to Lilly's suggestion and finished off the last of their meals. They all helped clear the table, and Aidan once again volunteered for dish duty. None of the others felt compelled to argue. Instead, they each started in on various tasks around the cabin, cleaning, organizing, and looking through the trunks in the bedrooms. Lilly came out of the girls' room with a couple of books, and Daniel had discovered a few more games in his and Aidan's shared room. Lilly grabbed them and put them and the books in the cabinet with the Mancala game. Once the inside of the cabin was in order, they split tasks for the gathering of foods.

Daniel told the girls where the blackberry patch was that he'd found, and they headed off with Aidan and a bucket to collect them. Daniel went out searching for wild animals. He'd given up years ago on getting Aidan to use his gift for hunting. And so Daniel left the cabin carrying his quiver and bow in search of dinner.

Roughly an hour later, all had returned to the cabin and Olivia started in on preparing the meats Daniel had brought back with him. Combined with the remainder of the pig from the morning, they would have enough to keep them busy for a while. Aidan built a crude meat dryer out in front of the cabin to help with the process. Using some of the supplies left behind by the previous tenants, Lilly helped Olivia salt the meat while Daniel and Aidan took the prepared strips outside and hung them. When they finally finished, all four collapsed into their chairs at the table. Thankfully, the presence of the two werewolf carcasses not too far off seemed to keep the other wildlife away from the fresh meat outside, so only occasional checkups were necessary.

"I need a nap," Aidan finally murmured, pushing himself up and shuffling to the back bedroom.

"I could use one too," Olivia announced as she, too, left for the comfort of her bed.

Lilly turned toward Daniel, her right eyebrow raised.

"Go ahead," he prompted her. "I'm going to stay up and keep an eye on the meat. I might even go take out one of those books you found earlier."

"Thanks," Lilly sighed and got up. "Holler if you need anything."

Daniel got up from his chair and wandered over to the cabinet. Taking down whatever was on top, he pulled his chair up to the table and sat down. Setting the book out in front of him, Daniel flipped to the first page and began reading, growing drowsier with each page.

Startled, Daniel sprung from his chair when he heard a door creak behind him. Aidan, rubbing his eyes, stepped through the bedroom doorway. "What?" Aidan asked, puzzled by the reaction.

"Sorry, I just...did you nap?"

"Yeah," Aidan replied. "It was a good one too. How's the meat?"

"Uh, I haven't checked on it. I guess I got wrapped up in the story I was reading. Doesn't seem like you were in there for very long."

Aidan crossed the room to the front door and opened it. "Don't worry about it. I'll check on it. Go back to reading if you want." Not wanting to make too much noise and wake the girls, Aidan left the door open. Daniel sat back down and kept reading. When Aidan returned, he poured himself and his brother some water. Sitting down next to him at the table, he placed one of the glasses in front of Daniel. "What are you reading?"

"Just something Lilly found in her room," Daniel replied. He closed the book and pushed it toward Aidan. "Pretty good story about dragons and knights and stuff."

Aidan picked it up and gave the cover a quick once-over before tossing it back on the table.

"Any good strategies in there we can use?"

"Not unless we need to fight a dragon," Daniel replied. "And even then, I don't think a story book is a good resource for battle plans."

"Fair enough," Aidan chuckled. "But seriously, you have any ideas for our attacks on Argyle's men?"

"I've put a few together," Daniel admitted. "Certainly not as many as I'd like. It should cover the basic places I think I'd like to catch them though. Besides, they probably won't wind up being exactly the way I imagine them. We just need to put together plans for whatever we can think of and make up the rest when we get there."

"Fine with me," Aidan replied. "I just can't wait to find those guys so we can have some more fun."

Daniel slammed his fist down on the table hard enough that Aidan jumped at the sound. "We're not doing this for fun, Aidan. That's not what convinced me to come here. I'm doing this to keep the three of you as safe as I can. I'm doing this to stop other people from being hurt. It's time Argyle and his men answer for their actions. It's time someone puts a stop to his kidnappings. We might not be able to stop all of them, but we can certainly make their lives a bit harder."

"Whatever you want," Aidan sneered. "I just want to do some more fighting."

Daniel rolled his eyes. "Just stay focused okay? It's not just your life that's in danger when we're out there. You need to think about Olivia and Lilly as well."

As if on cue, the two sisters emerged from their bedroom. Olivia paused and stretched her hands over her head and bent from side to side, stretching her back. With a satisfied groan, she plopped herself down at the table across from Aidan.

"So…?"

"Just discussing our goals," Daniel answered. "You two ready to go over plans?"

"Not yet," Lilly called from the kitchen. "Give me a chance to wake up first." She grabbed a kettle and placed it on the stove. "Let me light this and warm up some water for coffee."

"I'll get it," Aidan offered, getting up from his seat.

"Sit down," Lilly answered. "I know where it is. I can get it." Disappearing out the front door, Lilly returned with some firewood. She quickly lit the stove and sat down with the others to wait for the water to boil.

The four sat and chatted about nothing in particular, Aidan making jokes and the girls laughing at his wit. After a bit, Lilly returned to the kitchen and poured herself a cup of coffee.

"Anyone else want one while I'm in here?" she called to the others.

"I'll take one," Daniel replied.

Lilly poured one more and handed it to Daniel on the way back to her seat, moving slowly and shuffling her feet as she maneuvered about the room.

"Aidan and I were just discussing the basic plan of attack. I have some ideas regarding different locations we could engage Argyle's men, but as I was telling Aidan, we'll need to be able to think on our feet. Nothing is going to go exactly according to plan, so let's just throw out different scenarios and talk them out. The more we discuss the different things that can go wrong, the better we'll be able to react."

The others nodded their agreement.

"Good, let's get started then."

The four sat around for the next few hours going over various strategies. Lilly showed a remarkable insight into the details of fighting. She played devil's advocate in most scenarios, asking questions about placement, maneuvers, and retreat lines that sometimes resulted in the others deciding that the original plan had to be completely reworked. They finally decided to break it up when their hunger started getting in the way of clear thinking.

"Let's pause for dinner. I can't do this anymore right now," Olivia groaned. "I'll start up some stew." With that, she stood up and marched over to the kitchen, grabbed a large pot, and placed it on the stove. Aidan joined her and began fishing various roots and vegetables out of the bucket the girls had collected earlier. As he washed and cut them, Olivia put some water in the pot and began her search for any spices that might be lingering around, assuming they were still good.

While Aidan and Olivia made dinner, Lilly and Daniel grabbed the Mancala game and set it out on the dining table for a quick game. Daniel beat her three times in a row before she called it quits.

"I can see why Aidan got tired of playing with you," Lilly grumbled.

"Sorry," Daniel answered. "I've just played it a lot. You'll get better the more you play."

"I guess." Lilly grabbed the pieces and shoved them back in the box. "I'm gonna go check on the meat." After stacking the game back in the cupboard, Lilly went outside.

"Smells good," Daniel commented.

"It's not much," Olivia replied, "but we don't have much to work with in here. It should be better than raw roots and dried meat though."

"If it tastes as good as it smells, it'll be wonderful. Besides, I'm starving. How long until it's ready."

"Shouldn't be long now," Olivia said, wiping her hands on a nearby towel. "Why don't you get the table ready."

Daniel grabbed some spoons and glasses and set the table for dinner. When he finished, he plopped down into one of the chairs facing the room.

Lilly came strolling back in from outside. "Meat feels good," she announced. "It'll probably be ready tomorrow."

"Good," Aidan called from the back bedroom. "Then we can get out of here and start going after Argyle's men."

Daniel frowned. Olivia looked at him quizzically.

"Aidan's been itching for a fight. I told him we're not in this for the sport, but it seems he's still as gung-ho as ever to go."

"I can understand why he's upset," Olivia replied, grabbing the large kettle and bringing it over to the table. "They came and took away your parents. They tried to take you too." Olivia sat down next to Daniel and put her hand on his knee. "He just wants to try and make things right."

"I think he just likes to fight," Daniel said, casting a glance to the back bedroom to make sure Aidan wasn't in earshot.

"Why don't you give him the benefit of the doubt? He's going to need your support out there. We all will. It won't do us any good having you second-guessing him all the time."

Daniel let out a sigh, straightened up, and looked out the window.

"Agreed?" Olivia asked. She squeezed his knee.

"Agreed."

Lilly set a pitcher of water in the middle of the table and sat down. "Come and get it!" she hollered to Aidan. "Would you grab the stew on the way?"

"Sure thing," Aidan called back as he came out of the room while tucking in a new shirt. He'd gone to change after slopping stew on the one he'd been wearing while helping with dinner. Aidan grabbed the pot from the stove and brought it over to the table. After Aidan finished dishing out everyone's meal, they all dug in.

"This sure beats what we've been eating lately," Aidan commented. "I've already gotten tired of berries and leftover meat strips. And the roots Daniel keeps bringing back make my stomach turn just by looking at them." Olivia started, and Aidan realized his mistake. "They're fantastic in the stew though, they just need some spice and to be softened up a bit." Olivia seemed to relax a bit so Aidan scooped up a few more bites and let out an exaggerated moan. "Delicious."

Daniel smiled to himself and went about eating his dinner until Lilly set down her spoon.

"Now that we've got some food in our stomachs, why don't we go over the plans again. If we can work out the details tonight, we can pack up tomorrow and be on our way."

"Absolutely!" Aidan replied, wolfing down the rest of his dinner. "I'm ready."

"Well I'm not," Olivia said. She lifted her spoon to her

mouth and blew on the contents. "We can wait until after dinner, when we're all ready to talk. Aidan, why don't you go get yourself another bowl?"

Aidan's shoulders slumped but he got up from his seat and crossed over to the kitchen. "I don't see why we can't talk and eat at the same time," he called as he scooped up a large ladleful of stew and poured it into his bowl. "Ouch," he exclaimed. He stuck his finger in his mouth and licked the spot where the liquid had sloshed over the side onto his hand.

"Didn't your mother ever tell you not to talk with your mouth full?" Olivia replied.

"Yes."

"That's why we can't talk and eat at the same time."

Daniel snorted and started coughing. He choked down his mouthful of food and took a few sips of water.

"Very funny," Aidan replied sarcastically as he returned to the table, setting his dinner down gingerly in front of him. Light banter between the four continued throughout the rest of the meal. Daniel wound up having thirds, partially to fill up and help him heal, but mostly to drag out dinner and irritate Aidan. By the time he was finished, Aidan was practically bouncing in his seat.

They talked into the wee hours of the night, going over every possible detail they could think of, addressing things that might go wrong, and what they could do to prevent, or at least recover from them. Having exhausted every possible angle they imagined as well as exhausting themselves, the four retired for the evening with the intention of spending the next day getting everything ready for their travels. They planned on heading out the day after.

Once again, Daniel made a scrumptious breakfast for the others. Dragging themselves out of bed to the smell and sound of popping bacon and coffee, they woke up quickly and filled themselves with hot, delicious food. When they were finished, the four scurried about the cabin getting their things in order.

Daniel took charge of the food, allocating everything among the packs. Olivia and Lilly retrieved everyone's belongings and, along with the food, began filling the packs, making sure the bags weren't too heavy for their intended carriers. Aidan mended his shirt and pants before getting to work on cleaning the various weapons, taking special care of the rifle taken from Olivia's home as it appeared to have been a long time since it had been cleaned properly.

"How long do you think it would take you to run back to the girls' house?" Aidan called over to Daniel.

"By myself? A few hours I guess, why?"

"The bore isn't quite the same size as ours. They probably have a ball kit somewhere in the house. If you can get it, we can make balls the right size for this other rifle. Our rounds are too small for her to get any accuracy with them."

"It's in a box on the fireplace," Olivia said, looking up from her work. "You okay to run on that ankle yet?"

Daniel rotated his foot around. "Feels good. Besides, we need it. Your gun isn't going to do us any good if we don't have any ammunition for it. I'll take my bow and quiver with me just in case, but I don't think I'll run into anyone I can't handle." Daniel also grabbed a handful of meat on his way out the front door. "I'll be back in a bit," and he was gone.

By the time Daniel returned, the three others were napping in their rooms, the chores for the day completed, bags packed, and weapons cleaned. Daniel dropped his weapons near his bag and went back outside to grab some wood for the fireplace. Aidan came out just as Daniel got the fire started.

"You get the kit?" Aidan asked. Squatting in front of the fireplace, Daniel glanced over and tossed it to him. "Nice. I'll go grab some utensils to melt down." Aidan scavenged the kitchen while Daniel stoked the fire to get it as hot as possible. Aidan returned carrying a handful of forks and a bucket of water. "Is it ready yet?"

"It'll do," Daniel replied, reaching for the tools.

"I'll take care of it," Aidan said. He pulled his hand back from his brother's reach. "You go get some rest, I can make the balls. Grab a bite to eat first though. You get crabby when you get hungry."

Daniel smiled and stood up. "There should be a bag of silver in my pack as well." Daniel saw the confusion in Aidan's face. "I grabbed some of our silver before we left, figuring we might need to make more silver bullets at some point. Melt some of it down to so we've got both types of balls for both rifles. No telling when we might need it."

"I'll make as many of both as I can with what we've got," Aidan said as he started putting together all the tools he'd need for the first part of the process.

Daniel stood in the kitchen, grabbing handfuls of vegetables and fruits from the baskets that had been collected earlier. He munched on them as he watched Aidan work. Daniel could see the years of practice in Aidan's technique. While Aidan hadn't ever developed much of a desire, or need, to learn how to shoot, he'd been the one in the house who had always been in charge of making the balls for the rifle. His process was so much smoother than Daniel could imagine his own ever being. While a treat to watch Aidan's graceful movements, Daniel retired to his room for a much needed nap.

Olivia and Lilly awoke not long after Daniel had gone to bed and sat playing Mancala while Aidan continued his work. When he finished, he challenged the winner to a game. Lilly wound up being his opponent. Aidan beat her in a quick game.

"You're good," Lilly said. She pushed away from the table and stood up.

"I've had a lot of practice," Aidan replied. "Not as much as Daniel, but I've played my fair share with him and with my father before he was taken."

"You have enough in you for one more game before supper?" Olivia inquired, sitting down in the seat Lilly had just vacated.

"If you want," Aidan remarked and began setting out his stones.

"Don't sound too excited," Olivia grumbled with a frown.

"Sorry," Aidan replied. "It's just been a long time since

I've really enjoyed the game. Losing every time will have that effect."

"Well cheer up," Lilly interjected. "You just beat me."

Aidan smiled. "Yeah." Looking up at Olivia, he offered, "Ladies first?"

Olivia picked up the stones from one of her cups and distributed them on the board. Aidan followed with a move of his own. Olivia watched him closely and could see the joy in his eyes as he placed his stones. While his game with Olivia lasted longer than Lilly's, Aidan was victorious once again.

"Guess this game isn't so bad after all," Aidan said as he collected the pieces and placed them back in the box.

"You'll play with us from now on," Olivia announced. "You don't need to play against Daniel if you don't want, but I think you should play with me and Lilly."

"Um. Okay," Aidan answered.

"I can tell you like it," Olivia continued. "You just don't like losing to Daniel all the time. I can understand that. From now on you play us, and we'll play and lose to Daniel. That way we all get to play."

Aidan shrugged. "Works for me."

"Good. Now let's get started on supper. Let's make it a good one since it's our last night here. Why don't you go wake up Daniel, since he knows where there's a farm nearby. Maybe we can get some milk and bread from them."

Aidan nodded and went to go retrieve his brother. After a few minutes, both boys emerged from the bedroom.

"You ready to take Aidan to that farm?"

"Sure. You want anything else while we're out?"

"I don't think we'll need anything," Olivia answered. "I'm going to make that stew we had. With some bread and milk, I think that'll be a pretty nice dinner." Lilly nodded her agreement.

"All right then. We'll be back in a bit." Daniel grabbed his bow and quiver on the way out. "Just in case."

With the boys out of the house, the girls got to work peeling and cutting vegetables for the stew. Olivia retrieved another bucket of water from the creek and set the water to boil on the stove. By the time the boys returned home, the cabin was filled with warmth and the delicious scents of cooking venison and spices.

"Wow," Daniel exclaimed as he walked in the front door, "that smells incredible."

"Mmmmm-hmmmm," Aidan agreed emphatically.

Daniel set two pitchers of milk in the middle of the table and Aidan pulled two huge loaves of bread out of a pouch and placed them next to the milk.

"How did you get all that?" Lilly exclaimed.

"We told them what we wanted and asked if there was anything they needed. They told us they were running low on meat, so I went out and got them a deer. A big meaty doe. It was a bit larger than I think they were looking for, so they gave us extra," Daniel answered. Aidan's stomach grumbled audibly. "I don't think we'll have a problem with leftovers," Daniel laughed as Aidan ran a hand over his abdomen.

Olivia and Lilly served up the bowls and brought them to the table. Each of them tore a large hunk of bread off the loaf and then poured a glass of milk.

"Here's to the start of our journey," Daniel said, raising his glass. "May it be swift, may it be safe, may it bring pain and discomfort to Argyle and his army."

"Here, here," Aidan replied, raising his own cup to Daniel's. The girls joined the toast and all drank. "Hopefully we can find one of his little parties soon," Aidan added and shoved a stew-soaked chunk of bread into his mouth.

Olivia saw Daniel roll his eyes and used her own bread to hide the smile on her lips.

Their last meal at the cottage was a joyous and festive one. Jokes were shared, stories told, and all the food eaten. When dinner was gone, Daniel and Aidan pulled out a surprise. At the farm, they'd also managed to procure a blueberry pie. While not the dessert of kings, it was more than enough for the four youngsters getting ready to set out on a perilous journey.

Chapter Fifteen

The Hunt is On

Daniel woke first the next morning and took the opportunity to straighten up the place as much as possible. The fire from the night before had burned down to ashes, which Daniel scooped into one of the buckets and dumped outside, then took the bucket down to the creek and rinsed it out. A quick dip cleansed and refreshed him, and he was anxious to get started by the time he got dressed and made his way back to the cottage. He dropped the pails outside where he'd first found them and went inside to wake the others.

Aidan was quick to get ready, once his sleep-fogged mind registered what day it was and that they'd be setting out in search of Argyle's men. He was in such a hurry that he almost ripped his pants when he tried to shove both legs down the same hole. The two girls required a few more attempts to get going. Aidan had resorted to threatening to come in and pull them out of bed physically before they finally got up and dressed.

A small, quick breakfast was had before they each grabbed their packs and weapon and headed out. Closing and securing the door behind him, Daniel turned to Lilly.

"Where to?" he asked.

Lilly walked a ways away, turning first east and then back toward the west. After only a few moments, she turned back to her companions.

"There's a group of them west of us. I can't tell which way they're going, but they're there. I can't feel them very well, so they're pretty far off I guess."

"We can take King's Road west until we reach Exile. Once we're there, maybe we'll have a feel for which direction they're headed and we can set up our ambush," Olivia offered.

"Let's go," Aidan exclaimed, turning to lead the way north to King's Road. The two sisters followed next with Daniel bringing up the rear.

It took them two full weeks to complete the journey to Exile, and while a night at the inn would have been nice after sleeping on the ground for so long, there was no money for it. The four young travelers passed by the run-down town and turned south toward their upcoming battle. Roughly a mile south of the city walls, they set up camp for the night. All were tired from their day's journey so no fire was built. They ate their dried meat in the dark, drank from their water pouches, and retired early.

An uneventful morning spilled into a monotonous and unseasonably hot afternoon. Drenched in sweat, the youngsters trudged south through the woods and prairies, the oppressive heat hunching their shoulders and silencing their chatter. Aidan, still in the lead, stopped suddenly at the edge of the forest. Olivia, who hadn't really been paying attention, nearly bumped into him. Lilly was pulled off balance by Olivia's sudden stop.

"Hey!"

"Shhh," Aidan shot back, holding up his hand and urging Olivia to stay back. Looking around him, she saw what had caught his attention. Her breath caught in her throat.

"What's going on?" Lilly whispered in her sister's ear.

Olivia whispered back. "There's a unicorn."

Daniel caught up, and as the four stood at the tree line, amazed at the sight before them, Olivia tried to describe the scene to her sister. On the other side of the small clearing stood a unicorn, black as night and majestic. Not wanting to frighten it off, none of them moved. None had ever seen a unicorn. None of them knew anybody who had. Olivia leaned close and continued to describe the magnificence of the creature to her sister. The unicorn was once a rare and magical beast. It had been so long since anyone had actually seen one that it had now become just a legend, a fairy tale being. However, in front of them now stood a beautiful ebony unicorn. Though its coat was black as night, the beast's mane, tail, and horn were a brilliant silver. The impressively large horn shone and sparkled in the afternoon sun. Something seemed to catch its attention, as it suddenly stopped grazing and snapped its head in their direction. It regarded them for a moment before returning to its meal. Apparently it didn't feel they posed a threat. Daniel nudged Aidan.

"Can you make a connection?" he whispered.

Aidan shook his head and looked back at his brother. "I tried. It's...it's like trying to look into the sun." He shrugged and turned his gaze once more to the glorious animal in front of him. A breeze caressed its way across the glade, the long grass swaying lazily, and the long mane of the unicorn rippled against its elegant neck. Aidan's eyes caught a shadow moving across the clearing. What a beautiful scene, Aidan thought to himself, pushing his damp hair back from his forehead and enjoying the feeling of the cool breeze on this face. His eyes moved back to the unicorn when the hairs on the back of his neck suddenly stood on end. Something was wrong. Aidan's eyes scanned the area, searching for the source of his anxiety. He saw nothing to cause the alarm he felt. Still, the feeling would not leave him. Replaying the moment in his head, he realized what had disturbed the tranquility of the scene. The shadow crossing the field had moved in the opposite direction the wind was blowing. Looking up, Aidan was alarmed to see a large dragon circling the clearing. As it made its final turn, it dropped in altitude, racing just over the treetops as it approached the field. Looking back down, Aidan could see the unicorn was oblivious to the imminent danger. The dragon shifted in flight, its back legs coming forward, razor sharp claws gleaming and flexing in the bright sunlight. Aidan took a step forward.

"NO!" he shrieked.

The dragon pulled up out of its dive as if it had been dealt a furious blow. Alarmed by the sound, the unicorn bolted into the cover of the nearby forest. Pulling up out of its turn, the dragon scanned the field below him until it saw them. A violent roar shook the trees around them.

"Run!!" Daniel screamed. He grabbed the two sisters and shoved them back into the forest. Aidan turned and ran with them, dodging through the thick brush that choked the pathway they'd followed on their way in. Daniel scooped up Lilly in his arms and disappeared in an explosion of leaves from the forest floor. Aidan ran behind Olivia, urging her on when a fireball exploded in the nearby trees. Raising his left arm across his face to shield himself from the blistering heat, Aidan pushed Olivia forward. She screamed but ran on, tears beginning to stream down her face. The small trail they were following forked up ahead, and Aidan reached forward and nudged Olivia to the right, trying to take them off the line they'd been following. Another burst of fire hit behind them just as the passing of the dragon overhead blotted out the sun. Still they ran. Olivia staggered and fell.

"Get up," Aidan yelled, trying to pull her to her feet.

"I can't," Olivia cried. "I can't run any more." She choked and gagged as she collapsed back onto her knees.

"We've got to keep going," Aidan insisted. He knelt down next to her. "We've got to get out of here before it comes back on another pass." He tried again to lift her to her feet. She slipped from his grip and retched into a nearby bush.

Embarrassed despite the danger, Olivia looked up at Aidan. "Sorry," she gurgled, wiping at her mouth.

Another screech filled the woods as the dragon flew close overhead, searching for his prey. Pulling Olivia under the cover of the trees, Aidan shrugged out of his pack, pulled off his shirt and shoes and transformed. Now a large bear, Aidan hoped the brown coat would conceal them from the vigilant eyes of their pursuer. Aidan stood over her, hunched down to minimize any of her skin or clothing that might be seen. Aidan heard the dragon fly by overhead, low and skimming the treetops, before stepping to the side. He looked at Olivia, and then to his back, then back to Olivia, beckoning her to climb on. It took her a second to comprehend his actions, but then she scrambled to him, grabbing his fur and pulling herself onto his broad back. She wedged her rifle across her thighs and bent forward over it, trapping it between her legs and stomach. He lumbered forward. Olivia grabbed large tufts of his coat and squeezed with her thighs to keep herself from falling off as he lurched along. Closing her eyes, she pressed herself tightly against the mass of muscle between his shoulders, curling around it for better stability. She could hear him panting hard, feel the expansion and contraction of his broad ribcage as he struggled to keep going at full speed. She was rocked forward when he suddenly stopped. Looking up, she saw the problem.

"Oh, no," she whispered.

Aidan stood at the edge of a ravine, the sides of which were entirely too steep for them to climb down. Turning left, Aidan plodded along. His pace had slowed and Olivia sat up to look around. She looked down at the lazy river below, flowing and gurgling in the same direction they were currently headed. Following its path, Olivia saw where it turned onto a new course not far ahead. Her breath caught in her throat when her eyes rose just above the lip of the ravine. The dragon they'd run so far to avoid was hurling down on them along the narrow gorge. Her intended scream never escaped her lips when another fireball erupted on the ledge next to them. The force of the blast threw Olivia from Aidan's back and into the trees as the riverbank collapsed beneath Aidan. He clawed at the loose dirt, trying to pull himself to safety before plummeting into the icy river below. He bobbed to the surface immediately, paddling toward the water's edge. Olivia scrambled on her hands and knees to a nearby ledge, ignoring the fact that the dragon may be coming around for another pass. She watched as Aidan drifted farther and farther downstream, approaching the bend.

Daniel appeared next to her, hands on his knees and out of breath. He dropped Olivia's and Aidan's bags at her feet. A piece of Aidan's shirt poked out of the hole at the top. "What happened?" he gasped.

Olivia couldn't speak. She just pointed.

"That's Aidan?" Daniel asked. He stood up and pulled Olivia with him.

Olivia nodded.

Daniel pushed her back away from the bank and into the cover of the trees and bushes. "You stay here until I get back, okay? I'm going to go get him."

Olivia nodded.

Daniel took off at a jog, following the embankment downstream and around the bend. Olivia sat down and put her head in her hands, overwhelmed by the events. *Where is Lilly? Is Aidan going to be okay? Am I going to be okay?* These questions and more raced through her mind until she finally broke down sobbing. She crawled further back into the trees and hid behind the largest tree she could find, somewhat for protection, but mostly because she was ashamed of her tears. All she could do now was wait. Wait and cry.

Chapter Sixteen

Wet dog

Daniel rounded the curve in the river and slid to a halt. He gasped for breath as he strode carefully along the ravine, the stitch in his side causing him to wince with each intake of air. The banks down below were now thick with bushes and low growing trees. He'd never be able to see Aidan in there if he ran, so he moved only as fast as he was comfortable that he'd spot his brother's bear form if it were down there. He grew fearful the farther he walked. The river current was picking up speed and boulders were beginning to litter the bed. There was yet another turn in the river a short ways down, and although Daniel couldn't be sure there were rapids down there, it sure sounded like it. A steady roar of rushing water could be heard, growing louder as he walked. *I wonder if he can turn himself into a fish,* Daniel thought. He smiled to himself as he made the next turn with the river.

His smile froze on his lips. It wasn't rapids up ahead, it was a waterfall. Daniel ran to the edge, his heart hammering against his ribcage. Skidding to a halt, Daniel looked over the side of the cliff. The waterfall cascaded down a sheer face of rock and crashed violently onto boulders below. There was no way to survive a tumble down those falls. Daniel swayed at the sight before turning and moving upriver, pushing from his mind the possibility that Aidan had been swept away. He moved much more slowly and methodically now, searching everywhere the light would let him. Large shadows from the thick overhanging branches obscured much of the riverbank. Frustrated, Daniel climbed slowly down his side of the ravine and moved gingerly along the thin edge, careful to avoid being pulled into the currents.

"Aidan!" he screamed. Nothing.

Impatient at how long it was taking him to canvas the shore, Daniel slammed his fist into a nearby tree. A bolt of pain shot from his knuckles, through his wrist, and up his arm. Cursing, Daniel shook his hand as if the injury could be flung off like dirt.

"I don't see how punching things is going to help me."

Daniel spun at the sound of his brother's weak voice. Lying about twenty feet away, half in and half out of the water, his brother struggled to hold on to a tree root. Dashing forward, Daniel grabbed Aidan's arms and pulled him the rest of the way onto the shore. Flopping onto his back and coughing up a mouthful of water, Aidan choked out his thanks.

"Don't mention it," Daniel replied. "You alright?" Aidan nodded. "Good, and good job keeping Olivia safe." Aidan turned his head toward Daniel. "She's fine," Daniel added, seeing the concern in his brother's eyes. "I left her back up where you fell off the cliff. What happened up there?"

Aidan rolled over and pushed up onto his hands and knees before reaching up for a tree branch to pull himself to a standing position.

"I didn't fall," Aidan objected. "We came out of the forest and started to follow the river. I didn't even see the dragon, just the huge fireball that exploded next to us. She got tossed toward the forest and the ledge crumbled under me. I got pushed around by the current a bit. Good thing I finally managed to grab that tree. I'm glad you got here so quick. My arms were starting to get tired." Aidan shook them out to accentuate his point.

"Me too," Daniel remarked. He gave his brother an affectionate nudge. "By the way, did you know wet bear smells worse than wet dog?"

"Ha-ha. Why don't you save your breath and go get me some clothes? I dropped my pack back on the path on our way here."

"I got it," Daniel replied. "I found both yours and

Olivia's packs on my way here. I grabbed your shirt and shoes too. Wait here a second. I'll be back with your stuff."

Chapter Seventeen

Back to Work

Daniel had come, grabbed the pack, and disappeared without a word. Frustrated, Olivia paced the woods, awaiting their return. She jumped at the sound of the approaching boys and sprinting out of the woods, she threw herself at Aidan. When Daniel hadn't stopped to tell her anything when he'd come back for Aidan's pack, her imagination had gotten the best of her.

"Thank goodness you're okay," she blurted out. "I thought maybe something awful might have happened. You are okay, aren't you? You look..." Olivia broke off as her nose wrinkled up. "What's that smell?" she asked, taking a step back.

Daniel burst out laughing. "Wet bear. Nasty isn't it?"

Aidan frowned. "Shut up. I can't help it. I'll wash later. Let's go get Lilly, and then I'll worry about taking a bath."

"Now that you mention it, where is Lilly?" Olivia asked, her eyes darting to Daniel.

"When the dragon was chasing us, I took her and ran her to a safe place just north of here. Then I came back for you two."

"Safe? Where is safe?" Olivia inquired, looking back and forth between Daniel and Aidan.

"It's a little cave by a tributary that feeds the Styx River," Daniel replied. "I figured the safest place to be is in water. This place is about as close as you can get without actually swimming. It's a bit of a hike. We should be able to get there soon enough though." Daniel's stomach rumbled. Embarrassed, he looked to Olivia. "I know now isn't the time to stop and eat, but may I have some of your food? I'm starving."

Aidan gently grabbed Olivia's arm and turned her around. Digging into her pack, he pulled out a handful of dried meat. "Ask and ye shall receive," he said. He handed them to his brother who immediately shoved an entire strip into his mouth.

The three set out swiftly along the path, letting Aidan lead the way lest he tire from his adventures in the river. It wasn't long before they came to his shredded pants littering the side of the path. Aidan scooped them up and shoved them in his pack, but not before untying the small pouch from one of the belt loops and transferring it to the pair he was wearing.

"What's that nasty odor?" Daniel complained.

"I don't smell anything," Olivia replied quickly, shooting a pleading look at Aidan.

"I don't smell it either," Aidan offered. Olivia let out a sigh of relief. "Let's get moving."

"Let's!" Daniel agreed. "It stinks. It's worse than Aidan. It smells like someone threw up. I can't believe neither of you smells that," he remarked. He pushed past Olivia and Aidan. "Between that and wet bear, I think I'll take the lead. Yuck!"

"Thank you," Olivia mouthed at Aidan as she fell in behind Daniel. Aidan gave her a small bow and smile as she passed.

"How long until we get there?" Aidan called from the back of the line.

"About an hour, maybe two," Daniel hollered back over his shoulder. "We can sit down for lunch when we get there, and then start moving south again. Unless you've had enough for one day and just want to stay there and move out tomorrow. It's up to you three."

"I think I've had about enough for today if everyone else is okay with that," Aidan grumbled.

"I agree," Olivia added. "Let's just get there, set up camp, and relax. Almost being blown up by a dragon is more than enough excitement for one day."

Daniel kept a quick and steady pace, and they arrived ahead of schedule back at the cave where Daniel had left

Lilly. When they rounded the corner and entered the cave, Lilly jumped up from where she was sitting next to a campfire. She stumbled and bumped her way across the cave to her sister and gave her a big hug before turning and finding Aidan to give him a quick squeeze as well.

"I was so worried about you two," Lilly exclaimed. "Daniel snatched me out of there so fast I didn't know where you two went. What happened?" Lilly's nose twitched. "And what stinks?"

"That's it," Aidan answered. "You three can set up things in here. I'm going out to take a bath and wash my clothes out." Dumping his bag on the floor near the fire, Aidan opened it up, dug out a fresh set of clothes and left the cave. "I'll be back in a little bit," he hollered back over his shoulder as he stormed out.

"What was that all about?" Lilly asked, confused by Aidan's outburst.

"He stinks," Daniel replied with a laugh. "Having you point it out again I guess was the last straw."

"That was him that smelled like that?" Lilly gasped. "He get sprayed by a skunk or something?"

"That's wet bear smell," Daniel replied.

"Wet bear?"

Olivia could see the bewilderment in Lilly's face. "Aidan turned into a bear in the woods when we were trying to escape the dragon. I couldn't run any longer, and he changed so he could carry me. We came to a river and started to follow it when the dragon found us. It blew a fireball, knocking me into the woods and Aidan fell into the river. Wet bear."

"Gross," Lilly replied, scrunching up her nose. The girls burst into a fit of giggles. The sound of their mirth put a smile on Daniel's face as he unpacked some food from his pack and sat down on a rock near the fire.

"Sorry it's kind of damp and cold in here," Daniel offered as he took a bite of jerky. "Comes with being in a cave on the river I guess. Hopefully the fire will help dry it out at least a little bit. We can all sleep around the fire tonight and not get too wet."

"It'll be fine," Olivia answered and sat down next to him. "I'll go collect some more wood so we can make the fire bigger. The more heat we have in here, the better."

"I'll go grab it," Daniel answered. He stood up. "Aidan's still out there bathing, so he'll probably be a little less uncomfortable if I stumble across him."

Olivia nodded. "Anything we can do here while you're gone?"

"Nothing I can think of. I guess get some rest. It's going to be a cold night, and we've got a long hike ahead of us tomorrow if we're going to find Argyle's men."

It took a while to find dry wood, but finally Daniel returned with an armload that would last until nightfall. He'd make another trip later with Aidan to get more for overnight. Entering the cave, Daniel saw that Aidan had returned, his wet clothes draped over the rocks closest to the fire. Sitting on the ground and leaning back against a boulder, Aidan smiled as Daniel dropped the wood.

"I feel like a new man," Aidan announced. "Nothing like a good scrub and some fresh clothes."

Daniel piled some of the wood on the fire, stoking it as he went. The girls announced they were going to go bathe as well and disappeared with their bags. When the flame was high enough, Daniel sat down next to Aidan. Aidan closed his eyes and enjoyed the warmth of the blaze before him. When he opened them again, he glanced over at Daniel. Sitting cross-legged, Daniel's gaze seemed far away, as if lost in another time or place. He fidgeted with his ear unconsciously.

"What's wrong?" Aidan inquired, leaning forward and grabbing his pack. He pulled out a sewing kit and began mending his torn pants, every now and then glancing toward his brother.

Daniel started and turned his eyes to Aidan. "I was just thinking about this afternoon, when we saw the dragon. I don't know a whole lot about dragons, but how did he hear you? He was still pretty far away when you shouted. His reaction was like you'd screamed right into his ear."

"I guess it heard me more with its mind than with its

ears," Aidan answered. He poked himself with the needle. "Ouch!" He shoved the tip of his finger into his mouth and sucked on it.

"You're mind can connect with it?"

Aidan shrugged and went back to sewing. "Not like I can other animals," Aidan responded. "It's strange. I could feel it, but I couldn't control it, connect with it. I think it felt me when I shouted and that's what scared it. I get the feeling it doesn't like to be scared," he said with a smile.

"Do you think you could make a connection with it? Is it possible?" Daniel pressed, ignoring Aidan's attempt at humor for the moment.

Aidan cocked his head to one side and glanced at the ceiling. "Who knows? I guess maybe. Not the unicorn though. I couldn't really get anything from it. I guess it's kind of like werewolves, just the opposite."

"Makes sense I guess. As much sense as it can when talking about controlling an animal's mind I mean," Daniel joked.

"Funny."

Daniel stood up and started digging through his pack. "When the girls get back, let's go get some more firewood. We need to get some water too." He pulled a small pot from his pack along with his water pouch and set them on top. Aidan pushed himself up to a standing position and dropped the pants he was mending on a nearby rock. The two brothers paced back and forth in the cave, anxious for the girls to get back so they could leave. Aidan collected his own flask and flung it over his shoulder. When they finally heard the sisters' voices as they approached the mouth of the cave, Daniel grabbed the pot and pouch and the two boys headed out.

"We're going to grab some water to heat up for dinner and some more firewood. I want to make sure we burn the fire hot all night," Daniel said.

"Give me your water pouches," Aidan added. The two girls dug into their packs and handed them over.

"Bring the water back first," Lilly called back over her shoulder as the boys headed off. "Maybe we can put something together for dinner while you're out."

The boys did as they were told and were met with a warm meal upon their return with the firewood. They all dug in, talking about the events of the day as they ate. When dinner was finished, Daniel ran the bowls down to the river for a quick rinse. Aidan found his clothes, the mending finished, and shoved them back inside his pack with the sewing kit.

"Thank you to whichever one of you finished mending my clothes," he said to the girls. "The pants were a mess, but I guess the shirt needed a bit of work too."

"It's the least I could do for saving me," Olivia replied. "Looks like it wasn't the first time that you've had to change forms while still dressed. Your shirt was more stitching than actual fabric," she giggled.

"Yeah, it seems like that's happening more and more these days," Aidan answered with a smirk.

Daniel returned and Olivia rekindled the fire, sure to put enough wood on to keep it burning for a few hours while the others set up their beds in a circle around the blaze. Darkness came quickly outside, a deep chill creeping its way slowly into the mouth of the cave as the night wore on, only to be turned back when Aidan, who was sleeping closest to the exit, tossed the remainder of the wood on the fire and drifted back into a peaceful slumber.

The morning arrived unnoticed by the four youngsters because the mouth of the cave faced west, so the rising sun failed to rouse them. It was midmorning by the time Olivia awoke, shivering. She sat up slowly and rubbed her arms in an attempt to warm her flesh. Seeing the embers burning dully in the pit, she grabbed the few twigs that Aidan had missed and tossed them in. Her rustling awoke the others though Lilly merely pulled her blanket tighter around her and rolled away from them.

"I'll get up when the fire's going again," she grunted.

Olivia walked outside into the crisp morning air, pausing as she went to stretch. She spent the next few moments grabbing what little dry wood she could find before returning to her friends. Once the fire was restored, they boiled some water for coffee. The heat and smell finally roused Lilly from her slumber, and she sat up to sip from the cup Aidan handed her, still wrapped in her blanket.

"What does today have in store for us?" Lilly wondered aloud.

"Just another long hike I hope," Daniel offered. "We didn't get as far yesterday as I thought we would due to our little encounter. It's not like we're in a big rush though. We'll close in on Argyle's men as fast as we can do it safely. Once we catch them, we'll attack when we can find a good spot. Doesn't really matter to me if that's two days from now or three." Olivia nodded her agreement.

"Sure wouldn't mind running into them today though," Aidan mumbled. He thrust a branch into the fire as if it were a sword and the flames a servant of Argyle.

"We'll have our hands full with them soon enough," Daniel answered. "No need to rush into it."

With their meager breakfast finished, they packed up and set out. There were no unicorns or dragons on this day to break up the dullness of the walk. What little chatter there had been that morning died out as the weight of the packs and their quick pace began to take their toll. They stopped only once for lunch, pressing south toward where Lilly felt Argyle's men to be. All four slept well that night before setting out for another day's journey. The morning was uneventful, but around noon things started to liven up.

"We're getting close," Lilly announced as they crested a small hill. The others stopped and gathered around her.

"How close?" Aidan inquired.

"I can't tell you exactly," she answered, "but I've got a really strong attraction to them now." She pointed down the hill, and the others followed the direction of her finger to a small road that ran southwest and disappeared in the distance. "If we keep heading that way, we'll run into them."

"I'm going to go take a look," Daniel announced, handing his quiver, bow, and pack to Aidan. "You wait here. I'll be right back." A slight breeze blew back Lilly's hair as Daniel flew past.

"I guess we'll wait here then," Aidan joked as he dropped Daniel's belongings on the ground at his feet before sitting down. "Let's eat as long as we're stopping."

Olivia, Lilly, and Aidan sat around, chewing slowly on their jerky and rinsing it down with water from their pouches. A cool breeze dried the sweat on their brows, and Olivia closed her eyes and raised her face to the warm sunshine. She inhaled deeply, enjoying the smells of the grass and trees that surrounded them. The pine scents were strong in the late autumn air.

Daniel's voice intruded on her tranquility. "It looks like we might have a chance to test out our skills this evening," She started at his voice, always flustered at how he could get so close before she knew he was even there. He stood, hands on his hips, taking a few deep breaths. After a minute he continued. "There's a group of men coming north about an hour ahead of us on this road, just as Lilly felt. They don't seem to be more heavily armored than the last group we encountered, nor does there seem to be any more of them. It looks like they may be on their way back to the castle."

"Maybe they're a group that was already out when you attacked the other group. They haven't had a chance to hear about us yet," Lilly offered.

"I think you're right. There were at least ten kids with them, chained together. We'll have to try and draw the men away from them so they don't get hurt."

"I can take care of that," Aidan interjected. The other three looked at him expectantly. "Not the nicest way to do it, but I can try to scare them off. We're not going to have time to chat with them," Aidan said defensively when he saw the frown on Lilly's face. "It'll get them to move and move quickly. I'll apologize for saving their lives later."

"Sounds like a good idea to me," Daniel replied. "They've almost reached the woods again. If we hurry, there's a place where the trail slips out of the trees and runs along the base of the mountains. I saw it when I circled back to get a better look at their group. We can set up there, get the girls up in the boulders while Aidan and I attack from the trees. It looks like a good spot for our ambush, at least the best place I could find in a hurry. It should work though. We'll have to move quickly to get there ahead of them and still have time to set up."

The girls and Aidan jumped up and threw on their packs. Aidan handed Daniel the rest of the meat he'd been eating as well as a few small pieces of fruit he'd grabbed during their morning hike. "You need this more than I do, especially if you're going to keep it up during the fight."

"Here's the rest of mine too," Olivia said. She handed a strip to Daniel.

Lilly shrugged and blushed. "Sorry, I finished mine."

"Thanks, this should be enough. Give me a second to eat, and then we'll go. I'll carry Lilly so we can move faster. Aidan, can you carry her pack?"

"Sure thing," the younger boy replied. He helped Lilly remove her pack and threw it over his shoulder.

With that, the four set out, moving swiftly along the path before peeling off to the west to try and pass the soldiers unseen. While not fast, the four traveled quite a bit quicker than their quarry, and they arrived at the ambush point well ahead of them. Scrambling up the mountainside while trying to avoid starting an avalanche, the girls soon found a nice perch that provided Olivia a view of the path through the trees, and clear, uninterrupted sight as it ran past them. Cover was provided by a small earthen rim that had been formed by water runoff. The shallow ditch completely concealed the girls when they lay flat, and even when squatting only revealed their heads. Lilly loaded one gun while Olivia took care of the other.

Aidan spent the time scouring the nearby forest, searching for as many animals as he could find. Given the circumstances, he recruited the big and small, figuring the larger the numbers, the more advantage they would have in the attack. Soon the forest was alive with the scurrying and plodding of hooves and paws.

"Reminds me of the night I met the boys," Olivia whispered to Lilly.

"It's kind of spooky," her sister replied.

"It was. Just wait until they get quiet. It's creepy now

knowing they're all lurking in there, but when it's silent, it's even worse."

As if on cue, the forest below them fell mute. All that could be heard was the rustling of leaves and the occasional clatter of a rock down the mountainside. After a few minutes, the low murmur of voices could be heard. The volume grew steadily as the group approached. Raucous laughter and angry shouts announced the arrival of the gathering party. Olivia peeked up over the lip of the ridge, watching the first of the men appear. She shifted her weight slightly to try and steady herself for a better shot, but her foot slipped out from under her. A pile of rocks was dislodged and went tumbling down the cliff. Ducking back down, Olivia cursed silently under her breath. Both sisters could hear the shouts below and the sounds of someone climbing toward them.

With the crash and a string of profanity that made Olivia blush, the man below them went sliding back down the mountain. Olivia poked her head back up and saw a man, bloody and dirty, pushing himself up to his feet. Another man at the back of the party was swinging his sword wildly at nothing in particular, turning to and fro, his eyes wild as they jerked this way and that. Olivia, suspecting Daniel to be the cause of the man's alarm, set the barrel of her rifle gently along the top of a flat rock and fired.

Screams and shouts erupted at once. The soldiers drew their various weapons as their eyes searched in vain for their enemies. Sporadically, one or two of the men would drop where they stood, no movement seen besides their bodies slumping slowly to the ground.

Olivia had grabbed the other rifle and was setting up for another shot when she saw an enormous mountain lion emerge from the woods between the men and the kids. It moved slowly and deliberately at the child in front, baring its fangs. Olivia could only imagine the growl that must have been emanating from its throat. She watched as the children began backpedaling, tripping over one another as they scrambled back the way they had come, pulling the slower ones by their chained hands. Aidan closed the distance, ensuring their continued retreat. Olivia cringed at the terror so evident in the faces of the children even though she knew that Aidan was doing what needed to be done to keep them safe. Still, it was hard to watch.

"Why aren't you shooting?" Lilly yelled at her sister. Olivia snapped her head around to see her sister offering her the next rifle, already loaded.

Focusing her mind back on the task at hand, Olivia was scanning the scene for her next target when she spotted two men with swords who had moved away from the main group and now were sneaking toward Aidan. Whether they suspected the mountain lion was something other than what it seemed, or they were just trying to get the children back, Aidan was in danger. Swinging the rifle quickly to her left and lifting up, Olivia pulled the trigger. One man dropped to his knees. The other dove quickly to his right, landing about halfway into the brush. Bad idea, Olivia thought as she saw his legs kick and then get dragged quickly away.

The entire battle lasted only a few minutes at most. Though Lilly had reloaded again, her nimble fingers moving quickly through the process, Olivia wouldn't need the extra round. As before, the animals disappeared along with the bodies of their prey. Eventually, after all had fallen silent, Daniel walked slowly down the path, waving at the girls to come down. Aidan stepped out of the forest and stood next to Daniel as the girls made their way to the gathering spot, careful to avoid slipping and falling. When they reached the bottom, Daniel spoke, his eyes never leaving the point where the trail entered the trees.

"I think you two should go in and get them," Daniel murmured to the two sisters. "I don't want to scare them. If you two go in without your rifles, I think they'll be more receptive than if Aidan or I go in there. I'll move around to make sure you both stay safe. Agreed?"

The girls spoke in unison. "Agreed."

Daniel stepped immediately into the woods. Olivia and Lilly handed their rifles to Aidan and began marching along the path to where they'd seen the children disappear, Olivia leading the way, Lilly's hand on her shoulder as she followed. As they stepped into the trees, Olivia paused as the darkness washed over them. It seemed as black as night after leaving the bright hillside with its whitewashed rocks. Olivia squinted to try and make out the path as she shuffled forward. Finally, eyes accustomed to shadows, she began searching for signs of the group. The broken branches and trampled earth made for easy tracking. They finally found them, dirty, scratched up, and huddled together at the base of a fallen tree. It wasn't nearly large enough to conceal the group, but it was as much protection as one was likely to find in these woods. Approaching cautiously, Olivia extended her hands.

"It's okay now," she began. "It's over."

"Stop there," the boy closest to her demanded. He was tall and lanky with dark skin. Olivia could see his fist closed around a large rock. Not wanting to provoke him, she stopped and grabbed her sister's hand.

"We're here to help," Olivia answered. "We're here to take those chains off of you."

Olivia could see the hesitation in the boy's dark eyes. "Who are you?"

"I'm Olivia. This is my sister Lilly. What's your name?"

The boy glanced back at the others behind him before answering.

"I'm Atreyu," he announced.

"Nice to meet you," Olivia replied, taking a small step toward him and squatting down. "Are you from around here?"

"I...we...most of us are from Exile. We picked up the others later."

"I know you're scared," Olivia murmured. "I was, too, when I was freed from Argyle's men. But it's real. You don't have to be afraid. His men are gone." Olivia waved her hand back around her to accentuate the fact that they were alone. "My friends are the only ones still out there, and they won't come forward until I tell them it's okay. Can I tell them it's okay?"

Atreyu's eyes scanned the woods around them before looking back and whispering to the others. There was a brief moment of discussion before he turned back to Olivia.

"It's okay," he sputtered.

"You sure? You're still holding that rock pretty tight," she said, nodding her head toward his clenched fist.

"Oh, yeah." He let the stone fall from his hand.

"It's okay to come out!" Olivia yelled back over her shoulder, her eyes never leaving Atreyu's.

Daniel walked out from behind a nearby tree and casually leaned against it. Aidan appeared a bit further back and trudged forward to stand near his brother. Neither of them spoke.

"That's Daniel and Aidan," Olivia offered. "They're the ones that freed me. They also saved my sister from Argyle's men."

"We just barely got out before they got there," Lilly interrupted. "Now his men are after us!"

Olivia whacked her sister on the shin. "Sorry for the interruption Atreyu. My sister gets a little excited sometimes."

Lilly rubbed her leg. "Sorry."

"Anyway, they saved us. Now we're trying to save others like us. They took our parents, and they were taking you too. We think it's time someone put a stop to it. You probably shouldn't go back to Exile though, or wherever you're from, at least not yet. Like Lilly said, Argyle's men are looking for us, and they'll be looking for anyone that should have been brought in already. You should get as far away from here as you can and hide out."

Atreyu stood, shaking his head defiantly. "No," he replied. "My brother's still back in Exile. I'm going to go get him first. I've got to get him out. There's nobody left to protect him from Argyle's men. They took our parents. Then they took all the other healthy adults. It's just us now. We've got to look after one another." He yanked at his chains, pulling one of the other children off balance behind him. "Get me out of these. I've got to go back." His voice cracked with urgency.

"Relax," Daniel said. He stepped forward. "I don't think they're that close behind us."

Atreyu turned his attention to Daniel. "She said you were here to free us. Then do it!" He rattled the chains urgently, holding them out in Daniel's direction.

"I will. I just don't want you to panic. If you'd like, once we get these chains off of you, we can all go back to Exile together. We can get your brother and all set off together. You can join us if you'd like. Any of you are free to join us."

"I'm not going back there," came a voice from the back of the group. "I've got nobody back there. You set me free and I'll leave now, thank you." Others began muttering their agreement.

"Fine," Daniel answered. "Do as you will. You want to go, I'm not going to stop you. If any of you want to go back to collect your things, or to collect your loved ones, we'll go with you." With that, Daniel squatted down and picked up a large stone. Carrying it over to where Atreyu stood, he dropped it with a thud at the boy's feet. "I'll be right back." With a blink, he was gone. Atreyu swayed where he stood and shook his head.

"Wha?" he began. Daniel reappeared in front of him holding a broad axe.

"Kneel," Daniel ordered. Atreyu looked at him defiantly. "So I can break the chains," Daniel explained. Atreyu didn't move. "If I'd wanted to harm you, I'd have done it back in the clearing with Argyle's men." Atreyu glared at him suspiciously before kneeling down and placing his wrists on the rock.

He looked over at Olivia. She smiled. CRASH. Atreyu jumped at the noise. CRASH. Again he started, but looked down to see his wrists freed from their shackles. He rubbed at the raw red skin and then set the manacles around his ankles on the rock. Daniel continued the process until all were freed, wrists and feet, from their irons.

Daniel stood back and surveyed the motley group standing before him.

"Who wants to leave now and who wants to go back home to gather your things, or your family?"

"I'm going back," Atreyu stated, stepping forward.

"Anyone else?"

A few mumbled replies and glanced sideways at the others. There was a brief discussion. In the end the rest seemed content with striking out on their own.

"Very well," Daniel conceded. "If you continue south along this path, you'll arrive at Void by nightfall tomorrow. You should be able to get some food and drink there, maybe provisions for your journey if you're lucky. I don't think any of Argyle's men are down that way." Daniel glanced to Lilly. She seemed to know he was waiting for a response from her and shook her head slightly. "It's getting dark, but I'd advise you get moving," Daniel concluded.

As Daniel turned back to Aidan, Atreyu stepped up next to him and touched his arm. "When will we be leaving to go back to Exile? You said you'd go back so we could collect our things, so let's go. I know you think my brother Halem is safe for now, but I'd like to make sure with my own eyes. I'm his older brother. I need to take care of him."

Although he didn't respond, Daniel jerked visibly at the comment. "We can leave after we eat," Daniel grumbled after a moment's pause. "I need food, and you look like you could use some too."

Daniel sat down on a log and dropped his bag in front of him. He took out a handful of meat and vegetables and handed them to Atreyu before pulling some out for himself. Aidan joined them, followed by the girls. The four sat in a semi-circle around Atreyu, sizing him up when they thought he wasn't looking.

"What?" Atreyu finally asked. "Why do you all keep looking at me?"

"They're just trying to get a feel for you," Lilly answered. "You were the one who seemed to take charge of the group back there. You're also the only one willing to go back to Exile. If you'd like me to ignore you instead, fine." Lilly turned to face her sister, her back now to the new arrival. "Nice shooting back there, at least I think it was. We won, so it couldn't have been too bad," she commented, smiling and changing the subject.

"Thanks," Olivia replied, her eyes darting over Lilly's shoulder to Atreyu.

"Listen," he interrupted. "I'm sorry I snapped at you. I shouldn't be so rude and actually, now that I think of it, I haven't said thanks. Thank you," he said. He stood and gave a small bow, "to all of you. We never would have escaped on our own, so I owe you my life. Please, accept my apology."

"Apology accepted," Olivia answered. She smiled sweetly. "And you're welcome."

"Happy to help," Daniel muttered, gnawing at his venison.

Aidan leaned in toward Atreyu and whispered. "Don't worry about Lilly. She can get a bit hot under the collar. She'll settle down." Lilly overheard and stuck her tongue out at him. Aidan laughed at her gesture and leaned back against the moss-covered trunk behind him. "She'll be back to her charming self before you know it."

Packing up their things after having finished dinner, Daniel handed his water pouch to Atreyu who drank deeply. "We can move out now if we have to. The sun's going to fall behind the mountains soon though so I'd rather not go too far. We should camp out for the night and make the rest of the journey tomorrow, maybe the next day. You okay with that?"

"I don't suppose I can argue with you. I could go by myself, but it would probably be safer to stay with you. I'll trust you that Halem is safe for now."

"Great. Let's get moving," Daniel called to the others. "Not that I don't trust all of Aidan's little friends, but I'd like to camp in an area where we're not so...popular." Atreyu gave him a puzzled look. Daniel just shook his head. "You don't want to know."

"You really don't," Lilly agreed, catching a bit of their conversation as she walked by holding onto her sister's arm.

"And what's the deal with her?" Atreyu whispered, leaning close to Daniel.

"She's blind."

Shocked and unable to believe his ears, Atreyu raised his voice a little too loud when he responded. "She's WHAT?"

"She's BLIND," Lilly yelled back to him. "Not deaf." And she strolled off up the path with her sister.

Daniel chuckled to himself and glanced up into Atreyu's startled face. "You asked."

Daniel and Aidan snatched up their packs, and the group set out, this time headed back the way they'd come. By the time they'd walked a few miles, Olivia was walking with Atreyu, making small talk and being friendly while Lilly and Aidan walked behind them trading insults and smart remarks. Only Daniel was quiet, lost in thought, trying to find the errors in their attack to better prepare for the next.

They made camp after a couple of hours and stayed the night huddled close together for warmth. They rose with the sun and set out once more. The group traveled north, paralleling the White Mountains. Lilly and Aidan had moved to the front of the group and walked in silence side by side. As the sun settled slowly toward the peaks of the White Mountains, Lilly reached out and grabbed Aidan's arm, bringing him to a stop.

"Shhhh."

Aidan glanced over at her and pulled her quietly off the side of the path. The others followed suit, moving quickly into the cover of the brush.

"Can you hear that?" Lilly whispered to Aidan.

Aidan held his breath and strained to listen. He was silent for a moment before refocusing his attention on her.

"Come with me," Aidan said, as he led Lilly back down the path to where Daniel stood and waved at Olivia and Atreyu to follow.

"There's someone up ahead," Aidan whispered.

"Friendly?" Daniel asked, eyes narrowed with suspicion.

"I don't know. Whoever it is, it sounds like they're in trouble."

"Let's go take a look," Daniel replied. He started forward along the path.

"I don't think that's a good idea," Aidan said, stepping in front of Daniel. "I think there might be werewolves up there too. I'm not sure, but like last time, the rest of the animals have scattered."

Daniel surveyed the rest of the group.

"Why don't you all stay here, and I'll run up and check it out."

"Are you crazy?" Atreyu interjected. "There might be werewolves and you want to go to them?"

"Don't worry about me," Daniel answered. "Everyone else okay?"

"Be safe and come back quickly," Olivia said. She put her hand on Daniel's shoulder and gave it a light squeeze.

Daniel nodded and took off, leaving Atreyu stammering and confused.

"What just...?"

"You'll get used to it," Lilly laughed as she patted his back.

Atreyu was still looking back and forth at the others when Daniel reappeared next to Olivia.

"You're right Aidan," Daniel panted. "There's a pack of werewolves up there." The others took a step back. "The pack has a baby centaur cornered against the mountain. There's a grown centaur on a ledge above who's holding them off for now." He shook his head and looked at Olivia. "I don't know how much longer he can keep them away. He can't pull the baby up, and it doesn't look like he can get down to her."

"Let's go," Olivia said, pulling her silver bullet pouch out of her bag and dropping the rest. "The rest of you should stay here. I'll shoot while Daniel gets the baby."

Lilly and Aidan nodded and murmured their agreement while Atreyu stood silent, mouth agape.

"Let's get up some trees in case the werewolves come this way when the shooting starts," Aidan suggested as he reached up for a nearby branch. He pulled himself up quickly and reached down to help Lilly. Atreyu stood, watching Daniel and Olivia disappear along the trail.

"Hey!" Aidan shouted. Atreyu started and looked up at him. "Start climbing."

Atreyu scampered to a nearby tree and climbed up level

with Lilly and Aidan. He sat on a large limb, glancing nervously at the others while they awaited Daniel and Olivia's return.

Chapter Eighteen

Making Friends

As they approached the point where the trail turned toward the mountains, Daniel lifted Olivia into his arms and took off. Olivia closed her eyes to the blur of trees, trying to calm herself as the wind whipped through her hair. Daniel slid to a stop at the base of a tall pine.

"Climb up," he ordered. "You ought to be able to get a good view from up there. Once you can get the werewolves to back away a bit, I'll move in and grab the baby."

Olivia scrambled up the tree, careful to avoid dropping her rifle as she moved from limb to limb. Time was of the essence. About fifty feet up, she found a perch that offered an unobstructed view of the rocky outcrop Daniel had told her about. The baby centaur huddled in fear, trembling, at the base of the cliff. Roughly twenty feet above, an adult centaur trampled back and forth on a ledge, shooting arrows into the trees and bellowing at the top of his lungs.

Scanning the forest floor, Olivia could see six or seven werewolves moving through the trees, keeping the small centaur pinned where she was. Olivia could also see one werewolf lying motionless on the forest floor. She couldn't tell what had happened to it, but she assumed it to be dead, maybe as a result of an arrow wound. She couldn't be sure. Steadying herself, Olivia loaded a silver bullet and took aim at the werewolf closest to the centaur. The round hit her target in its flank and dropped it to the ground. It struggled briefly to try and get back to its feet before collapsing.

Olivia reloaded, keeping an eye on the rest of the pack that had been distracted by the shot. As she loaded her gun, Olivia watched Daniel appear next to the baby centaur. She watched him bend down and say something to the little half-girl. She nodded and Daniel scooped her up in his arms. He shouted something up to the adult who nodded and yelled back.

Refocusing on her job, Olivia watched the wolves creep closer to Daniel's position. Another shot hit its mark, and Daniel snapped his head around. Seeing the approaching wolves, Daniel ran. He moved at a much more human speed due to the cumbersome load he was carrying. As the wolves closed the distance between them, the centaur above rained arrows down on them as fast as he could draw and release. Olivia saw two go down.

Must be silver arrowheads, Olivia thought to herself as she pulled out the ramrod, took aim and fired. Her target fell and slid to a stop, kicking up a cloud of dust around it that drifted lazily after Daniel as if trying to continue the pursuit. Olivia pulled out another cartridge but put it away when she saw the remaining werewolves scatter.

Not sure if it was safe to come down yet, Olivia watched Daniel slow to a stop and set the little girl centaur down. She clung to his neck and Olivia smirked while she watched him kneel, give her a hug and pry her hands loose. He stood up and took a quick look around to make sure the wolves hadn't turned back. Olivia, too, surveyed the woods and saw nothing to alarm her.

Olivia waited, impatiently, perched in her tree until she heard voices approaching below. Recognizing her sister's voice, Olivia made a slow descent and waited for them on the path before leading them to Daniel.

"Well, that ended well," Aidan observed, glancing at the wolf body that lay up ahead. He punched Daniel in the shoulder and then turned to Olivia. "Nice shooting. Thanks for keeping Daniel's butt attached to his body."

Olivia blushed. "Thanks. And you're welcome."

Aidan pointed to the small figure cowering behind Daniel. "So I see you saved the little one. Where's the other?"

As if on cue, the sound of galloping hooves announced the approaching centaur. He was enormous, his chest broad and muscled. The short white coat of his body matched that on his head, which was cut close to his scalp. He had an air of authority about him that made the young group take a step back and drop their eyes. He slowed only when he reached them and immediately snatched up the little girl. They both cried as he covered her face in kisses and held her to his chest.

"I don't have the words to express my gratitude for saving my daughter," the large man/horse boomed. He wiped the tears from his eyes as the little girl buried her face in his chest, her long auburn hair falling across and hiding her face. "My name is Shon and this is my daughter Samantha."

Daniel introduced the group, pausing on Olivia to add that she had helped in the rescue.

"I am in your debt, young Olivia," the centaur acknowledged, giving a low bow. "You," he continued, pointing at Daniel, "are very strong and fast for a human."

"It's a gift," Daniel replied with a shrug.

"I have another gift for you, young Daniel. My bow. My arrows." He took off his quiver and handed it and his bow to Daniel. "It is a very special weapon," Shon went on. "There are no others like it. A normal man wouldn't be able to use it." He paused and his eyes twinkled. "I have a feeling you're no normal man. I'd like for you to try. If you can draw and shoot, it's yours."

Daniel hesitated and then took the offering. The bow was extraordinarily light. It was like nothing he's ever felt. The dark brown wood gleamed as if polished, and he turned it to and fro, inspecting the workmanship and celestial carvings that marked its surface. Taking an arrow from the quiver, he nocked the arrow, drew, and let it fly at a nearby tree. Shon's eyes sparkled as he watched.

"Beautiful," Daniel commented. He admired the bow in his hand while he ran his fingertips over the symbols carved into its side. Aidan wandered over to the tree to try and pull the arrow out.

"Uh, Daniel?" Aidan called over his shoulder. Daniel looked up at him. "You may want to see this."

Daniel, continuing to caress the smooth curved surfaces

of the bow, meandered over to where Aidan stood. Looking up, his mouth dropped open. The arrow had not only stuck in the tree, it had penetrated clean through. Roughly six inches of the shaft was visible on the opposite side of the tree, while the fletchings were still visible, barely, where the arrow had entered. Daniel looked back to the centaur. A broad smile filled his face.

"It is settled. The bow and arrows are yours."

Daniel took one more look at the arrow, fingering its gleaming silver tip. "Remarkable," he muttered before returning to the others.

"I can't accept this," Daniel said, offering the bow back to Shon. "It's the most exceptional bow I've ever seen. I can't take it."

"You can, and you will," Shon insisted. He pushed the bow away. "I am a bowyer as my father was. This is the finest bow you will ever find. I want you to have it. You gave me something far more precious," he continued. He pulled his daughter to his side. "Now, the sun is setting, night is almost upon us. I pray you will come back with us to our village, that you might eat with us and stay the night."

Daniel glanced to the others who merely stared blankly back at him.

"We can offer hot food, shelter, and protection for you and your friends. I can also refill your quiver. I'm guessing you don't have any silver arrowheads in yours. As we saw today, they might be useful to you. Come young ones. Do not be afraid. You will be safe. You can rest knowing that my clan will protect you from any that would do you harm."

"What about Halem?" Atreyu asked. "We need to get back to him."

"You'll travel faster with a hearty meal and a good night's sleep," Shon answered. "We'll set you back on your way first thing in the morning. You need rest. You can either do it in comfort or curled up in the forest. The choice is yours of course."

"Very well," Daniel replied after another glance toward the others. "We'd be honored."

"The honor is mine," Shon said. Giving another low bow, Shon grabbed his daughter's hand and added, "Follow us."

The small group of young travelers fell in behind the two centaurs. They paralleled the mountains north for a bit before turning toward them. The sun had already disappeared behind the tall peaks and a cold wind blew down off the slopes. Olivia shivered and crossed her arms in front of her.

"Where are we going?" she whispered to Daniel. "I thought the centaurs lived in the forest, not the mountains."

Daniel shrugged. "I have no idea. I've never been here before."

The group trudged along, too tired to complain. Soon they came to the base of an imposing cliff, the face extending upward until it disappeared from view.

"Um, Shon?" Daniel stammered, "We can't climb that."

"No need," Shon replied, "just follow me." Letting Samantha go first, Shon followed and disappeared behind a large boulder that rested at the foot of the cliff. When he didn't appear on the other side, Daniel walked around to see where they had gone. A large fissure, invisible from the other side of the rock, stood before him. The others came around the corner and stood with him.

"Let's go," Daniel muttered and began shuffling into the crack. He could see the deep depressions made by the hooves of Shon and Samantha. They walked single file, as the walls of the mountain were only about three feet apart. The opening wound its way through the mountain. While some light might find its way down to the bottom during the day, it had grown very dark. Moving to his left, Daniel placed his hand against the wall, telling the others to follow suit. Eventually the path began to widen, and they all wound up walking side by side. It also seemed a bit lighter, and they picked up the pace, figuring they were near their destination. As they rounded the last switchback, they all stopped at once. It was beautiful.

A lush green valley opened up beneath them. In the middle of the valley, a large lake glistened in the light of the full moon that had appeared overhead. Three waterfalls plunged from the cliffs to their right and fed the river that dumped into the lake. Between them and the mountains beyond, a lively village welcomed them. A trumpet sounded at their arrival and what seemed like the entire village came out to meet them. Shon and Samantha came galloping back up the trail and beckoned them onward. Daniel took a hesitant step forward and the others followed. Soon they were surrounded by centaurs, all laughing and welcoming them to Alustria, their home.

"I apologize for all the commotion," Shon said, "but they were very excited by the tale."

Daniel looked at him questioningly.

"I told them what happened. Granted, not the whole story, but enough."

With that, Daniel and Olivia were raised up high and onto the shoulders of the centaurs before being carried off to the village. Aidan, Lilly, and Atreyu were picked up as well and, while not hailed as heroes, were welcomed graciously to the town. The two champions were placed near a roaring fire in the center of the village, and the others placed in nearby seats, too exhausted from their journey to question the celebration.

"To our honored guests!" came a toast from a nearby centaur. Goblets of a shiny gold liquid were passed around. Although the fact that the fluid seem to be smoking gave most of the youngsters pause, after a small sip the cups were drained immediately, each savoring the sweet and tangy drink. One of the women centaurs laughed and brought a pitcher to refill them. After draining two more glasses in as many minutes, they settled into their seats, watching the festivities. Aidan stifled a large burp and smiled sheepishly when Lilly giggled. She shifted her chair closer to him and sat back down.

"Sorry," he muttered, but she'd already focused her attention elsewhere, her ear cocked to the sounds that surrounded her.

"Tell me what's happening," Lilly asked. She searched out Aidan's hand with her own. He smirked slightly when her hand found his and leaned close to tell her everything he saw.

Music played, coming from a circle of centaurs near the fire. They played what appeared to be lutes, something similar to a guitar, which Aidan had seen a picture of in a book once, but this one had a much longer neck, and two of them pounded large drums that hung from straps around their necks. The band was lively, playing a song with a quick pace and beautiful melody. Many of the other centaurs joined in and danced, circling the band and laughing while clapping or stomping to the beat of the drums. Olivia and Daniel were given seats of honor near what appeared to be the chieftain.

"So tell us, young ones," the chief boomed over the ruckus, "what happened out there with our noble Shon and little Samantha?" The commotion stopped, the music tapered off as all eyes focused on the two guests of honor, all ears strained to hear their answer. The crowd tightened around them, only the occasional cough breaking the silence.

Daniel and Olivia exchanged a nervous glance.

"You tell them," Olivia whispered. She was blushing furiously and brought her hands up to her hot cheeks.

"Um..." Daniel shifted uncomfortably in his chair. "We were coming up the path on the other side of the mountains when we heard a cry for help. I went to see what was going on while the others stayed back." Daniel looked over at Olivia. "When Olivia heard what was going on, she insisted that we help. She brought her rifle and climbed a tree to find a good perch. When she fired, the werewolves were distracted, and I ran in and grabbed Samantha. Shon and Olivia protected me as I escaped with Samantha, and the rest of the pack eventually scattered."

"So you risked your lives to help two cherished members of our community?" the chieftain bellowed, more of a statement to the surrounding crowd than an actual question.

"I...I guess," Daniel stammered. The centaurs erupted in applause. They hooped and hollered and stamped their hooves, clinking their goblets together to toast the young children.

"I think there is another important thing everyone should know about this brave young man," Shon announced, stepping forward out of the crowd. The yelling and clapping stopped as he turned and stood in front of Daniel. "As you all know, I make the finest of bows and arrows." Heads everywhere nodded furiously. "And you all know the strength it takes to draw those bows, which are made for our noble centaurs and beyond the abilities of mere men." Again, agreement from every side. "Well I've given my own personal bow and quiver to this fine young man. He has proven his worth and his strength. He is no mere human." The stunned crowd looked from Shon to Daniel. "A demonstration!!" Shon hollered.

Grabbing Daniel by the arm and lifting him to his feet, he dragged Daniel to a nearby archery range on the outskirts of the village. The centaurs gathered and lined the sides of the range. From the shooting spot down to the target, the rails were lined with expectant faces. The trampling of hooves was deafening. Handing Daniel the bow and an arrow, Shon smiled and stepped back.

"Show them, young Daniel, your gift."

Daniel nocked the arrow and drew. Holding his breath, he took aim and released. In a blur, the arrow flew, finding its home in the center of the bull's-eye at the far end. The crowd exploded in applause, and he was once again lifted and carried around the town until they finally settled down and set him back in his chair. The dancing resumed, and soon supper was served. Large plates of hot food were handed to each of the five guests as they enjoyed the festivities.

"Jugged hare, haggis, cabbage, and bread," Shon commented as he handed Daniel his plate.

"What is jugged hare and haggis?" Daniel inquired.

"Probably best you don't ask," was the response. "Just eat it. It is both delicious and healthy."

Daniel frowned slightly and slowly lifted a forkful of jugged hare to his mouth. While expecting the worst, he was not prepared for the exquisite taste that filled his palate. The tender rabbit meat seemingly dissolved on his tongue. Scooping as fast as he could while still retaining a shred of dignity, Daniel polished off first the hare, then the haggis and vegetables. He then used the bread to sop up the juices before shoving it into his mouth. The others also appeared to be enjoying themselves, as the only time they stopped eating was to take a swig from their goblets before shoveling more into their mouths. Seconds were brought for each of them, thirds for some, and Atreyu even managed a fourth plate before collapsing back into his chair, a swollen belly protruding in front of him, a content grin lingering on his lips.

The party raged on for hours until only the full moon and stars shined down from above and the coals of the fire glowed up. Finally, Shon reappeared and offered to guide them to a small lodge where they would be welcome to stay the night. Lilly had fallen asleep in her chair, so Daniel lifted her gently and carried her to their accommodations. Three rooms had been arranged for their use. Atreyu took one, Daniel and Aidan another, and Olivia and Lilly shared the other. Daniel set Lilly on her bed and removed her shoes before pulling the covers over her.

"Good night," he whispered to Olivia.

"Night," she whispered back as he left the room. She closed the door and collapsed into her own bed.

The sun had risen high in the eastern sky by the time the children awoke. Shuffling from their respective rooms, they eventually all stumbled into the main dining area. Fresh fruit and juice had been left out on the table for them. As they served up their breakfast, there came a knock. Atreyu, who happened to be sitting closest, got up and opened the door. In walked Shon and Samantha carrying coffee and milk respectively. Setting them on the table, they each bowed.

"A very good morning to you all," Shon exclaimed.

"A very good morning," came the greeting from Samantha, barely louder than a whisper.

"Good morning," replied the others.

"When you are all finished with breakfast, we will be at

my workshop. It's across the plaza, next to the fish market. Please come by when you are ready, and I will assist you with anything you need."

They finished up quickly, again gorging themselves on the delicious food brought for them, and, with directions from their host, bathed and washed clothes for the next leg of their journey. Shon had made sure they were brought additional supplies for they were beginning to run low on food and silver bullets. When they finished their packing, they walked across to Shon's workshop where Daniel stocked up on silver-tipped arrows. Quiver full, they followed Shon back out into the middle of the square to say their goodbyes.

"Where will you be going from here?" the chieftain inquired.

"We're hoping to get back to Exile by this evening," Daniel responded. "Atreyu's younger brother is there, and we need to get to him before Argyle's men do."

"Argyle's men?" the chieftain asked, confused by the reference. "What danger do they pose to someone his age?"

"Well," Olivia interjected, "the last group we attacked came through Exile first. That's where they took Atreyu. Then they went south and took some more children down near Void. We think they were on the way back to the castle when we attacked them. We figure that Argyle will send some of his soldiers back through there when his slaves don't show up. We don't think they'll be very gentle with the townsfolk when they arrive, so we need to get Halem out before they show up."

"I'd be surprised if they showed up before tomorrow night, maybe the morning after. It'll probably be later than that, but to be sure we'll push hard today to get there by tonight," Daniel added.

"Maybe they'll get there while we're still there. I wouldn't mind another chance to attack Argyle's men," Aidan muttered.

Daniel shook his head and scowled at his brother. "Anyway," he continued, "we'd better get moving if we're going to have a chance at making it by tonight. Thank you again for the bow and arrows," he said, shaking Shon's hand.

"And for the delicious meals and our rooms," Olivia added. She, too, shook Shon's hand and bent down and gave Samantha a kiss on the forehead. "I'm pleased to have met you," she told the little centaur. Samantha latched on to one of her father's forelegs. With her cheek pressed to her father's leg, she looked up at Olivia and smiled before hiding her face.

"Whenever you need help, you will always find it here," Shon said. He grasped Daniel's forearm, Daniel doing the same to his, and they shook. "Always."

"Thank you," Daniel replied, trying to hide his discomfort at Shon's intensity.

When all the goodbyes were said, the band of travelers followed the path back the way they'd entered. Seemingly every centaur in the village lined the path, thanking them for their bravery and wishing them a safe journey. Once again the trip through the crevasse was dark and difficult to navigate. Exiting from the shadows, they each paused, squinting into the blinding morning light.

Chapter Nineteen

Near Death

Once they could see, Atreyu took the lead and led them back to the trail that would take them to Exile. He set a fast pace and held it. The day's travel was difficult but uneventful, and they arrived at the gates of Exile just as the sun dropped behind the peaks of the White Mountains. The sky turned a deep and ominous red as the sun retreated. Looking west, Atreyu shivered.

"I don't like the looks of that," he grumbled.

"What's the problem?" Lilly asked.

"A sunset like that is a bad omen. It means sickness."

"It's just a red sunset," Daniel interrupted. He gave a sideways glance at Atreyu and pushed to the front of the group as they approached the entryway of the town. "Nothing more."

He stopped at the large gates and called out. "Hello?"

"Who goes there?" a voice shouted from above.

Looking up in an attempt to locate the man he was addressing, Daniel yelled back. "I travel with Atreyu, who was taken from this town a few days ago. We have freed him and have come back for his brother." Turning to Atreyu he whispered, "what's your brother's name again?"

"Halem."

"Halem," Daniel shouted. "Please open the door so that we may see Halem."

The large gates rolled back on their hinges, groaning and creaking all the while. The group proceeded slowly into the streets of Exile. Atreyu walked quickly to the front and led the way through the nearly empty streets, winding this way and that until he came to a small grocery store. The windows were dirty and the door swung loosely on its hinges. It looked all but abandoned. Atreyu entered quickly and walked straight to the back of the store, opened yet another door and started up the staircase.

"Halem," he called up the stairs. "Are you up there?"

A soft voice cascaded gently down from above.

"Oh, no," Atreyu moaned. He took the rest of the stairs three at a time, and barged into the room at the top. He took a quick right and entered an extraordinarily small bedroom. Atreyu dropped to his knees beside one of the two beds that nearly filled the room. Aidan stopped in the doorway, preventing the rest from entering.

A small figure lay huddled in the bed moaning quietly. His brown skin was drenched in sweat and he was flushed with fever, his long hair matted against his head and face. A sudden coughing fit shook not only the boy, but the entire bed. Sitting up and gasping for breath, it sounded as if his very lungs would be expelled from his chest. Finally, the spell passed, and he collapsed back onto the bed, clutching the sheets to his neck.

Atreyu rose and pushed the others back into the main living area and closed the bedroom door behind him.

"He's sick."

"How bad is it?" Olivia whispered. She grabbed Daniel's arm and pulled him close. Daniel smiled and tried to hide the color rising in his cheeks. It really didn't matter as everyone's attention was focused on Atreyu.

"I'm not sure," Atreyu responded. "My guess is it's Witch's Breath. I don't know for sure. He does have puss oozing from the corners of his eyes. I don't know of anything else that causes that. He's my brother, so I've got to take care of him. It's probably best if everyone else stays out of the bedroom until he's better."

"We've already had it," Aidan pointed out. "Even if it's Witch's Breath we can't catch it again."

The others nodded their agreement.

"I'm sorry for this," Atreyu remarked. "I wouldn't have brought you here had I known he was ill."

"Don't apologize," Olivia responded. "We're all here to help one another. We'll stay here until he gets better and then take him with us. We won't leave you here alone with him knowing Argyle's men may be coming. Will we?" Olivia looked to the others. "Will we?" she probed, waiting for someone to speak up.

Aidan stepped forward. "Of course we'll stay, and if Argyle's men show up, we'll protect you and your brother."

Although he thought Aidan was being a bit dramatic, Daniel raised his voice as well in agreement. "We're here for you Atreyu. Whatever you need, just let us know."

Putting her hand on Aidan's shoulder Olivia mumbled, "Why don't you and Daniel go out and bring back some water, Holy Basil, and Eucalyptus. Lilly and I will stay here and straighten up a bit and see what we can put together for dinner."

"What do we need Eucalyptus for?" Atreyu inquired.

"It'll help clear his chest so he can breathe better," Olivia answered. She turned back to Daniel and Aidan. "Now hurry."

Aidan grabbed Daniel and pushed him out the door in front of him. "Let's go."

With the two boys gone, the sisters helped Atreyu clean up the living area and kitchen. When they finished, they searched the kitchen for food before giving up and going down to the market below. The pickings were slim. But, with some searching, they found enough for a full meal and headed back upstairs to heat it up. Daniel and Aidan eventually returned and took over dinner while Olivia prepared some home remedies for Halem; Holy Basil tea and Eucalyptus paste. She handed both of them to Atreyu.

"Get him to drink as much of the tea as you can. It'll help to bring his fever down. Rub the paste on his chest. It'll help clear up his congestion so he can breathe better. It should help with his cough as well." As Atreyu crossed the room, Olivia called to him. Scrambling for a cup, she poured some cold water into it. "And put this by his bed. He needs to drink as much water as he can keep down."

"Thank you," Atreyu said and returned to his brother's bedside carrying the medicines.

Dinner was eaten in silence, and they all retired early.

Atreyu stayed with his brother in the small bedroom that they had already been sharing before Atreyu was taken. Olivia and Lilly slept in the other bedroom, which had once belonged to Atreyu's parents. Daniel and Aidan slept in the living area. While Aidan had found a comfortable chair to sleep in, Daniel had to resort to laying out a blanket and using his pack as a pillow. He set up in front of the door to ensure nobody could get in without him being alerted.

Halem gradually improved over the next couple of days, turning from a coughing, sweating lump on the sheets into a pale, kind-faced boy. The group took turns bringing him food and drink to aid in his recovery, and they frequently stayed to keep him company as he'd yet to regain enough strength to move around on his own. Still, his spirits were up, and he improved steadily. On their third evening together, Daniel carried Halem out to the kitchen table so he could join the others. Daniel had gone out on a couple of occasions to hunt. He'd brought his kills back to the town and traded some of the meat for other supplies, so the food was plentiful, the chatter lively, and the company warm. After supper that night, Daniel and Aidan cleaned up while the others shared stories and got to know one another. Daniel washed and stacked the dishes, and Aidan dried and put them away. When Aidan finished, he turned and saw Daniel staring out the window at the darkness beyond. Aidan knew it was serious, because he could see Daniel's fingers kneading his earlobe.

"What's on your mind?" Aidan asked under his breath, moving close to Daniel's side and leaning against the counter.

Daniel shook his head. "Nothing. We can talk about it later."

"You wondering how long it'll be until Argyle's men get here?" Aidan guessed.

Daniel's shoulders slouched. "I can't help but worry that they're closing in. I don't want to scare the others, but I don't think we can wait until Halem's healed. We're going to need to move him while he's still sick, or fight. It'll be another week before he'll be ready for travel, and I have a hard time believing Argyle's men will take that long. I'm surprised they haven't shown up already."

"Then let's fight," Aidan growled.

"I don't think the people here will be very happy if we turn their town into a battlefield," Daniel replied.

"You have a better plan?" Aidan mocked.

"I was thinking we'd take the fight to them," Daniel retorted. He straightened up to his full height and looked down at his brother. "Rather than waiting for them to come to us, we can move out and intercept them before they get here. That way, hopefully, Argyle and his men will stay focused on us and not come back and punish the people of Exile. We'll have to make sure we let one escape to go back and report to Argyle what happened and where."

Aidan's eyes gleamed in anticipation. "When do you want to leave?" he inquired.

"The sooner the better. I'd like to leave tonight if possible. We should talk to the others and see what they think. Let's do it after Halem goes to bed. There's no point in worrying him about this. There's nothing he can do about it anyway."

"Agreed." Aidan pushed himself up from the countertop and wandered back into the living area where he sat down on the floor next to Olivia. Olivia glanced down and saw the smile on his face.

"What?" she asked.

"Nothing,"

Olivia frowned and shot an inquisitive look over her shoulder at Daniel. He just shook his head. "Later," he mouthed. Olivia returned her attention to Halem, who was telling a tale of flying horses and giant spiders. When he finished, Daniel picked him up and carried him back to his bed.

"You've been up long enough," Daniel explained. "Time for you to get some sleep."

"Thanks for the story," Lilly called after Halem, as Daniel entered his bedroom.

"I've got plenty more," Halem yelled back. "Goodnight, everyone."

After getting Halem situated for the night, Daniel returned to the living area. He had an air of urgency about him now, and the others stopped what they were doing to listen to him.

"Aidan and I spoke earlier," Daniel began. "We're concerned that Argyle's men are getting too close." He waited for that to sink in before continuing. "I don't think the people here will want to get involved, so we can't wait for Argyle's men to arrive here. I think we need to pack up and go out to meet them before they get too close. I'd rather have more time to plan and pick a place for the attack, but I don't think we have it. We've got to cut them off before they get here."

Olivia looked over at Aidan and saw the same sly grin on his face as he'd been wearing earlier. "How far away do you think they are?" Olivia asked.

Daniel shrugged. "I would have thought they'd have been here by now." He turned to his brother. "You have any idea how far off they might be?" Aidan shook his head. "Lilly, anything?" She dropped her eyes into her lap.

"Half a day maybe," she mumbled. "It's hard to pin it down more than that."

"Well then I think we should get our things together and move out as soon as possible. We don't want to wait around until Argyle's men come crashing through the gates. They're on their way right now, probably trying to find the gathering party. They know something went wrong, so they won't be happy, and they won't be gentle. If we're going to help the people of Exile, we need to cut off Argyle's men before they get here." Turning to face Atreyu, Daniel placed a hand on his shoulder. "I'd like for you to fight with us. The more we have, the better off we'll be. Do you have any weapons?"

"What about Halem?" Atreyu asked with a glance back at the closed bedroom door.

"He'll be fine for now," Daniel reassured him. "If we're successful, I'm hoping to be back by morning. If we're not, it won't matter if you're here with him or not. I imagine they'll destroy the whole town."

Opening a drawer in the cabinet next to him, Atreyu pulled out a small length of cord with a cup in its center. "I have my shepherd's sling," Atreyu announced. Seeing Daniel cringe at the crude weapon, Atreyu added, "It works better than it looks. I might not be able to do a lot of damage with it, but maybe I can keep some attention on me while you...uh...do...your thing."

Daniel looked to the others, eyebrows arched as he checked their opinions. Olivia shrugged and inspected the rifles. Aidan chimed in when Daniel's eyes met his.

"The more the merrier," Aidan offered. "It may not be the prettiest thing I've ever seen, but if he knows how to use it, I think we should let him."

"Let's go then," Daniel replied.

Everyone went to work preparing for the trip. Olivia took the pouches of cartridges out of her own sack, as well as Aidan's, and shoved two into her pants pockets. She handed the other two to Lilly who did the same. Daniel left his old bow and quiver in the corner of the kitchen, opting to take his newly acquired weapon with him. Aidan shoved his shoes into his pack, knowing that he may need to transform quickly and not wanting to ruin yet another pair. He also removed his shirt and shoved it in with his shoes. As each of them finished gathering their gear, they assembled at the door.

Atreyu was the last to join them, having gone back into the bedroom to check on his brother. His eyes glistened as he exited the bedroom. He wiped them quickly on his sleeve and pushed through the others standing in his way.

"Let's go."

Chapter Twenty

Night Journey

Daniel gave a quick glance Aidan's way and saw his lips curl up at the corners. His eyes flashed, and he moved quickly to Atreyu's heels, his thirst for a fight burning in his chest. Daniel allowed the two girls to exit in front of him, and he closed the door softly behind him before descending the stairs. Down in the market, Daniel hustled to catch up with Atreyu.

"Is there a secret way out of town?" Daniel asked.

Atreyu cocked his head to the side. "Why?"

"I just want to involve as few people as possible in this. If the guard at the gate sees us leave, he might realize it was our group when he hears of the fight with Argyle's men. If someone here knows we...you were involved, the town will be in danger. If we can sneak out and take care of what needs to be done without anyone seeing us, I think it'll be safer for us all."

Atreyu still didn't look convinced, but turned north toward the back end of town instead of south to the main entrance. After weaving their way through the dark and deserted streets, the small clan ran into a dead end.

"What the...?" Aidan began.

"Shhhh," Atreyu replied, putting his finger to his lips. Atreyu leaned down and pulled at a few stones that had been piled in the corner at the end of the street. Moving them out of the way, he squatted down and began pushing at the rocks on the other side. When they shifted out of the way, the others could see the moonlight bouncing off the surface of the pale stones on the other side. Atreyu slid quickly through the hole, followed by the others. When Daniel had pulled himself back up into a standing position,

Atreyu quickly set the rocks back in their places. From this side, it was impossible to tell there was an entrance there. They were standing in a small culvert that ran the length of the walls of the town. The entire waterway was filled with identical bone-white rock. Without Atreyu, Daniel doubted they'd be able to find their way back into the town via this route even though they now knew it was there. It was just impossible to see amongst the identically colored stones.

Now that they were out of the village, Daniel again took the lead, taking them into the forest for a while rather than using the main road where they'd be at risk of being seen by the gate guards. Once out of view of the town, Daniel moved them back to the road.

"I'm going to go scout up ahead," Daniel announced. "Keep to the road. If you hear anything, get into the forest quickly. You'll be able to hide and fight better in there. And Aidan," Daniel continued, turning to face his brother, "you may want to start gathering some of your friends as you go."

Aidan nodded. "I've already got six or seven coming this way that I'll be able to bring with us," Aidan answered. He ignored the bewildered expression on Atreyu's face.

"And why don't you fill Atreyu in on our gifts. He needs to know what he's gotten himself into, and with whom."

Daniel gave them all a quick pat on the arm before vanishing.

"How does he do that?" Atreyu questioned.

"Come on," Lilly giggled. She grabbed him by the arm and pulled him along. "I'll fill you in on all the interesting quirks of our little circle of friends."

Olivia took the lead, followed by her sister and Atreyu, while Aidan and friends brought up the rear. Whenever Aidan felt another animal presence in the vicinity, he tried to bring it into the fold before it could get back out of his range of influence. By the time Lilly had finished her summary of everyone's skills, Aidan had assembled a support team of six wolves, two mountain lions, four wolverines, two badgers, six deer, and a colony of bats. Custos had also rejoined the group and was lumbering along through the trees to the south.

Atreyu and Lilly kept chatting as they walked, Atreyu asking an occasional question about the others as they popped into his head. Olivia stayed alert at the front, scanning the road as far out as she could see when they crested small hills. Aidan focused his attention on gathering more animals for the impending fight. He'd had some luck when they first left the village, but they seemed to have hit a relatively uninhabited area. The concern that he wouldn't get enough warning if werewolves approached crossed his mind more than once. They trudged along, mindful of their surroundings until Daniel came jogging up the road toward them.

Olivia put her arm around his shoulders and led him to a nearby boulder. He sat down, out of breath and sweaty. Olivia pulled her canteen out and popped the top off. Daniel took a long pull from the flask before choking. Spewing water on Lilly, who happened to be standing in front of him, Daniel gasped for air between lung busting coughs. When he finally caught his breath, he looked up at Lilly.

"Sorry about that," he said.

Lilly stood, still dripping. "Gross," was her only reply as she raised her arms from her sides and flung them about like a dog trying to shake water from its tail.

Olivia chuckled to herself before looking back to Daniel. "Did you find them?"

Daniel nodded. "They're still a ways off," he replied, "and there's a good spot for an ambush up ahead. If we hurry, we can get there and set up before they arrive."

"How many are there?" Atreyu asked from behind Aidan.

Daniel craned his neck to see around his younger brother. He locked eyes with Atreyu before answering. "There are fifteen of them."

Daniel watched Atreyu's mouth fall open. "Fifteen?! How are we supposed to fight fifteen of Argyle's men? We're only children! We can't win a battle like that." Atreyu dropped into a sitting position in the middle of the road. "Impossible," he muttered, picking up a small rock and throwing it into the bushes.

"No," Olivia remarked, her voice full of defiance. "Not impossible. I watched Aidan fight ten of Argyle's men by himself and win. I've fought with Daniel, Aidan, and Lilly, and we've won. We can win this one too. Now get up off the ground Atreyu and act like you care about fighting back, about defending your town, about defending your brother."

Atreyu rose slowly to his feet. "Fine," he mumbled. "Whatever, let's go. Yay," he commented, twirling his finger in the air.

"Listen," Olivia growled, "if you don't want to fight, that's one thing. If you WON'T fight, that's another. Your brother is back there, and if we don't stop Argyle's men, what do you think will happen to him?"

Atreyu kept his head down and shuffled his feet. "I'll fight. I just don't see how we can win."

"Well then watch. You're about to see it firsthand." Olivia looked over at Daniel. "Lead the way."

The walk was quiet and hurried. Daniel kept the pace swift, glancing over his shoulder occasionally to make sure nobody was falling behind. Just as Atreyu was about to ask for a break, Daniel halted.

"Here we are." Daniel pointed to a field to the left, littered with fallen trees. "Olivia and Lilly, you two will be in there. Find a good spot and keep your heads down until they come around that curve up there. When they get to about where we're standing now, that's when I want you to start firing. That gives them the least amount of cover. Atreyu and I will move a bit farther up the road here and hide. Once they pass, we'll be able to cut off their retreat. Aidan, you and your...friends can stay out of sight back down the road a little where all those boulders were, remember? Once Olivia starts things off, you can move in. Oh, and look!" Daniel added with a sweeping gesture of his right arm, indicating the forest that lined the southern border of the clearing. Aidan, Olivia, and Atreyu peered into the gloom.

"What about it?" Aidan asked.

"Notice all the bones?" Daniel asked, the excitement

building in his voice.

Aidan stepped a little closer, his eyes squinting as he tried to see into the shadows. Daniel saw one of his eyebrows lift and a smile form when Aidan made the connection.

"Assassin vines," Aidan almost laughed. "Perfect!"

"They stretch pretty far along this edge, so everyone be sure to stay away from them. Once the fighting starts, we'll have too much to do to fight off plants too."

"Assassin vines?" Atreyu asked hesitantly.

"Creepy creepers," Olivia answered. "Stay away from them. They'll eat you."

Atreyu's eyes bulged.

"Just don't go in there. I'll give you a closer look on our way to our hiding spot so you know what they look like and can stay away from them." Daniel looked back to the others. "Everyone clear on their roles? Let's go."

"What am I supposed to do?" Atreyu blurted out. "You've got a magical centaur bow and arrow and can disappear and reappear whenever and wherever you want. He can talk to animals," he went on, cocking a finger in Aidan's direction, "and they have rifles. All I've got is my sling and you want me to cut off the retreat of fifteen of Argyle's men while keeping an eye out for killer plants?"

"You're with me," Daniel said patiently. "I'll put you in a safe place. Make sure you stay out of sight as much as possible. I'll make sure they don't get near you. Just sling away. The more confusion we can cause, the better."

Atreyu looked about to retort, but bit his lip instead. Daniel looked to the others. "You ready? They'll be here soon."

"Be safe everyone," Olivia mumbled before grabbing her sister by the arm and trotting off into the field to find a good location from which to shoot.

Aidan slapped Daniel on the back. "See you soon," he chuckled. He dropped a quick wink before running back the way they'd come.

Daniel watched him disappear around a bend before turning back to Atreyu. "Follow me."

Daniel and Atreyu took a closer look at the assassin vines so Atreyu could identify them. Daniel kept his knife out just in case, but either they weren't close enough for the plant to notice them, or maybe it was full. Either way, both boys moved a little faster than needed as they moved away from the carnivorous vegetation. They jogged up to where the forest again lined the sides of the road. Here, the trees were large and thick enough that the light of the moon could not penetrate the canopy that had grown together overhead. The path loomed like an open mouth, black and forbidding. Daniel peeled off to the north and entered the trees quietly, slowing to allow Atreyu to catch up and grab his shirt. No point in risking getting separated. Daniel only moved a few steps into the trees before squatting down. In the process he bumped his quiver and sent his arrows spilling out into the darkness. Daniel hissed in frustration.

Atreyu hunkered down next to him. "What is it?"

"I dropped my arrows."

"What do we do?"

"We'll have to come back for them later," Daniel replied, "after the fight."

"Later? You don't have any arrows!" Atreyu retorted.

"I'll be fine, now quiet. It shouldn't be long until we see them coming up the road," Daniel whispered. "They're carrying torches." He smiled. Atreyu frowned. "We'll be able to see them," Daniel explained, "but they won't be able to see us in the dark."

"Oh," was all Atreyu could find to say.

Both the boys focused their attention on the path winding its way through the woods. Soon, a flickering glow announced the arrival of Argyle's men. Atreyu held his breath, the light growing brighter. He let out a huff of air when the first man rounded the corner. Daniel elbowed him sharply. "Shh."

Atreyu and Daniel pushed themselves against the tree as the group of men passed. With the exception of the stomping of their feet and creaking of their equipment, not a sound was made. No talking, no laughing. These mercenaries were here for business and business only.

When the last one passed, Daniel crept around the tree he'd been hiding behind, keeping it between him and the men before peeking out. After a few seconds, Daniel beckoned Atreyu to him.

"Stay in the trees if you can," Daniel whispered. "Some of them have crossbows and the trees will give you cover. Remember, sling as many rocks as you can as fast as you can. Understood?" Atreyu nodded. "Good. Remember to wait for Olivia to take a shot. That will be your signal, okay?" Again Atreyu nodded and squatted down. He fumbled around in the dark before picking up a few stones. Daniel picked up a thick branch. "I'm going to go introduce myself. I'll see you when it's over. If each of us is careful, we should all come out of this in one piece. Think about Halem. He needs you to fight, and he needs you to live."

As Daniel had requested, Olivia waited until the small unit of men was centered in the clearing. Taking an easy breath and slowly releasing it, she sighted in on one of the men, the only one who carried a rifle, and squeezed the trigger. He collapsed to the ground and the other men scrambled in all directions. Olivia dropped behind the moss-covered log and exchanged guns with Lilly. Popping back up, she searched for another target.

"Not good," she muttered, taking aim and firing again.

"What is it?" Lilly asked as she pulled the ramrod out and again traded rifles with Olivia.

"There are a few moving this way. They know we're here."

"You're right, not good," Lilly responded. She worked to reload quickly.

Aidan meanwhile had again transformed into his favored form of a mountain lion and was working with his animal friends to deal with the men who had continued forward along the path when Olivia had started the assault. He moved quickly in and out, searching for weak points in their improvised defenses. They had huddled together in a tight formation facing out when Aidan had first attacked. He'd peeled off at the last second and dashed into the nearby trees as an arrow whizzed just over his sleek back.

For the most part, they were at an impasse. The men couldn't move much farther down the road, pinned in by the circling pack. Nor could the animals move in to attack across the relatively open terrain without risking being shot. Aidan dashed to and fro, circling the men. He let out periodic growls to keep the men guessing as to where, and how many, animals were out there.

On the opposite side of the clearing, Atreyu began his assault as instructed, waiting for the first report of a gunshot before letting loose his first stone. It caught one of the mercenaries squarely over the right ear, dropping him to the ground in an unconscious heap. A small trickle of blood oozed out of the enormous knot forming just behind his temple. Atreyu quickly stepped behind a nearby tree while reloading his sling. Taking a quick peek to check for his next target, he swung the sling around his head before leaping out and firing. His shot again found its mark, this time between the eyes of one of the other men who'd been carrying a crossbow. Atreyu also noted the two additional men who lay prone at the edge of the road, only their legs sticking out, their torsos hidden in the tall grass that lined the trail. One of the bodies began sliding slowly toward the forest.

The assassin vines must still be hungry, Atreyu thought to himself before realizing what was about to happen. He grimaced and tried to refocus on the battle. He scanned the scene and saw the two men working their way toward Olivia's position. He watched as one of the men pitched forward and collapsed, disappearing into the grass.

Olivia, still hidden behind the log at the northern edge of the clearing, was about to fire when the man she'd been aiming at slumped to the ground. *Daniel,* she thought to herself. Frustrated that he'd taken out her target instead of the man's companion, she shifted her weapon toward the remaining mercenary advancing on her position when she saw him fire his crossbow. A scream caught in her throat, and she squeezed her eyes shut, sure the arrow would find a home in her bosom. Nothing. She opened her eyes, shocked to still be alive, and saw the man redrawing his bow.

Confused, but with instinct taking over, she pulled the butt to her shoulder, sighted her weapon and fired. He dropped. Olivia collapsed against the log, shaking violently, the scream in her throat threatening to break free. A whimper fought its way out.

"What happened?" Lilly asked, alarmed. She shuffled forward, searching the ground with outstretched hands until she found Olivia. Lilly grabbed her sister and pulled her to her chest, holding her close.

"I don't...don't know," Olivia choked out. "I should be dead. I should...he shot me." Her chest heaved as she held on to her sister and trembled.

Lilly ran her hands over her sister's body. "You've been shot? Where? Is it bad?" Her hands continued their search, finding nothing to indicate her older sister was wounded in any way. She was frantic and breathing hard, but her sharpened senses picked up the rustling sound of someone or something moving their way. She pried herself free of Olivia's grasp, picked up a rifle and sprung up, ready to aim and fire. She was unlikely to hit whatever was headed their way, but she might be able to buy some time. Lilly was blind, but Argyle's men didn't know that. A second's hesitation on their part might make the difference between life and death. Instead of a mercenary, Atreyu stopped dead in his tracks and raised his hands.

"Just me," he stated. "Don't shoot me please. It's Atreyu," he went on when he realized she might not recognize his voice.

"Is there anyone else?"

Atreyu scanned the clearing. "Uh, no."

"Come here," Lilly commanded before dropping back down to her sister's side.

Atreyu raced around the end of the log and squatted down beside the two girls.

"What's wrong with her?" Atreyu asked, his voice suddenly filled with concern. "Is she hurt?"

"No," Lilly answered. "I don't know. She said he shot her but she wasn't hit by anything that I can feel. I don't know what happened. Where are Daniel and Aidan?" Lilly asked.

"No idea," Atreyu replied as he straightened up and looked around.

"Wasn't Daniel with you?" Lilly asked, agitated.

"He started with me," Atreyu answered defensively, "but you try keeping an eye on him." He realized his mistake and was about to apologize when she cut him off.

"Well why don't you go look for them," Lilly suggested stiffly, "while I try to figure out what's going on with Olivia."

Atreyu trotted off in the direction that Aidan had been sent before the fight started. As he jogged along, he heard the snarls and howls of an array of animals. He could also hear yelling and shouting. Oh no, Atreyu thought to himself, they're still fighting over here. He picked up the pace until he came over a small rise in the land and halted at the scene before him. The remainder of Argyle's men stood huddled together in the middle of the path, a few lying on the ground at the perimeter. A variety of wild animals moved in and out among the trees and boulders that bordered the road. As Atreyu tried to figure out where he should be and what he should do, another of the soldiers collapsed. The men hollered and pulled in closer, their heads swiveling in an attempt to locate their attacker. Atreyu picked up a stone, loaded his sling, and let loose. It wasn't as accurate as his earlier shots, but it got the attention of the three men. Having finally found a target—a reasonable target—the men attacked. In unison, they charged toward Atreyu, swords drawn, ugly sneers on their lips, and violent gleams in their eyes. They didn't even make it halfway up the hill before being taken down from behind by the pack of wolves. Atreyu looked away, not wanting to witness the carnage before him. He waited, hoping for a quick end to the sickening noises behind him, when a hand patted him on the shoulder.

"Sorry for that," Aidan chortled as Atreyu nearly leapt out of his skin. "Good job though," Aidan added. "I was having a tough time getting close to them until you drew their attention. Thanks."

"Happy to help," Atreyu replied dryly. "Where's Daniel?"

Aidan swiveled his head and called out. "Daniel!"

"Over here," came a weak reply.

Aidan and Atreyu followed the voice through the rock field, weaving this way and that among the boulders. Aidan paused briefly to grab his clothes and get dressed before continuing the search. Atreyu spotted a bloody handprint on one of the stones, and rapped Aidan on the arm. "Look."

Aidan followed the direction of Atreyu's pointing finger until his eyes found the crimson palm print. "Daniel!" Aidan shouted. He moved frantically among the boulders following the drips of blood on the ground as well as the intermittent smear on the rocks. He finally saw Daniel's feet sticking out from behind a boulder and ran to his brother.

Daniel sat slumped against the stone, pale and ashen. Aidan's attention immediately fell to the arrow still stuck in his right arm. The sharp end had pierced clean through Daniel's bicep, the slick tip resting against his chest. Having to hold his arm forward to allow for the arrow shifted his shoulder forward in an unnatural position. The blood slid slowly down his arm and pooled between his wide spread legs. His head wobbled as he looked up at his younger brother with eyes that didn't seem to hold their focus.

"Catching arrows is dangerous business," Daniel slurred.

"What?" Aidan asked, shaking his head, sure that he'd misheard.

"One of them shot at her. I tried to catch it." He paused and moaned as he shifted his arm. "I tripped as I reached for it. Missed the catch. Remember when we used to go do that with Father? I never missed then. I guess there's a first time for everything."

"Quiet now," Aidan instructed as he stepped to his brother's side. "Don't waste your breath and energy."

Atreyu made the connection. "That's what Olivia was talking about back there," he exclaimed.

Aidan had knelt down next to Daniel and was examined the wound. He turned slightly to glance back at Atreyu.

"What was she talking about?" Aidan prompted, refocusing his attention back on Daniel's arm as he gently rotated it back and forth to determine the extent of damage that had been done.

"She was saying something about being shot. Daniel saved her."

Daniel's head flopped to the side as he looked up at Atreyu. "Go get them," he commanded. "Have Lilly find my bow and arrows and then bring them here. We need to get back to Exile and get your brother out." Daniel looked back to Aidan, struggling to focus. "How bad?"

Aidan glanced up. "It's not pretty," he commented. "We need to get you back to Exile. I'll need some supplies to fix this up. You're bleeding pretty bad." Aidan stood and removed his shirt. "Let's get this cleaned up as much as we can before the girls get here." He waved at Atreyu to go before squatting back down. He snapped the end with the fletchings off as close to Daniel's arm as he dared. Checking for jagged edges that might catch on Daniel's arm, he found none. "You ready?"

Daniel grabbed Aidan's rolled up shirt and stuffed it between his teeth. He nodded. Aidan gave a quick pull on the arrow, forcing it the rest of the way through Daniel's arm. Daniel jerked and let out a muffled scream before collapsing back against the boulder. His chest heaved as Aidan removed his shirt and tied it around the gory wound.

Aidan sat down between Daniel's feet. "You all right?" he asked.

Daniel gave a loopy nod. "Thirsty."

Aidan unplugged his water and leaned forward to pour some in Daniel's open mouth. When Daniel had taken his fill, Aidan used what was left in the pouch to clean away the filth on Daniel's arm. He then tossed a couple handfuls of dirt on the stain between his brother's legs for good measure.

"No point in alarming the girls," Aidan said, noticing Daniel's cocked eyebrow. "Sounds like Olivia's scared enough as it is. Your bandaged arm isn't going to help, but we don't need blood stains all over the place to make it worse."

Daniel nodded. "Thanks," he mumbled.

"What are brothers for?" Aidan answered.

Aidan stood as he heard the sound of approaching footsteps. "We're here," he called out to the others. Atreyu led the two girls to where Daniel sat, leaning heavily against the rock.

"What happened?" Olivia cried, falling to her knees beside Daniel.

"Just a little scratch," Daniel answered. He pulled his feet under himself and tried to push up into a standing position. Atreyu caught his uninjured arm and helped him. Olivia looked unconvinced.

"What happened, Aidan?"

"Nothing that can't heal, and nothing we need to stand around here discussing." Aidan turned his attention to Daniel. "You ready to walk?" Daniel nodded and Aidan ducked under his brother's arm. "Then let's get started."

Atreyu and Aidan took turns helping Daniel along as Olivia followed behind, the worried crease in her forehead never smoothing. Not far into their trek, Daniel collapsed, panting hard and unable to continue. Aidan transformed into a bear and Daniel made the rest of the journey slumped over on Aidan's broad back. They reached the walls to the city just as the eastern sky turned a fiery red, announcing the beginning of a new day. Aidan shifted back and helped Daniel navigate the uneven surfaces of the culvert as Atreyu located the entrance and shifted the rocks out of the way. Aidan went first, followed by a wobbly Daniel. The two girls were next and Atreyu last.

"Take him back to the rooms while I put this back together," Atreyu urged. Aidan turned and pulled his brother along with him. Daniel's strength was again diminishing quickly, and by the time they reached the market, Olivia had positioned herself on Daniel's right side to keep him from stumbling out of Aidan's grasp. They bounced their way down the aisle to the back of the store before Atreyu caught up to them. It was with maximum effort that the four younger members of the group hauled

Daniel up the stairs and dropped him clumsily into Atreyu's bed, careful to avoid waking Halem. Aidan stayed and tended to Daniel's arm while the others retired from the bedroom and stumbled to their own beds before collapsing into dreamless slumber.

Chapter Twenty-One

Get Moving

Halem awoke the next morning feeling almost back to his normal self. He sat up and stretched, swinging his feet over the side of the bed and standing before he noticed Daniel was lying in the bed next to his. He frowned, not knowing why Atreyu would offer up his bed to a stranger. Halem leaned over, intent on shaking Daniel awake, when he noticed the blood-soaked rag tied around Daniel's arm. Still not sure what to make of the situation, Halem snuck out of the bedroom and into the main living area where he found Atreyu and Aidan sprawled on the floor snoring loudly. Both were dirty and were sleeping in their clothes. It also appeared as if they'd dumped all their gear in the middle of the room at some point as it was littered with weaponry. Scanning the living area, he also noted the closed door to his parent's old bedroom. *That must be where the girls are sleeping,* Halem thought to himself. He scowled as he tried to piece together what had happened the previous evening after he'd gone to bed. They'd obviously gone out without him. Where had they gone and what had they been up to? He racked his brain, but came up with nothing, so he gave up and decided to make his brother a proper welcome home breakfast like their mother used to make.

Halem snuck down the stairs to the market, grabbed a bagful of items, and headed out the front door. Stepping out into the cool morning air, Halem paused and inhaled deeply. After having been stuck inside for almost a week while ill, the crisp clean breeze was heavenly. He moved quickly through the streets and left the town via the front gates, pausing long enough to give a small package of sausage to the sentry on duty. He jogged down to the nearby springs and took a quick dip to rinse off the filth that had accumulated over the last few days. Feeling human again, he dressed in a clean shirt and pants he'd brought with him before returning to town. He made a few quick stops, bartering away the items he'd taken from the store. He smiled broadly as he meandered back through the narrow streets to his home.

Halem had the eggs cooking, the coffee brewing and was preparing to drop the bacon and sausage on the griddle when Atreyu and Aidan finally awoke.

"You two have been sleeping like the dead," Halem joked. "I've been hauling wood in from outside and banging pots and pans together and you two didn't even move."

"Hmmph," Atreyu grumbled, still groggy from not enough sleep.

"What did you guys do last night anyway?" Halem asked as he continued to prepare breakfast. "Daniel's in your bed with a hurt arm, you two are obviously exhausted, the girls haven't come out of their room, and there are slings and arrows all over the place."

"We went out and fought Argyle's men," Aidan chimed in.

Halem just about knocked the coffee off the stove as he wheeled toward them. "You what?!"

Atreyu nodded his head. "They were coming here. If they find us, they'll kill us. We decided to go and meet them on King's Road. That way we'd have an advantage. I still can't believe we did it. I thought we were goners when Daniel said there were fifteen of them." Atreyu looked over at Aidan who was leaning back with a smug look on his face. "We did it though. We won."

"We sure did."

"And Daniel?" Halem replied.

Aidan's self-satisfied air disappeared at the mention of his brother. "Well, he took an arrow through the arm saving Olivia and Lilly."

"How bad is it?" Halem asked.

"Not as bad as it looked at first. He bled a lot, and the walk back last night didn't help him any, but he'll be fine I think. He just needs some time to rest and heal, that's all."

"And Olivia and Lilly are both okay?"

Atreyu nodded. "They're fine. Olivia got a good scare, but nothing physical."

Halem finally turned back to the stove, peeling off pieces of bacon and dropping them into the griddle next to the sausage. "Why don't you go wake the girls then. Breakfast is almost ready."

When the meat finished cooking, Halem filled two plates with food and headed to his bedroom. "You all can serve yourselves. I'll eat in here with Daniel." He opened the door with his foot and stepped inside. Daniel rolled over and mumbled something unintelligible before the smell of bacon and coffee woke him up. His eyes fluttered open, and he started at the sight of Halem standing in the doorway.

"It's just me," Halem stammered, "Halem. I've brought you breakfast." He lifted one of the plates out in front of him. "Are you hungry?"

Daniel settled back into the mattress as he looked around the room and got his bearings. He nodded and pushed himself into a sitting position, cradling his right arm to his side protectively in the process. When he'd gotten situated in a comfortable position, Halem set Daniel's plate on his lap and sat down on the bed next to him.

"Thanks. I'm starving."

"So you went out and fought Argyle's men last night," Halem commented.

Daniel nodded, picking up a piece of bacon and shoving it into his mouth.

"Your idea?"

Daniel nodded again.

"Why would you do that?" Halem asked. "Why attack his men and bring his wrath to your door, OUR door?"

Daniel looked Halem in the eye and swallowed. "I don't have a door any longer, thanks to Argyle. I fight his men to free slaves, slaves like your brother was going to be. We freed him during our last battle and brought him back to get you. Last night, we fought not for slaves, but for lives, including yours. If we'd waited, the fight might not have ended in our favor, and I am fairly sure some of your townsfolk, some of your friends, would have died."

"He wouldn't send anyone here. Why would he? There's nothing left here he could want."

"Revenge," Daniel countered. "That's all the reason he needs. He can't let what we're doing go unpunished, or the whole kingdom will rise up against him."

Halem blinked and looked down at his plate. "Oh," Halem replied softly. "I hadn't thought about it like that. I guess I should say thank you." He grabbed a few slices of bacon and shoved them into his mouth.

"No need to," Daniel answered. "What Argyle's doing is wrong. I don't think making it right is doing anything special. It's just doing what should have been done a long time ago."

"How long do you think you can keep fighting his men?" Halem inquired. He scraped his fork across his plate and stuffed some eggs into his already full mouth. "He'll come after you eventually with more men than you can win against," he mumbled through his mouthful of food.

Daniel shrugged. "I imagine he will. One advantage we have is we can also run. We don't have a fort to defend, or a castle on a hill. We can move about through the mountains, the woods, the prairies. We can decide when and where to meet his army. It's been working for us so far. Besides, we also don't have an image to defend. If we lose, who cares? If word gets out that he's losing, well that's a whole different problem for him, isn't it?"

Halem chuckled. "Yeah, I guess it is."

Daniel focused his attention back on his plate, clearing it before Halem was even halfway done with his. Halem fetched Daniel a refill and grabbed him another cup of coffee in the process. Daniel again cleaned his plate, washing it all down with a large mouthful of coffee. He leaned back against the wall, full and content.

"Thank you. That was delicious."

"You're welcome." Halem looked down at Daniel's bandage. "How's the arm feeling?"

Daniel started to flex his bicep before stopping with a

hiss. "Hurts," Daniel replied.

"Take it easy," Halem suggested. "You don't want to get it bleeding again." Daniel nodded his agreement. "We should probably clean that up a bit more too," Halem continued. "If it gets infected, you'll be in real trouble. There aren't many places to get medicine these days. I'll be right back." He returned a short time later with a bowl of hot water and some clean rags. Halem cleaned and dressed Daniel's wound quickly, careful to avoid reopening the injury. When he was finished, Halem helped Daniel stand and supported him as he walked into the next room to join the others. Aidan stood so Daniel could have his chair.

"It's good to see you up and around," Olivia commented. "I was afraid..."

"It's nothing," Daniel interrupted. "I'll be fine. Just a scratch." Daniel gave her a quick wink and a smile to lighten the mood.

Olivia wiped a tear from the corner of her eye and smiled back. "Well, thank you anyway."

"I'm glad I was there," Daniel said pointedly. He leaned forward and stared intently at Olivia. "It could have been ugly." She shuddered. Daniel broke the gaze and straightened up. He made eye contact with each of the others as he continued.

"We're going to need to leave soon," Daniel announced. "The plan was to leave one man alive to go back to Argyle last night. I guess I got a little caught up in the action, and I didn't. Did anyone else?" The others glanced around the room at one another, some shrugging, none answering. "I didn't think so. In that case, this place will probably be crawling with his men in the not too distant future. I think it would be best to be gone when they arrive. Everyone agree?" The others mumbled their assent. "Good. We'll head out tomorrow morning."

"What about the rest of the people?" Halem asked. "If they're coming here, won't the town be in danger?"

Daniel shook his head. "There's nothing we can do about that now. We can't stay here to guard everyone. Hopefully they fight back against the first of the men to show up and then leave. Argyle can't chase everyone around the forest. We'll have to hope that everything turns out for the best. Sorry."

"But it's our fault Argyle's men are coming here! How can we just desert them knowing what those men are going to do?"

"Because we can't stop it from happening. We can warn them before we go, but that's the best we can do. Staying here is a mistake."

"We should warn them now," Halem insisted.

"You can go tell them whenever you'd like," Daniel answered.

"Where are we going to go?" Lilly inquired.

"I think for right now we should head north into the forest. We've been doing most of our damage to the south of here. They'll probably start looking for us there. We'll head north to give us some time to heal," he motioned to his arm, "and to come up with a new plan of attack. Any other ideas?" The others just shook their heads. "Good, we'll pack up our things today and leave tomorrow morning. I think we should leave the back way, Atreyu. The less the people here know about our comings and goings, the better."

"I'd rather go fight, but I guess we could use a break. Besides, we'll be able to kick more butt if everyone's healthy and we have some time to plan our next move." Aidan stood. "I'm gonna head out and visit with Custos. He's feeling a little lonely. Be back in a bit."

"Custos?" Halem asked.

"Don't ask," Lilly said. "I'm sure you'll find out about him soon enough," she giggled.

"Whatever," Halem grumbled. "I'm going to go tell everyone they need to get out of here." He got up and stormed from the room.

"He'll be okay," Atreyu said. "He just needs time to get a grip on what's happening."

After spending the day relaxing and chatting, the rest went to bed early to make sure they were well rested for their journey. Everyone rose before the sun and headed out into the calm morning air. Once they snuck out of town, they found a footpath that headed north into the woods. Daniel took the lead and meandered slowly along the trail. With no real goal to their march, the pace was an easy one, and they took frequent breaks to sit and talk amongst themselves. Atreyu and Halem were brought up to speed on the gifts and talents of the various members of the small clan. Halem mumbled that he wasn't good at anything. Aidan and Daniel gave each other a knowing smile that something might develop in the aftermath of his brush with Witch's Breath. Although there was no way to know if he'd receive a gift, or what it might be if he did, the potential was exciting. Not wanting to let everyone down if nothing happened, the two brothers remained silent to the possibility.

As the sun hung high in the sky marking midday, the group trudged along, stirring up the dry dust from the path and making Aidan sneeze. Having had enough, he jogged to the front of the group.

"I'm tired of sucking in the dirt you all keep kicking up," he yelled back over his shoulder. "Your turn." He unplugged his water pouch, took a mouthful, swished it around, and spat into the grass that lined the trail. "Blech."

He then took a few more gulps of water, enjoying the cool refreshment as the sun beat down on his upturned face. He poured some over his head and rubbed it into the back of his neck before plugging the pouch and returning it to his side.

A short time later, they all stopped for lunch at the top of a small hill, taking advantage of the sparse presence of trees, to plan the next leg of their hike. To the north, they could see the White Mountains turn west and cross their path and continue their line to the Great Lake to the east. The Styx River could be seen emerging from a wide gap in the mountains, having carved its way through over hundreds or thousands of years. In the distance to the northeast, the towers of Argyle's kingdom could be seen shimmering in the heat.

Overhead, the sky was clear with the exception of a few cotton ball puffs of clouds moving slowly across the sky, one lazily transforming from what looked like a flower to a shape resembling a short-legged horse. Aidan lay on his back watching the development when he caught movement out of the corner of his eye. He sat up quickly, scanning the landscape to the north for what he'd seen. Circling low over the treetops, he spied a dragon. He couldn't be sure it was the same dragon they'd encountered previously, but the markings and coloring appeared to be the same. He tapped Olivia on the shoulder and pointed out the animal.

"Oh, no."

Daniel looked up from his lap. "What?"

Olivia nodded in the direction Aidan had pointed. "He's back."

As she spoke, the dragon dropped from view, rising back up a moment later with what appeared to be a horse in each of its claws. It looped slowly around for a moment as if searching for something else below before turning in a large circle and flying west toward the mountains. Its large body landed in a rocky outcropping at the base of a tall cliff and then disappeared.

Aidan looked over at his brother. "I'd like to go take a look."

Daniel choked on a mouthful of water. "What for?" he asked. He saw the crease form in Olivia's brow as she realized what Aidan was suggesting.

"I want to see if I can make contact again. Last time something happened, but I didn't have time to see if I could really communicate with it. I want to try again."

"And what happens if it tries to torch you again?"

"Well," Aidan continued. He had to choose his words carefully. "We leave everyone here, and only you and I go. If it doesn't work and the dragon comes after us, we can run. It can't keep up with you, so you should be fine. I'll just transform into something small so it can't find me or so you can carry me easier. As long as it doesn't somehow follow us back here to the others, we should all stay safe."

Daniel glanced over to Olivia. She looked at him, her right eyebrow raised. "I hate to say this, but I think it would work," she offered.

Daniel knew they should stay away, be safe, and focus

on the battle with Argyle's men. But he, too, was curious to see if Aidan could make contact. "Okay," Daniel agreed, then turned to the others. "You four stay here. Aidan and I are going to try to find that dragon and see if he can communicate with it. If you see it headed your way, hide. Get into the trees and stay out of sight. We'll be back in a bit."

Aidan sprang to his feet, excited by the prospect of trying his gift on the dragon again. "Should I change?" Aidan asked. "We could travel out there a lot faster if I'm in a different form."

Daniel waved his hand at him as if shooing a fly. "Whatever you want is fine with me." Daniel grabbed his water pouch and put his pack and weapons behind a nearby tree. Aidan walked over to the same spot, checked to make sure he was out of sight of the others, and undressed before transforming into a deer. The two boys set off together in pursuit of the dragon.

It didn't take them long before they arrived at the edge of the forest below where the creature had disappeared and Aidan shifted back to his human form. They stood, eyes scanning the rocky mountainside above them for signs of where the beast may have landed.

Chapter Twenty-Two

Try Again

"There," Aidan pointed out.

Daniel followed Aidan's gaze and saw what his brother was looking at. Among the rocks and boulders was a spot where the white surfaces darkened with soot. Moving cautiously forward, the two brothers climbed slowly upward and further north to try and get a better angle.

"We're going to have to stay fairly close to the forest," Daniel murmured to Aidan. "I won't be able to get to you quickly if I have to climb too far through this stuff, not to mention getting both of us back out. I can't get very good footing and with my bad arm it's even harder."

Aidan nodded but said nothing. He moved even more slowly than Daniel, careful to avoid sharp edges with his bare feet. Eventually, the entrance to a large cave came into view. The hole in the side of the mountain wasn't as large as the size Aidan had expected for a dragon lair. It seemed too small to hold such a large creature, but he could feel the dragon's presence inside. Aidan climbed slowly along the rocks until he found what he was looking for. He stood on a large flat boulder looking up toward the mouth of the cave, staying somewhat close to the trees in case they needed to make a quick escape. Daniel crouched behind it, peeking out, but tried to stay hidden. For a while, nothing happened. Aidan stared intently into the blackness, his eyes squinting as he concentrated on trying to make a mental connection to the beast he knew to be hiding within.

Daniel heard it before he saw it. A low grumble emerged from the darkness followed by a scratching and clawing sound as the monster pulled itself into the light. Its large head poked briefly out of the hole before squeezing the rest of its body through. It sniffed at the air and shook its head quickly as if casting off a dizzy spell. When it finished, the emerald green eyes locked immediately on Aidan. Never looking away from the boy, the dragon moved swiftly down the mountainside, slithering more like a snake than walking. It covered about half the distance before pulling up and stopping. It was now close enough that both of the boys could see the smoke rising from its nostrils before being caught by the cool afternoon breeze and swirling away.

Daniel's muscles tensed as he prepared to grab Aidan and run at the first sign of aggression. His heartbeat hammered in time with the throbbing of his still-healing bicep. The dragon stood, its head cocked to the side as it seemed to examine Aidan. Daniel could see the pupils dilate and contract as it swayed its head back and forth to look at Aidan from different angles.

Daniel had no idea if this was the same dragon they'd encountered with the unicorn. The coloring was remarkably similar, and instead of staying alert to signs of danger, Daniel found himself admiring the beauty of the beast.

Two golden horns swept back from the top of its head, pressing flat when the beast extended its long neck toward the boys. Deadly looking spines, the same color as its horns, ran from its lower jaw to its throat and then along its back where they then continued down to its tail. They contrasted beautifully against the chalky white color of the dragon's skin. The large scale-covered back smoothed out gradually into an almost leather-like underbelly. Lethal and razor-sharp golden talons tipped the fore-claws. Daniel couldn't see the dragon's hind feet and could only assume they looked the same.

Most impressive of all, however, were the beast's wings. They were leaf-like in appearance, large veins visible throughout the thin membranes that connected the fingers. The skin was almost translucent as Daniel could see the outline of the scales underneath the folded wings.

Suddenly the dragon snorted and lifted itself to its full height. Daniel saw Aidan's hand go up in a "stop" gesture before he could react. The beast glared down at the naked boy on the rock in front of it, shook its head violently, and huffed out a small fireball at the base of the boulder on which Aidan stood before retreating back up the mountain and into its cave, pausing to cast one last glance back at Aidan before disappearing into the hole from which it had crawled.

Aidan turned to face Daniel, a goofy smile plastered across his face. He hopped down from the rock and swaggered over to where Daniel stood waiting.

"So?" Daniel asked when Aidan didn't immediately volunteer information.

"I think it went rather well," Aidan bragged.

"It shot a fireball at you!" Daniel exclaimed, exasperated by Aidan's flippant attitude.

"Believe me, if it had wanted to hurt me, it could have done a lot more than just singe the hair on my toes."

"I still say you're lucky that thing didn't kill you."

"There was no need for violence."

"It could have been hungry," Daniel suggested.

"She. But she wasn't," Aidan replied. He turned and started strolling back in the direction of their camp.

"What?!" Daniel jogged after his brother.

"She. The dragon is a female. She'd just eaten those two horses after all."

"Okay, she," Daniel conceded. "So what happened when you tried to connect with her?"

"Well, she wasn't real happy to begin with," Aidan said through a chuckle. "She didn't like me intruding into her thoughts. Once I convinced her I didn't mean any harm and only wanted to introduce myself, she settled down a bit. That's when she came walking down the mountain." Aidan skipped over a log on the trail before continuing. "The rest of the time was just me telling her about myself. I'm not sure if she believed me when I told her I could change forms though. That's when she broke the connection and stormed off back to her cave." Aidan looked at Daniel, the excitement obvious on his face. "I can't wait to do it again. It's not like with other animals where I just pick up on feelings. I can actually talk to her! I've got to try and share some water with her. Imagine if I could change into a dragon!"

Daniel rolled his eyes, uncertain that Aidan's gift extended to such a magical being. "Was she the same one we ran into back at the clearing with the unicorn?" he asked.

Aidan stopped and turned to face him. "You know what? I don't know. I didn't even think to ask." He started walking again. "I was so excited at having made contact with her, it never crossed my mind that she might be the one that almost had me for lunch." Aidan chuckled. "I don't think it really matters, but I'll have to ask her next time." Aidan started jogging. "C'mon, let's get back to the others and tell them what happened."

Aidan transformed in an instant and took off toward camp. Daniel followed.

When they arrived back at the clearing, Aidan quickly dressed and emerged from behind the tree with an air of triumph, as if he'd just returned from battle. The others dropped what they were doing and ran over, gathering around the two brothers and asking questions over one another.

"Did you find it?"

"How big is it?"

"Could you communicate?"

Aidan finally raised his hand to silence the others. "Let's sit down. I'll tell you all about it while we finish lunch."

The group moved back to the crest of the hill where they'd been eating. Between bites, Aidan told the others of his and Daniel's exploration of the cliffs and the dragon's cave. Daniel watched the others with amusement as Aidan told them of the dragon's trip down from her cave and their subsequent "conversation." As the others asked questions, Daniel became bored with hearing the story over again and went in search of more fruits and roots to satisfy his hunger. Between the wound in his arm and chasing Aidan around half the day, he was famished. When he returned, the others were talking animatedly amongst themselves, retelling the story with various "what ifs" thrown in. Daniel grabbed his things and picked up Olivia's pack.

"We should get going," Daniel remarked, helping her

into her pack when she stood. He grabbed Lilly's as well and helped her put it on. Daniel picked up his bows and frowned.

"Halem," he called out. The younger boy looked up. "You know how to use this?"

"Sort of," Halem replied. He pushed himself up to a standing position.

"There's no point in my hauling around two of these all the time. I can't use them both at the same time, and you don't have anything. Why don't you take this one?"

Daniel tossed his old bow and quiver to the younger boy. Seeing how awkwardly Halem handled the weapon, Daniel walked over and put a hand around his shoulder and led him away from the others.

"If you'd like some pointers on how to use it," Daniel whispered, "you and I can do some shooting together."

Halem nodded. "Thanks. I only shot one of these a few times, and it's been a while."

"We'll get you shooting bats in the dark in no time," Daniel answered and clapped the younger boy on the back. Halem smiled. "Alright everyone, let's go," he called out to the others.

The troupe traveled north, being sure to give the dragon's lair a wide berth. While Aidan may be safe, the rest weren't sure they wouldn't wind up a mid-day snack if they ventured too close.

They approached the Styx River to the east, and they could hear the faint roar of the water as it flowed down from the White Mountains and made its way to the Great Lake. The forest became thicker near the base of the mountain range ahead of them. Daniel looked up and judged it to be roughly a two-day walk to the cliffs. They'd find a place to camp there and heal up before planning their next foray against Argyle's men.

The next day, as they continued their march north, Halem came to a sudden stop. Olivia ran into him.

"Hey," she started, but Halem cut her off.

"Daniel, Aidan!" he called softly. "Come up here."

Daniel and Aidan exchanged a worried glance before

trotting up to where Halem stood. The others stepped off the path and into the trees, Olivia readying her rifle and Atreyu his sling.

"Listen."

Daniel and Aidan shushed the others and moved farther along the trail they'd been following. The sounds of battle could be heard faintly from up ahead. Very vaguely the cries, hollers, and grunts could be made out.

Aidan herded the others farther back down the path while Daniel listened for a while longer. When he joined the group, Halem looked worried.

"What's wrong with you?" Atreyu asked his younger brother.

"I'm not sure I'm ready for this," Halem answered, his eyes downcast.

"We don't have to fight," Olivia interrupted. "We can move west from here and avoid whatever is going on up there." Atreyu gave her a quizzical look so she continued. "Daniel's arm isn't in any condition for us to be fighting. We don't know how many men are involved or if it's even Argyle's men. Halem needs more training before he's ready. I think we should get out of here before someone comes down the trail and sees us."

"I'm not running away from any fight," Aidan countered. "I don't care who's ready to fight and who's not. I'm going up there."

"Hold on," Daniel said. He grabbed Aidan by the elbow and pulled him back closer to the others. "Why don't we have Aidan transform? He can go take a look and tell us what we're getting ourselves into. Nobody will notice a deer or something in the middle of a battle. We can decide when he gets back if we want to get involved. Agreed?"

"Agreed," Aidan answered immediately, starting to walk off into the woods to undress and change.

"But," Daniel continued, "if we decide that we're not going to attack, that means none of us." Daniel leveled his gaze at his younger brother. "Nobody."

"Sure, whatever." Aidan disappeared behind the trunk of a large tree. It wasn't long before a wolf appeared and ran in the direction of the commotion. Daniel and the others waited, pacing the trail, anxious to hear what was happening up ahead. It didn't take him long.

He walked out from behind the tree before anyone knew he was even back.

"It's a war between some fairies and gnomes," Aidan announced as he tied his pants. He could see he caught everyone off guard. "The gnomes have axes, and it looks like they've been trying to chop down some trees up there. I guess they're the fairies' homes because they're all over the place attacking the gnomes. It doesn't seem to be going well for them. The gnomes have armor on, and the fairies don't look like they can penetrate it with magic or weapons."

He shrugged and, after grabbing his bag, continued toward the trees on the other side of the trail.

"We can take a shortcut through the woods and pick up the trail later on. No point in getting involved in that squabble."

"You're kidding right?" Halem said, stepping into Aidan's way. Aidan stopped short to avoid running into him. "We can't leave the fairies to fend for themselves. Don't you remember the story of King Javi? Of how the kingdom originally started." Aidan stared at him, confused. "He and his men helped the fairies in their war with the goblins. They gave him the Scepter as a thank you. That's what kept the kingdom strong until Argyle destroyed it." Halem looked back to the others, now pleading his case with everyone. "I may not be as ready as I'd like to fight, but I think we have to do this. It must be a sign or something. What are the chances we'd come across something like this? You've fought Argyle's men and won. Don't you think you can fight some gnomes? They're nothing compared to what you've already done, what you're doing. They wouldn't leave us in peace if they came across us out here," he continued with a wave of his hand. "They'd be on us in a heartbeat, killing us and taking whatever we had on us. Dirty creatures. We should get them before they get us, and we can help the fairies at the same time. Who knows, maybe they'll give us a gift too."

Daniel and Olivia looked at one another. Atreyu had already stepped to his brother's side and taken out his sling.

"I like you," Olivia smiled as she took out a cartridge and readied her rifle. Lilly followed suit.

Daniel looked over at Aidan and drew an arrow from his quiver.

"I thought you didn't run away from any fight," Daniel chided.

Aidan's nostrils flared and he frowned. "I'll be right back," he muttered as he pulled off his shirt and again vanished behind the large trunk.

He didn't even wait for the others. Once transformed, this time into a bear, he charged up the trail snorting and huffing as he went, and the sound of Custos barging through the brush to their left could be heard as he moved in to protect his friend. The others followed after, spreading out as much as they could to allow one another to shoot if given a target.

Chapter Twenty-Three

A Pivotal Battle

As they approached the scene of the ongoing battle, a few gnomes called out a warning and retreated back into the trees. Aidan and Custos charged in after them. The fairies cheered and collected together at the base of a large oak, congratulating one another and flying the injured up into the thick foliage above. Daniel grabbed Halem by the back of his shirt as he ran by chasing after Aidan.

"Don't bother," Daniel told him. "Aidan will be back in just a moment. He's not going to waste a bunch of time chasing gnomes in the forest. They're probably all underground by now anyway. Stay here and keep your arrows ready and your eyes open."

As if on cue, Aidan emerged from the forest and barreled toward them. He slid to a halt near Daniel and the others and started nudging them into the trees and bushes.

"What's the matter with him," Lilly asked, pushing back against the cold nose that kept nudging her arm. "Get off of me. That's disgusting." Olivia grabbed her arm and pulled her back behind some nearby bushes. Olivia dropped her pack and pulled her sister's off as well.

"I don't know," Daniel answered, "but it can't be good. Everyone get ready. Something's coming."

With his group under cover, Aidan transformed once again, this time into a large bat. One powerful beat of his wings and he disappeared into the treetops. The others stood, weapons at the ready, scanning the forest before them.

They heard them before they saw them. The rustling of leaves and snapping of branches and twigs announced the arrival of a foe using the cover of the trees above.

Daniel tried to draw his bow and failed. Pain shot in both directions from the still healing wound in his arm, down to his fingertips and up through his shoulder and into his neck. Olivia watched as he winced and dropped the bow to his side. She shook her head as a fresh bright red stain spread on the bandage. Daniel saw that she was studying him and turned away from her.

"Get ready," he stated. "Make sure both rifles are loaded." He turned to Atreyu and Halem. "You too. Halem, just do the best you can. Atreyu, keep him close."

Daniel shoved his arrow back in his quiver and picked up a nearby stick. He pounded it on his palm a few times to check its sturdiness. Satisfied with his primitive weapon, he disappeared in a swirl of leaves.

Olivia's gaze returned to the trees, trying to locate a target. She caught a glimpse of something scampering through the branches toward them. Halem let loose an arrow. Although it didn't come close, the creature did pause long enough for Olivia to get a look at what it was. It was a tree goblin. It was about half the size of an adult human, with thin, spindly arms and legs. Its skin was a dark hunter green to help the creature blend in with the leaves through which it swung. Its large yellow eyes met hers. It bared its wicked fangs and hissed before leaping up into the higher branches and disappearing.

"The goblins must be behind the gnome attack," Olivia called to the others. "Gnomes are too stupid to organize something like this on their own. Keep an eye out for the goblins up top. The gnomes may come back too, now that they have a bit of help and have had a chance to organize, so don't ignore the ground. Just...keep your eyes open."

Atreyu and Halem nodded their understanding, their eyes never stopping the back and forth scanning of the forest in front of them. Halem had an arrow nocked and at the ready. Atreyu had his sling loaded and was occasionally stooping down to pick up more rocks which he shoved into his pockets.

"There!" cried out Halem, pivoting toward a cluster of bushes on the far side of the clearing. A couple of bearded faces peered out from between the leaves. They growled and charged out of the foliage, battle-axes lifted over their heads. Halem let loose his arrow. Though he didn't get a clean hit, he did manage to nick the thigh of one of the attacking gnomes. He tripped and fell to the ground, his axe dropping from his hand and bouncing away. Olivia fired at the other just as he leapt behind the large oak. She saw an explosion of bark where the bullet clipped the tree. She'd missed. She grabbed the other rifle from her sister and brought it up to her shoulder, preparing for another shot at the now retreating gnome. He'd grabbed his fallen companion and was dragging him back toward the bushes.

"Eeeeeyaaaaaaahhh," came a cry from above. Olivia turned toward the source of the sound and saw a goblin dropping from the limbs overhead, a deadly-looking dagger clutched in both hands as it plummeted toward Halem. The young boy turned, but there was no way he'd be able to defend himself. Olivia knew she wouldn't have time to aim either. As Halem fell to the ground, his arms outstretched to defend himself, a large black bat swooped down through the trees and snatched the goblin just as its feet touched Halem's forearms. The creature cried out and slashed downward with the blade before being lifted up and vanishing into the leaves.

Olivia rushed over to where Halem was now lying with his hand clasped over his left forearm. Olivia could see the blood oozing out from between his fingers. He looked up at her, the fear obvious in his young eyes.

"He...he stabbed me," Halem stammered, his eyes welling up with tears.

"You'll be okay," Olivia said in a soft voice. "It's not too bad."

"It burns," Halem cried. "My whole arm burns."

Olivia could see red lines forming around the wound, slowly moving outward from the gash. *Poison*, she thought to herself. *The nasty little buggers poisoned their blades.*

"Lilly!" Olivia screamed. As her little sister stumbled forward, arms outstretched, Olivia barked out orders. "We need to get Halem against one of those trees. Clean and bandage up his arm, and then have him watch the tree above you. Atreyu and I will take opposite sides of the tree and help defend you. You get that?" Olivia called over to Atreyu as she and Lilly leaned Halem against the trunk.

"I heard," he yelled back, moving to his right and into position while staying focused on the trees ahead.

"I think the goblins put something on the blades of their knives," Olivia whispered in her sister's ear. "Try to keep him calm. We don't want it spreading any faster than it is already. We'll try to figure out what it is after the fight." Lilly nodded her understanding.

There was movement in the brush to his right and Atreyu let loose a stone. A hollow thump was heard before a stumpy gnome fell face first from the bush and into the dirt. A pair of dirty hands reached out from the brush, grabbed the creature by his long grungy beard, and pulled him back into the foliage. Atreyu slung another rock into the bushes and was awarded with a curse in a language that he couldn't understand. He looked back to Olivia, and she saw a quick smile play across his lips before he pivoted around to keep watch.

Olivia listened and waited, trying to find another target. It was difficult as Halem was groaning in pain. She chanced a quick look over at him and was horrified to see the dark red lines had spread and now disappeared under the sleeve of his shirt. She could even see the beginnings of the lines appearing just above his collar, evidence that the poison was spreading far faster than she'd anticipated. She cringed, hoping they'd be done soon enough to save the young boy.

A rustle of leaves in the trees to her left gave away the position of their next attacker. Bringing her rifle around and aiming at the spot, she waited. A glimmer of light off of a piece of metal gave her the only target she needed. She aimed and fired quickly before dropping to her knee to reload. A goblin fell from the tree and landed with a grunt in the bushes. She scrambled to reload as the thing stood and unsheathed its knife. It hobbled toward her, favoring its right leg. Blood ran down the creature's thigh, so dark green it was almost black. It dripped on the fallen leaves that crackled underfoot as it approached. Olivia ripped open the cartridge, primed the pan, dumped the powder and ball into the barrel, shoved in the paper and rammed it home. She brought the butt of the rifle to her shoulder and got the goblin in her sights.

It suddenly spun in a circle, its lanky arms twirling out from its sides, and fell over. It didn't move. Olivia frowned and stood up, staying hunched over as she moved forward toward the goblin. She kept the rifle at the ready in case it was some sort of ploy, but standing over it, she saw the reason for its collapse. A large knot behind its ear rose up so fast she could see it growing. *Daniel*, Olivia thought to herself as she backed up, sweeping her rifle from side to side, *he must have clubbed it and kept going.* There was another loud howl from overhead. As she raised the gun to the source of the sound, she realized it was getting softer instead of louder. *And now Aidan's turn.* Olivia smiled.

Olivia started back to join Lilly, Halem, and Atreyu when the sound of a twig breaking overhead caught her attention. She caught only a glimpse of the cold yellow eyes before they disappeared. The falling of a single leaf above her sister's head revealed their course, if not their destination.

"Look out!" Olivia yelled at the others. She brought the rifle up, shifting it back and forth, searching for a target but finding none. She moved forward slowly, certain the goblins lurked in the nearby trees, hidden and waiting for their chance.

"Look out for what?" Lilly called back. She dropped to the ground when Olivia had screamed, but now started to stand back up at the sound of her sister's approaching footsteps. "Is everything okay?"

"I saw some goblins. They scrambled right over me. Did you hear anything?"

"I heard a couple of twigs snapping. I heard Halem moaning and I heard Atreyu—"

Her words were cut off with a scream when a goblin dropped out of the trees and grabbed her. Olivia brought her gun up just as the creature pulled her younger sister behind the trunk and began clambering up into the canopy.

"Lilly!" Olivia shrieked. She ran to the tree and looked up at where her sister had disappeared. Nothing.

"Over here," Atreyu hollered. He stood off to the north and pointed up into the treetops. "There were three of them. They just passed by. They're still headed north."

"You come take care of Halem, I'm going after my sister!" Olivia took off at a sprint, catching occasional glimpses of her sister or hearing a muffled cry. "I'm coming for you!!! Daniel! Aidan! Where are you? They took Lilly!"

Olivia ducked and dodged through the trees and bushes, panicking as she fell farther and farther behind. She came across a single gnome standing in her path and dispatched him with a swift kick to the chin. *Must have thought he'd scare me off,* Olivia thought to herself. *Not with my sister in trouble.*

"Daniel!"

Olivia stopped in a small open area, uncertain of which way to go. She'd lost track of her sister.

"Oh, no. No, no, no. Lilly!"

Olivia spun in a circle, desperate for any sign of her little sister.

"Which way were they headed?" Daniel asked.

She screamed and jumped away from him. Realizing it was Daniel, she grabbed his arm. "You've got to help her. The goblins grabbed her and pulled her up into the trees. They've been headed that way," Olivia said, pointing north. "We've got to get her back."

"We will," Daniel answered, holding on to her shoulders. He gave her a soft shake. "Look at me." She stopped jerking her head around and met his gaze. "We will. I need you to calm down and do something for me."

"Anything," Olivia sobbed.

"About a hundred yards east of here is a clearing. Go stand in it and flag down Aidan. He's circling overhead, looking for goblins to pick up. Let him know what happened. He's our best hope for getting to her in the trees. Got it?" She nodded. "Then go!" He gave her a little push and disappeared.

Aidan saw her as soon as she emerged from the woods. He'd just returned from dropping off a goblin and her timing couldn't have been better. Another few seconds and he'd have been over her head and searching the woods. He dropped down quickly as she flailed her arms and screamed at him to land. He pulled up just in front of her and hovered, waiting for her message.

"They took Lilly. Some tree goblins. They grabbed her and pulled her up into the trees. They headed that way," she yelled, pointing off to her left. "Please find her. You've got to save her."

Aidan launched himself into the air and took off, skimming the treetops as he went. He stayed as low as possible, both to see better and to get an even stronger connection with the animals in the area. He hadn't been searching long when he felt Lilly's presence through a nearby squirrel. Aidan dove down into the trees, pulling up just before hitting the soft forest floor. He transformed himself into a bear and let out a deafening roar, mostly to get Daniel's attention, but also to try and scare the goblins carrying Lilly. Reaching out with his mind, Aidan found Custos and sent him ahead to try and slow down the goblins. He also sent the few other squirrels and birds he could find in the area to keep an eye on things until he and Daniel could get to her.

Daniel appeared next to him, so he shifted back to his human form.

"They're up there a ways," Aidan panted. "They're still up in the trees. I've sent Custos up there. We need to hurry. From what I've been able to get from the animals that have seen her, she's not moving."

"You find them and bring them to the ground. When you do, I'll be there. Get going."

Aidan shifted quickly to a small bat and sped off through the trees, dodging this way and that to avoid the branches and limbs speeding by. He caught a glimpse of Lilly's clothes through the leaves just up ahead. He pushed himself harder to catch up.

Two goblins were pulling her along, each with one

filthy green claw hooked under her arm, the third following just behind. Her legs dangled under her, slapping against the branches and leaves as they dragged her toward some unknown destination. Her head wobbled loosely as they bounced her to and fro.

Aidan's blood turned to ice. Weaving his way through the trees around them, he tried to come up with some plan to force the group to the ground. None of the larger animals he could transform into would be able to move as quickly through the trees as the goblins. The smaller ones wouldn't be able to stop them. Only one choice, Aidan thought to himself. He pulled up and over his prey before shifting back to his large bat form. He followed from above and awaited his opportunity. There! There was the break in the trees he was waiting for. Just as the goblins passed through it, Aidan dove. He streaked toward the group, his claws stretched out in front of him. He heard the shriek of one of the goblins as his claws closed around Lilly's shoulder. He pulled her to his body and wrapped his wings protectively around her as they plummeted toward the ground. Aidan turned as they fell, putting himself between her and the ground. They hit hard and the air exploded from Aidan's lungs. He ignored the pain the best he could and changed back to his human self.

"Daniel! Over here! I've got her," Aidan screamed, gasping for breath, and shifted into a bobcat. He could have taken a larger shape, but he wanted to draw the nasty creatures down to the forest floor. Custos showed up nearby, but Aidan held him back, having his friend instead circle around behind his foes.

The three evil creatures dropped to the forest floor just as he'd hoped. Each pulled a wicked dagger from its sheath and grinned, their lips pulling back from their rotting pointed teeth. The middle one hissed something to the others, and they started to separate, one to his left and the other to his right. Aidan backed up a step closer to where Lilly's body lay behind him. He felt his back paw touch her foot and bared his own teeth at their attackers. He let out a low growl. Their grimaces only grew larger as they closed in on his position. The one to Aidan's left raised its blade and screamed its battle cry. It didn't even have the chance to take a step when the twang of a bow announce Daniel's presence nearby. The creature slumped to the earth without a sound. The goblin that had been in the middle, presumably the leader of the three, paused and made some other gurgling sound that brought its companion to a halt. The lead goblin glanced at the arrow embedded in a nearby tree, covered in dark green liquid. Its eyes closed slightly as it frowned. It turned back to face Aidan when another arrow appeared seemingly out of nowhere, also stuck in the tree and also covered in the same green fluid. The beast's eyes widened in surprise, and it, too, crumbled to the ground. Aidan turned to the sole surviving member of the goblin party only to find that it was scrambling as fast as it could move into the surrounding forest.

Maybe some other time, Aidan thought, *or maybe Daniel will get him too.* He transformed back to his human form and knelt next to his fallen friend. He rolled the young girl onto her back, brushing her long brown hair from her face. Placing his ear to her chest, he heard the soft, steady beating of her heart. He let out a huge sigh of relief and felt her chest rise as she took another breath. She was alive. At least for now. He did a quick check of her body, searching for wounds or broken bones. Her legs looked pretty battered from the trip through the treetops, but other than that she looked okay. Daniel appeared next to him.

"She okay?" Daniel asked, leaning down on her other side.

"She's alive, just unconscious. I'm not sure what happened."

"Let's get her back to the others. We'll make sure the area's safe and then figure out what we can do. I'll carry her. Meet us there?"

Aidan nodded and took off into the sky, again taking his bat form. Once he cleared the trees, he turned south. He arrived just after Daniel, having been delayed by stopping to put on his pants. Daniel had Lilly leaned up against the tree next to Halem who, Aidan noticed, looked horrible. Thick black lines covered his face and arms. Aidan could imagine what the rest of him looked like. Halem convulsed briefly and then collapsed back against the trunk of the tree. His breathing was shallow and fast. Not good. Olivia was already at her sister's side, checking her over.

"We think she's okay," Daniel was telling her. "Aidan didn't find anything. Maybe she fainted. But I'm worried about Halem. Did you see the attack?"

"Yes, it was a tree goblin." Lowering her voice and turning her back on Halem, she whispered to Daniel, "I think the knife blades were laced with poison. I'm not sure he'll survive."

Custos came charging through the clearing, bellowing at the top of his lungs before disappearing into the bushes at the far side.

"Looks like we've got company," Daniel announced. "Get ready."

Atreyu peeled his eyes away from his dying brother and started spinning his sling, ready for any target that showed itself. Olivia moved a short distance from her sister, shouldering her rifle while Daniel and Aidan moved a bit farther out. They heard another loud roar and a gnome yell that cut off a bit too quickly for there to be any doubt as to what just happened. Custos came trotting casually back to where Aidan stood.

"I guess we're good," Aidan said.

"For now," Daniel replied. "Keep your eyes open. I don't think we've seen the last of them."

The two boys snuck forward together, searching the forest for any signs of goblins or gnomes. Aidan sent Custos out ahead of them to utilize his sense of smell.

"You're right," Aidan whispered. "There're still quite a few hanging around, mostly goblins."

"Let's get 'em," Daniel answered.

Aidan glanced over and smiled. "Absolutely." In a flash, Aidan had transformed into a bear and charged into the woods after Custos. Daniel followed.

Backing up to her post, Olivia glanced around to again check on her sister. She froze at what she saw. Lilly had fallen onto her side while what appeared to be at least a dozen fairies worked on Halem's arm. He thrashed in pain as the fairies removed the bandage from his arm and inspected the wound. Olivia watched in wonder as each of the pixies removed a small vial from their belts and poured the contents over the open gash on Halem's forearm. With a wisp of smoke, the slash gradually closed in on itself. The evidence of the poison also disappeared, the black veins withdrawing down his face and neck, slowly turning red before collapsing in on the rapidly shrinking cut on his arm. Within a minute, the only indication that he'd ever been injured was the bloody rag now draped across his leg. He flexed his hand as if to test its strength before standing and picking up his bow and arrow. He smiled at the fairies around him and choked when his brother wrapped him in a hug.

"It's the least we could do for him," came a pleasant whisper in Olivia's ear. Olivia started and whipped her head back to the left as she leaned right and away from whoever had snuck up on her.

"The little girl will be fine as well. I apologize for alarming you. I can assure you that I mean you no harm."

Olivia blinked once, twice, trying to make sure she was seeing what she thought she saw. Although she didn't NOT believe in fairies, she had never expected to actually see one. This one hovered in front of her, close enough to reach out and touch if she dared move.

The fairy glanced over her shoulder at the trees behind her. "There are more coming our way," she warned. "I will help you see them." The sprite grabbed a handful of powder from one of her tiny pockets and flew toward her. Olivia gazed up at her as she sprinkled the dust down into her eyes. Although it didn't hurt, Olivia rubbed them anyway out of habit. When she again opened her eyes, the forest had transformed. All of the colors had become so much sharper than she had ever experienced. What was most remarkable though was the aura she could see surrounding Halem and Lilly. Halem was surrounded in a beautiful purple haze while Lilly's was more of a golden yellow.

"Beautiful, isn't it?" the fairy observed, watching her look around in awe. The small creature flittered down and hovered next to Olivia's ear. "You may want to turn around now though."

Olivia spun and could now see the same type of cloud in the trees above, but this time is was a nasty reddish black.

"Those are the goblins you see," the pixie told her. "And there to your right you'll see three disgusting little gnomes."

Glancing up at the sprite, Olivia looked where she pointed and saw the brownish aura that surrounded them.

"You can see them because the leaves and branches don't block the aura. Please do what you must to defend yourselves and our home. I must get back."

The others must have received the same treatment as the battle took a sudden and dramatic turn. The goblins and gnomes were no match for the clan once the fairies blessed them with their magic. With the last of their opponents scattering into the forest in all directions, Daniel returned to the others who were standing around Lilly, who was finally coming around and rubbing the back of her head.

"Aidan and Custos should be here shortly," Daniel announced as he walked up. "I passed Aidan headed back for his clothes just now."

Daniel walked up to Halem and grabbed his arm, rotating it this way and that. "What the—," Daniel said. "Where is your injury? You've got blood on your shirt and I saw the poison making its way through your body. What happened?" He turned to the others, looking for answers.

"He was injured. It sounded like it was pretty bad, too," Lilly replied. Daniel looked at Olivia, confused.

"The fairies fixed it. It was incredible. After Custos took down that gnome, I was going back to my post when I turned and saw a bunch of fairies surrounding Halem. I watched them as they took off the wrap and poured something on the cut. It smoked and then disappeared. The poison, too."

Daniel glanced around at the others. "Well a little more of that stuff would be welcome about now," Daniel muttered as he pulled at his own bandage. "The only thing we got was some stuff to help us see the gnomes and goblins better. I'd rather have gotten my arm healed," he grumbled.

Aidan came trotting up the path and joined his friends, out of breath but excited. Custos lumbered after him and sat down at his side.

"What happened to his arm?" Aidan asked, watching as Halem stood and rotated his hand back and forth. "He was cut right?"

"The fairies healed him," Olivia explained.

"Ah, that makes sense. We saw them too. They came and sprinkled some powder in our eyes that showed us their aura, not that it did me much good when I was in a bat form. You guys get it too?" he asked.

Atreyu and Olivia nodded.

"What did you do with them anyway?" Olivia asked. "The goblins you grabbed when you were a bat?"

Aidan laughed. "Other than the three that took Lilly, none of them ever saw me coming. Not one of them. I just swooped down and grabbed them and then dropped them in the river," Aidan replied. "I figure they'll be well downstream by the time they can swim their way to the bank, if they even make it to the bank. They can be someone else's problem for…"

Aidan trailed off. A ring of twinkling lights was slowly descending from above. The circle encompassed the entire group of children as they stood together under one of the trees that had been attacked by the gnomes. The children shot nervous and curious glances back and forth at one another as the ring lowered to roughly shoulder height before stopping. One of the shimmering lights moved forward, steadily, toward the children who huddled closer together, unsure of what to make of the display. Lilly, oblivious to what was happening around them, sensed the change in mood and reached out for her sister. Finding her arm, she pulled her close.

"What's going on?" she whispered in her sister's ear.

"I'm not sure," Olivia whispered back. "The fairies are coming out. There are a lot of them. It's incredible."

One lone fairy glided up to where Daniel stood, his

mouth agape at the beautiful creature hovering before him. Her gowns where pure white and made of such fine material that the light from her twinkling wings reflected on its surface. She put her tiny hands together and bowed her head. "Queen Iris would like to thank you for the deed you have done here today. As such, she invites you to join us this evening for a meal and presentations."

Daniel looked back at the others, unsure of how to reply. Everyone looked back at him, awaiting his reply.

"We would be honored," he finally answered.

The shimmering lights of the ring grew brighter and the fairies sang with delight. The band of pixies began to rotate around them. It moved not only in a circle, but up and down as well. The children stared in awe at the demonstration before them, and Olivia did her best to express to Lilly what she was seeing. The halo began flickering with other colors from the visible spectrum. A glitter of red, a sparkle of blue. The display grew more grand with each passing moment, the song of the sprites growing louder in their ears until the children's eyes began to droop. Their limbs grew tired, and they leaned against one another for support before slowly dropping to the ground. The lights went out as their eyes closed, and they fell into a deep and peaceful sleep.

Chapter Twenty-Four

A Fairy Party

Olivia was the first to wake. She blinked her eyes rapidly, trying to get them to focus. It took a moment for them to cooperate. She sat up, rubbing at her eyes, and tried again. This time she was successful, and she watched as the sun fell behind the White Mountains bringing nightfall quickly to the lands below. When she looked around, there were glowing lights everywhere. The trees themselves seemed to glow in the growing darkness. A faint music filled the evening air, a very relaxing and peaceful tune. She rose to her knees before looking down and noticing her clothes had been changed. The old blouse and pants she'd been wearing previously had been removed, and she was now dressed in a beautiful silky top that buttoned down the front and matched the dark green trim of a silver wrap on which she'd been sleeping. She also wore an exquisite pair of emerald slacks with matching shoes. As she stood admiring her clothes, it also finally dawned on her that she wasn't standing on the forest floor, but a wonderfully downy surface. Glancing down around her, she saw what appeared to be a giant pillow on the ground beneath her. Surrounding her were the other children in identical clothes and sleeping peacefully on their own cushy beds.

"Please follow me," whispered a sweet angelic voice in her ear.

Olivia followed the fairy, careful to avoid waking the others. When she'd successfully navigated the obstacle course of sleeping bodies, she found the pixie waiting for her. The pixie was female in appearance, though Olivia couldn't say for sure as she'd never seen one until today, with long wavy brunette hair, bright blue eyes, and an outfit identical to Olivia's, minus the wrap.

"I'm sorry about the sleeping charm we cast on you. We just thought it best to make sure you were all rested, cleaned, and healed for tonight's events. You being asleep made that easier for us. Do you feel better?"

"I feel...remarkable." Olivia was surprised, actually, by how fantastic she felt. No aches and pains in her muscles, no stress about what may happen tomorrow, and like she'd just woken from a full night's uninterrupted sleep.

"I'm glad to hear you say that," the fairy commented. "Now, if you'd please come this way, Queen Iris would like to extend her thanks."

Olivia shuffled along behind the fairy as it floated gently down the trail and between two large elms. Olivia had to duck a little to avoid the low hanging branches as she wound through the dense brush. In front of her, the trees and bushes opened up into an enormous glade, punctuated in the center by the largest oak tree she'd ever laid eyes on. She didn't think it would have been possible. The silvery light was even brighter here, each leaf of the tree seemingly glowing with its own internal luminescence. She followed the golden twinkling of the pixie's wings to the center of the clearing and base of the oak.

"If you please," the pixie requested, indicating a small cushion resting on the ground.

Olivia sat cross-legged and waited as her fairy guide rose up into the cover above. Olivia stared after her, trying to follow the path of her flight. She quickly gave up trying to track the glitter of her wings among the radiant leaves and branches. Soon enough however, Olivia heard a change in the tune that had surrounded her since she'd woken. The song grew louder, more powerful. Every bit of foliage seemed to pulse with the beat. Fairies appeared from out of the woods surrounding the clearing, pausing at the perimeter and hovering in the cool air. An air of expectation filled the night. A collective sigh arose from the fairies, causing Olivia to look back up into the tree above her.

Drifting down from the tree came a parade of pixies. An ornamental guard of some sort led the procession as it glided toward her. She could see the miniature arms carried by the sentries as they took their places before her. Behind them came, Olivia guessed, their queen, dressed in a long flowing emerald gown with silver trim. Her blonde hair floated around her face as if she were underwater. Olivia straightened her clothes and smoothed her own hair self-consciously. The music dropped to a barely audible level.

"I am Queen Iris," the fairy confirmed. "I would like to thank you for your part in defending our settlement. It has taken us quite some time to rebuild and organize after our last home was destroyed by the goblins. You and your friends provided protection in a time when our defenses were still weak. For that, you are to be honored. You and yours are hereby granted the titles of Fairy Guardians." A soft cheer arose from the tree line as Queen Iris floated forward, landing gently on Olivia's right knee. "As you can see, we have replaced your clothing with a gauchlian, something a bit more suitable for your new rank. It is made of fairy silk. It will keep you warmer than normal clothes, it will never tear, it need never be washed, and it will identify you to any other pixie community you may encounter. You shall always be welcomed and cared for wherever fairies reside. We also gave you a manta, a cloak to help keep you warm on the coldest of nights." Another cheer went up. Queen Iris raised her hands in a request for silence. "Additionally, for your bravery, I would like you to accept this gift."

Queen Iris flitted away with a quick flutter of her wings, extending her left arm out to her side and guiding two male fairies down to where Olivia sat. Between them they held a square leather sack. It was a little larger than her water container, yet still smaller than her pack. They dropped the gift gently onto her lap and disappeared back up into the tree above. Olivia lifted the pouch and examined it, turning it back and forth in her hands. It seemed to be fresh leather, showing no signs of wear or aging, and was decorated in an intricate pattern that gave the impression that ivy was crawling across its surface. Two strong drawstrings secured the top.

"It's beautiful," Olivia gasped, still studying the elaborate design on the leather. She couldn't quite make them out, but there also appeared to be words woven into the stems that wound their way to and fro across both sides. Opening it and inspecting the interior, Olivia discovered the same designs adorned the inside as well.

"It is an endurtaka," the tiny queen explained. "Anything you put inside it will replicate. One loaf of bread becomes two. One water pouch, the same. I'm certain that you will find it useful in the journey ahead of you."

Olivia's eyes just about popped out of her head. "Really?" she stammered. "Anything I put in here? May I try it out?" she asked excitedly while bouncing up and down on her cushion.

Queen Iris smiled. "Of course, dear."

Olivia searched the ground around her, opting for a nearby leaf to test her exciting gift. She examined it first, checking it for identifying marks before placing it gently in the pouch and pulling the strings to close it. She looked up at Queen Iris.

"Go ahead, it happens as soon as you pull the strings to close it."

Olivia opened the pouch and peered inside. A smirk crept across her lips as she reached inside and pulled out two identical leaves. She inspected them both and, sure enough, one was an exact replica of the other. Her eyes twinkled with excitement when she glanced back up at the queen.

"A small token of our gratitude."

As the others woke, the process was repeated until all six had received the same gift. They all sat together on their cushions, excitedly chatting back and forth, putting various objects into their pouches before pulling out two, laughing, and showing them off to the others.

A fine meal was then served consisting of a variety of vegetation served in plain wooden bowls.

"Forgive us the dinnerware. We are unaccustomed to having humans as guests. We have done our best to make your dining a pleasant experience. Please excuse us if the experience does not live up to your standards," Queen Iris apologized.

"No need for apologies," Daniel replied. "The food is delicious. And we would be extraordinarily ungrateful if we were to complain about the type of dishes on which you served our meal. Besides, it is we who should be thanking you for all you've done for us," he said lifting his healed arm. "You did as much, or more, to help us as we did to help you."

"And the food is delicious too," Halem added, shoving another forkful of greens into his mouth.

The queen smiled at the repetition. "Well then, I'm glad to hear you are enjoying yourselves. Please let the servers know if you desire another serving. We have more than enough." Queen Iris flitted away, drifting upward into the cover of the canopy overhead.

The children chatted amongst themselves, retelling the story of the battle with the gnomes and goblins, filling each other in on the details of the fight the others might have missed. Daniel and Aidan did most of the talking as the other four had stuck together through most of the engagement. Aidan had spent most of his time plucking the goblins from their perches high in the trees and dropping them in Styx River. Daniel, on the other hand, had focused his attention on the wandering gnomes, only catching the occasional goblin that had fallen to the forest floor, like the one Olivia had fought.

They laughed and drank, then laughed some more. The clan stuffed themselves with greens, mushrooms, roots, nuts, and berries. When dessert was finally served, they all drank deeply the sweet nectar served to them in silver goblets. The group settled into their seats, finishing off the last of the juice and thanking the pixies that removed the empty cups.

"That was exquisite," Olivia whispered to Daniel who was now gazing up into the glow of the leaves overhead.

Daniel nodded. "And I don't feel nervous about what I just ate," he joked. Seeing Olivia's confusion, he explained. "When Shon handed me my plate in Alustria, he told me to eat and that it would be best if I didn't ask what it was."

Olivia stuck out her tongue in distaste.

"I'm sure it was fine," Daniel went on, "but still, I was relieved when the fairies brought out fruits and vegetables instead of some unidentifiable meat."

"I'm glad you didn't tell me," Olivia groaned. "I don't think I could have eaten the food back in Alustria, if I'd heard that."

Daniel smiled at Olivia and then turned his attention back to the tree. His eyes wandered back and forth, drifting lazily among the lights flickering above. The music eventually died down, but the fairies didn't leave. The glow grew more intense as the children whispered among themselves, speculating as to what would happen next.

Queen Iris again descended from her kingdom in the treetops and hovered above the youngsters.

"I'd now ask that you present to me your leader, that I may honor that person with one final gift."

All eyes immediately fell to Daniel, who stood and stepped forward from his cushion.

He hesitated before announcing, "I am Daniel, son of Troy. I have the honor of leading this clan."

"Very well, Daniel," Queen Iris continued. "I would like to bestow on you this artifact as a symbol of our recognition for what you have done. I pray you understand the significance of that which is being offered."

With a deep curtsy, the queen glided away as a group of six fairies descended from above. They held a scepter, elegant in its design and shimmering in the glow of the forest. The fairies placed it carefully in Daniel's outstretched hands. Raising it in front of him, four empty slots were apparent in the crown that ornamented the top.

"Do you know what you hold in your hand?" the queen inquired, gliding slowly back to Daniel.

Daniel stared in disbelief. "I...I think it's the...it can't be," he stammered. "Wasn't it destroyed when Argyle took over?"

"The jewels were removed and sent back to different lands as a reward to the mercenaries they provided. The

Scepter was removed from the altar and cast into the Styx River. It eventually made its way back to us, compliments of Kyrie, the Queen of the Lake."

Daniel glanced back at the others, searching for some clue as to how he should answer.

"This gift was given to you humans once before, a long time ago, when Javi stepped in during our time of need. He saved our colony just as you did today. This is the Scepter that was given to him. It was a blessing from my ancestors. It brought peace and prosperity to your lands, which formed the foundation of the Kingdom of Castiglias. That tranquility has since been destroyed, as has the magic carried in the Scepter, by King Argyle."

"Just Argyle," Aidan interrupted. "That devil is no king of mine."

"Well spoken, young Aidan," the queen remarked. "That magic was destroyed by Argyle when he removed the stones. Without them, this golden staff is but a memory of a better time. A time when all men were free and lived in harmony with fairies. Take it, as a wish that the days ahead of you and yours are filled with serenity. May your lives be long and joyous."

Daniel ran his fingers down the smooth surface of the Scepter, admiring its beauty, even though it was missing its four stones.

Aidan stood. "But what if we found the stones?" he asked. "What if we found them all and put them back in the Scepter?"

The queen's eyes blazed. "What if?"

~

If you enjoyed *Scepter* and would like to read more about the adventures of Daniel and Aidan, Book Two will be available soon.

Get updates on this and the author's other current projects on his Facebook page (Scott L Collins).

About the Author

Born and raised in Southern California, Scott and his wife relocated to Colorado after the birth of their first son. He currently resides just south of Denver with his gorgeous wife and two energetic boys. After publishing his debut novel in the fiction thriller genre, Scott has switched to YA fantasy in order to combine his passion for writing with his children's love of reading.

5420574R00134

Made in the USA
San Bernardino, CA
06 November 2013